W9-AAS-679

# THE RANCHER'S HEART

# THE RANCHER'S HEART

## C. H. ADMIRAND

**FIVE STAR**

*An imprint of Thomson Gale, a part of The Thomson Corporation*

**THOMSON**

**GALE**

Detroit • New York • San Francisco • New Haven, Conn. • Waterville, Maine • London

**THOMSON**

**GALE**

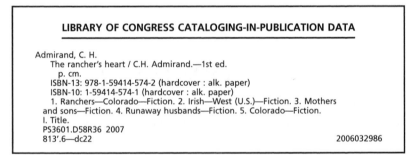

**LIBRARY OF CONGRESS CATALOGING-IN-PUBLICATION DATA**

Admirand, C. H.
  The rancher's heart / C.H. Admirand.—1st ed.
    p. cm.
  ISBN-13: 978-1-59414-574-2 (hardcover : alk. paper)
  ISBN-10: 1-59414-574-1 (hardcover : alk. paper)
  1. Ranchers—Colorado—Fiction. 2. Irish—West (U.S.)—Fiction. 3. Mothers and sons—Fiction. 4. Runaway husbands—Fiction. 5. Colorado—Fiction. I. Title.
  PS3601.D58R36 2007
  813'.6—dc22                                      2006032986

First Edition. First Printing: February 2007.

Published in 2007 in conjunction with Tekno Books.

Printed in the United States of America on permanent paper
10 9 8 7 6 5 4 3 2 1

This book is dedicated to love of my life, DJ, and our three awesome "adult" children, Phil, Jessi and Josh. Though they may grumble at times, their support is absolute and unconditional.
Thanks, guys, for always being there. I love you!

# ACKNOWLEDGMENTS

Thanks to my amazing editor, Alice Duncan, for everything!

Thanks to my BB for allowing me to use his lyrics and song in the opening of this book.

To the three generations of feisty Irish-American women in my family: Garahan, Flaherty, Daly, and Purcell. Your sharp tongues, hard heads, and big hearts have kept our family strong (though your decisions to marry stubborn men of English, Welsh, and German descent are questionable, it must be the reason I chose to marry a stubborn Dutchman with just enough Irish in him to be his saving grace).

A very special thank you to: Terri Brisbin, Jennifer Wagner-Schmidt, Lyn Wagner, MaryLou Frank, Susan Stevenson, Terri Castoro, Madeline Archer, Mary Stella, Elizabeth Keys, Emily Baker, and Madeline Hunter. You kept me sane, and helped me survive rejections. Who knew copious amounts of French martinis and chocolate would be the cure-all?????

# OFF TO AMERIKAY
## LYRICS BY DEAN M. DOBBS

A long time ago in a place far away, a son told his
father, "Da, I'm goin' away.
There's no future for me here, there's not enough
work to go 'round.
You plow the fields, till the soil, but there's more
rock than dirt to our ground."

Seamus he got his first glimpse, of the land of
Amer-i-kay.
As he stood at the top of the gangplank, getting
ready to go ashore,
he was thinking of his father and mother standing
at the cottage door, and he was saying—

Chorus:

Oh my da, I'm off to Amer-i-kay, I'm sorry to be
leavin', but you know I cannot stay.
There's no work for me here, there's no future so
they say, so oh my da, I'm off to Amer-i-kay.

# PROLOGUE

*Colorado Territory, Late 1860s*

Bridget O'Toole's hand shook as she reached for the pen. Tears of joy blurred her vision.

Wiping them away with the back of her hand, she drew in a deep calming breath. Dipping the pen into the inkwell, she steadied her hand and put pen to paper.

Michael Garahan O'Toole, born this 17th day of September in the year of our Lord, Eighteen Hundred and Sixty-Six.

She looked over to where her week-old son lay fast asleep in his cradle by the warmth of the fire. Love for him welled up within her, blotting out the sharp slice of sorrow that had been her constant companion since her baby's father had walked out the door nine months ago and not returned.

Desperate emotions churned within her, until her head pounded and her stomach began to ache. She reached for the O'Toole family Bible, flipped to the back page, and lovingly traced the flowing curves of her husband's handwriting, the only words of his that she had left.

The key to happiness is in the hands of the one who holds my heart, M.O.T. 3 * 3 * 1 8 5 0.

Michael's written words had been a balm these last nine

months, but the date following his initials truly was a puzzle. She had been born in 1850, but not in March. She shook her head, remembering one of his quirks, the inability to remember numbers without first committing them to paper. *It hadn't worked this time either.*

The baby's lusty cry of hunger interrupted her thoughts.

She closed the Bible with a snap, snagging the edge of her nail on the loose thread that bound the leather covering in place. Running her fingertips over the slight bulge in the lower corner near the binding, she marveled that her husband had felt strongly enough about his family's treasure to repair the cover when it had apparently come undone the year before. It was all the more precious to her because of its imperfection.

Baby Michael's cries became more insistent, causing a tingly sensation in her breasts; they suddenly felt full. Lifting the squalling baby into her arms, she settled in her grandmother's rocker. The soothing motion of rocking back and forth, with her baby suckling at her breast, went a long way toward healing the jagged hole in her heart.

"We'll be just fine, angel face," she whispered, brushing the tips of her fingers across his forehead. The downy hair stood up then fell back against his head.

"Your papa will come back."

Bridget's promise rang through the empty cabin as she lifted the baby to her shoulder to rub his back.

Where was Michael? Why had he left without a word?

Just then, the baby let out a lusty, bubbly burp, and she forgot all about Michael and the nights she'd spent at the cabin door, waiting, watching. Enthralled with her tiny son, she pressed her lips to the top of his head and breathed in his scent, catching a whiff of the soap she had laundered his sleeping gown in, mixed with the lavender she used to keep her linens smelling fresh.

Stroking the edge of his ear and the curve of his eyebrow, she whispered nonsense words to him, hoping to soothe him. He opened his eyes, and when his dark blue gaze fixed on hers, a wave of love swept over her. He was going to have his father's eyes, the shape of them, if not the color.

A lone tear slipped past her guard, as she thought of her handsome husband, gone these last months. A fragment of an unanswered question thrust its way into her drifting thoughts. Where had she left her mother's cameo? Had she put it with her father's gold pocket watch and their marriage lines? Both had gone missing months ago, around the time Michael left.

She felt the baby's mouth go slack and looked down at his little body, replete with milk, solidly in the grasp of whatever dreams his baby's mind could conjure. Kissing the top of his head, each tiny closed eye, and the tip of his nose, she laid him on his full tummy in his cradle, tucking her grandmother's crazy quilt around him. She smiled and touched the tip of her finger to a faded square of blue—Gram's favorite dress—and one of equally faded red plaid—Granddad's favorite shirt. The pieces had been stitched alongside one another, as her grandparents had lived the whole of their lives: side by side. Comforted by thoughts of them, Bridget climbed up into bed, but stretched one hand out to gently rock Michael's cradle, all the while, envying him his innocent dreams.

Bridget's dreams were tortured with nightmares of his father never coming back, entwined with thick black smoke and flames licking the length of the cabin's walls.

The baby's screams awakened Bridget from a dead sleep. Unable to shake herself free of the nightmare, she scrubbed her hands across her face in an effort to clear her vision, but the smoke remained—thick and black. She drew in a breath, and her lungs protested violently. Coughs wracked her body, hampering movement.

Dear God in heaven! This was no dream!

A roar rumbled off to the left of her as the entire north wall of the small cabin erupted into flames.

Terror for baby Michael galvanized Bridget into action. Grabbing the baby, tossing Gram's quilt over his face, Bridget pulled him tightly to her breast. A wicked fit of coughing had her reaching out to steady herself. Her hand landed on the bedside table and the book she always kept there. Another roar of flame sounded, this time from behind her. Half of the cabin was engulfed, floor to ceiling, in wicked red-orange flames. The smoke from the fire rapidly filled the room, making it impossible to see.

Bridget grabbed her baby and the Bible, tucking them protectively within her arms. Ducking her head down, she sprinted for the door while tears began pouring from her swollen, smoke-filled eyes. Unwilling to shift her precious burden to wipe them clear, Bridget closed her eyes and prayed they would make it to the door.

# CHAPTER 1

*Twelve Years Later*

"Where are you off to, Mick?" Bridget gathered the remnants of her flagging strength, lifted her heavy head up from the pillow, and waited, listening. The creaky floorboard near the front door told her that her son had heard her rasped question and paused.

The floorboard creaked again before he answered, "Hunting."

Her son's terse reply hurt, but she ignored the feeling and asked, "At this hour?" Mick was growing like a weed and was moody as a bear with a thorn stuck in his paw. She wracked her brain for something to say that would draw him back to her side, but her boy had changed. He was no longer the sweet little toddler who followed her everywhere, nor was he the laughing young boy with the high-pitched, squeaky voice who worked tirelessly by her side planting their garden. She thought of their sun-baked garden, and missed the way he had trustingly put his hand in hers; looking down at their shriveled-up plot of vegetables, asking how they would eat, knowing she would somehow find them food.

"I'll be back." His words broke through her troubled thoughts. "Don't worry, Ma."

Good Lord he sounded just like his father, with the same deep rumbling timbre that seemed to spring up from deep inside of him. After all this time, she still missed the way her husband's voice reverberated from deep within his chest when she would lay her head against him.

For a heartbeat neither of them spoke or moved. The low hoot of an owl nearby drifted in through the open window, jarring her back to the present.

Bridget had to get a handle on her drifting thoughts and useless wishes. She might be weak from fever, and what her son termed a "mysterious illness," but she was still aware enough to know when her boy was up to no good. Worry for her only child speared through her like a hoe through freshly turned earth.

"But Mick, I thought—"

"I love you, Ma."

The puff of air from the softly closing door blew out the stub of a candle Mick had thoughtfully placed on the table next to her bed.

As her only source of light winked out, darkness closed in on her, leaving her alone with her tortured thoughts.

*Where was he going? Who was he meeting?*

*Would he leave her and not come back as his father had?*

Too weak to get out of bed and chase after her son, Bridget gave in to the hopelessness and fatigue plaguing her, closing her eyes. She had one option left to her, and she would use it.

"Lord, please watch over my boy . . . he's all I have left."

Her prayer did not go unheard.

"Jest kill him and leave him for the coyotes," one of the rustlers ground out.

"No!" the scrawny-looking boy shouted. "I did what you asked."

"Then why is the hair on the back of my neck standing up?" the one with the black eye patch demanded.

"Maybe ya need to use more soap—" the boy began.

"Don't sass me, boy," the one-eyed rustler growled. "Everybody knows it's a warning; I inherited the sight from my Scots granny."

James Ryan inched another step closer, then crouched low to hide behind the jagged boulder, never taking his eyes off the rustlers or the young boy surrounded by them. Here was trouble he hadn't bargained for. All he'd intended to do tonight was stop a mangy group of cattle rustlers from stealing any more of his herd. He'd have to change his plans. The boy was in deep trouble, probably his own doing. But the boy needed his help, and he couldn't ignore the boy's pleas. Now it looked as if he'd have to stop the rustlers from hurting the poor boy shaking in his boots.

"Naw, jest cut off his nose and his lips," the one with the scarred face snarled. "That'll teach him he can't poke what he don't have into nobody else's business."

Ryan's gut clenched in reaction to the gruesome threat. He flexed his hand then slowly drew his Colt from its holster.

"Yeah," another gruff voice shouted, "without his lips, he won't be tellin' tales."

"No, stupid. He can still talk without lips. Ya need to cut out his tongue—"

"Help!" the boy screamed as the rustler with the eye patch slid a wicked-looking Bowie knife from his belt and held it up to the boy's lips.

The high-pitched keening sound raked jagged fingers up and down his spine, causing the hair on the back of his neck to stand at attention. The eerie silence that followed was quieter than last Sunday when the preacher had given his twice-yearly hellfire and damnation sermon.

"Bloody buggering eedjit," Ryan mumbled. No one was going to lay a finger—or knife—to that poor boy while there was breath left in Ryan's body.

"Are ye after savin' the lad then, Jamie?"

"Aye," Ryan whispered. "Somewhere he's got a mother worrying herself sick over him. "Ready, men?" Ryan turned to look at the four men riding with him. All four nodded in unison. "Wait for the marshal's signal. Shoot to disarm."

Off to Ryan's left the marshal gave the signal. Ryan and his ranch hands stepped out of the darkness into the firelight, guns blazing. The black powder was clearing by the time Ryan had a hold of the boy's arm.

"Let me go!" the boy shouted, though Ryan thought he heard the boy's voice wavering.

"Is that anyway to talk to the man who saved yer skin?" one of Ryan's men demanded.

"Let it go, Murphy." They didn't have time for this now.

"Doesn't seem grateful, does he lads?"

"That'll do, Flynn," Ryan bit out, watching as one of the rustlers tried to sneak off without being noticed. "See if you can help Marshal Turner over there. I want to talk to the boy."

The boy struggled to free himself, so Ryan let him go. The boy stumbled back and landed hard on his backside. Recognizing the boy's embarrassed pride, he didn't offer his hand in help, knowing it would more than likely be refused. "Are you hurt?"

The boy shook his head and brushed himself off as he got to his feet.

Getting a better look at the youngster, he wondered just how old he was and how he got mixed up in the attempted rustling. "What are you doing with the likes of them, lad?"

Ryan watched the boy, waiting for an answer, but before he had the chance, one of the rustlers called out, "Don't tell him a thing, Mick!"

The boy's head swiveled away from Ryan toward the threat. *So, his name's Mick.*

"I'll cut your throat ear to ear!" A stream of brown tobacco juice splattering the boy's left boot accompanied the second threat.

Anger surged through him. "Enough!" Ryan watched Mick bend down to wipe the spit off his worn boots.

"Gag 'em," the marshal ordered, coming to stand alongside Ryan and the boy.

Taking pity on the boy, who was starting to shake something fierce, Ryan hunkered down next to Mick. "You want to save your mama from having to watch you hang?"

The quietly spoken words had an empowering effect on him. Mick nodded and pointed to the man with the eye patch. "I don't know the name of the man they rustle for, but that one's called One-Eyed Jack."

"Well now, Jamie," Flynn said with a nod, "the lad's not as dumb as we thought."

"I'm not stupid!" the boy snapped.

"Aren't you?" Murphy pushed back his Stetson and scratched his head, "Sure and it's a smart lad who knows to stay home instead of taggin' along after cattle rustlers."

Mick opened his mouth to speak then shut it.

"Tie 'em up," the marshal ordered.

"And lay them face down over their saddles," Ryan added.

"How will you get them to town then?" Mick asked.

"We're going to tie their horses' reins together," Marshal Turner said, pulling bits of rope out of his saddlebags and tossing them to Ryan's men, who began tying the outlaws' hands and feet together.

Satisfied that orders were being followed, he turned back to Mick and asked, "Why?"

More than one muffled curse sounded, and Ryan was afraid the boy would balk and run. But Mick only looked over at the men, obviously to judge whether or not they were securely tied, then drew in a deep breath and stood up straight. "I did what I had to. For my ma."

Ryan wondered where the boy's father was, but knew better than to ask that just yet. "We'll stop by my ranch on the way to jail."

Still a bit wobbly, Mick took a step closer to Ryan so they stood toe to toe and braved, "Am I going to jail, too?"

"You'll not be goin' off to jail tonight, lad."

"He's broken the law, Ryan. He'll have to answer for that—"

"Oh, let him alone, Marshal—" Flynn began, but Ryan interrupted.

"I think Mick will be invaluable in capturing the head of the rustling operation." Ryan turned toward the boy. "Won't you, Mick?"

"I swear I don't know the man's name, but I know we were to meet him tomorrow night up by the abandoned mine shaft."

"I need to take the boy into town for questioning," Marshal Turner insisted.

Ryan's gazed locked with Mick's, and he would later swear the boy was seeing his own ghost—he looked that petrified about going with the marshal. Ryan remembered just what that fear could do to a person . . . what it had done to him.

"I'm sure you can ask Mick anything you want, tomorrow after breakfast."

"Ryan—" the marshal began.

"You have enough to keep you busy until then, Marshal Turner." Ryan patted the boy's shoulder. "He won't be going anywhere anytime soon."

More muffled curses sounded from behind them as he watched Mick mount his horse. "Follow me back to the ranch."

"All right."

One of the rustlers managed to loosen his gag and threatened, "I'll cut your mother's heart out the minute I break out of jail!"

Mick's cry was heartfelt and terrified. He squirmed to get

down off the horse, but Ryan anticipated the reaction and was there to steady the boy, keeping him from leaping from his saddle.

"No one's escaped from the Emerson jail in ten years," he assured Mick. "It's not likely to happen with Marshal Turner in charge."

"Aye, lad," Flynn said. "Don't mind them. They're just anxious to test the length of rope the sheriff has waiting for them over at the jail."

"But I thought the marshal—"

"Marshal Turner is here for another reason," Ryan said quietly, meeting the lawman's gaze over the top of Mick's head.

"I'll find her, Ryan," the marshal vowed. "You have my word."

Ryan nodded, trying not to think about his missing sister. Maggie should have arrived over a week ago.

"What about my ma?" Mick demanded.

Ryan's thoughts shifted back to the present. "She won't be following after you will she?"

Mick shook his head as they started riding toward the Ryan spread. "Naw, she's too sick. The doc won't see her anymore, and we needed the money. That's why I—"

Ryan put a hand on top of the one Mick placed on the saddle horn, and squeezed once before letting go. "I'd never fault a boy for trying to take care of his mother, would you lads?"

The group riding with Ryan and the marshal closed ranks, with the exception of the one who led the string of rustlers' horses they'd tied together; he concentrated on the task of keeping the train of mounts together.

"Nay, I'd not," Flynn agreed.

"Well sure an it's a grand thing."

"No lad should desert his ma, 'specially when she's ailing," Murphy sagely added.

"Right you all are, and sure it's himself that'll be the one to save the day."

Ryan wondered at the odd look in the boy's eyes, and he looked around at his men. Nothing out of the ordinary there, but maybe through a scared boy's eyes they might look a bit rough around the edges.

"Does this mean you'll help me?" Mick finally got up the gumption to ask.

"Do I have your word that you'll not try to steal from me?" Ryan countered.

Mick's jaw dropped. Before he had a chance to close it, the marshal bit out, "He broke the law."

"He's just a lad. Misguided at that," Ryan insisted.

"Why would you be willing to help me?" Mick demanded. "No one else would."

"And there's yer answer," Flynn said.

The marshal sighed loudly then added, "He's in your custody, Ryan. Keep him out of trouble."

"Are you certain you won't change your mind?" Mick asked him as they urged their horses into a canter.

Ryan let his gaze slide off the gangly young man riding at his side. He was younger than Ryan had first thought. He shook his head. Nothing would make him change his mind.

"Well all right then. About my ma . . ."

"I promised you, we'd send a wagon—"

"You don't understand—"

Ryan's skin started to itch. There was more here than just a boy out on a midnight cattle raid. "What don't I understand, lad?"

"She's so weak . . . so sick . . . and the doctor . . ." Mick's voice trailed off, and Ryan pretended not to notice the way the boy used the edge of his sleeve to swipe at his watery eyes. "I'm all she's got left."

Mick's bleakly whispered statement went right to Ryan's heart.

"So you've chosen me to trust enough to help you?" Though quietly asked, Ryan's question did not go unheard.

Mick nodded. "I have to trust someone. I failed my promise to watch over my ma . . ."

"But Mick, lad—"

"I promised her the first time I found her lying on the floor all beat—"

Ryan's stomach lurched. He clenched his jaw tight enough to grind wheat into flour. His gaze swung over to the young man who carried the weight of responsibility for his gravely ill mother on his broad, but still bony, shoulders.

Even in the pale moonlight, Ryan could see the way the boy's shoulders were hunched over. Mick looked as if he were drawing all of his past hurts within himself, hoarding them. The one tentative request to trust another was being withdrawn before Ryan's eyes.

He couldn't let that happen. He knew his next words were crucial to getting the lad to confide the worst of his past to him. Ryan went with his gut feeling and began, not noticing when he slipped into the familiar lilting brogue. "I left me mother, da, and younger sister to fend for themselves as soon as the boat docked in New York Harbor."

Mick's shoulders shrugged. Not impressed.

"Me da hadn't fully recovered from the gunshot wound he received fightin' the—"

"Who'd he fight?"

Ah, a bloodthirsty lad. Just as Ryan had hoped, Mick's interest was riveted on him. Ryan had never felt less like talking, but he knew he had to. "Oh, Da often skirted trouble back home in Ireland. He believed in freedom and fightin' those who'd oppress us . . ."

He let his words drift off, saying just enough to encourage Mick's interest and just enough to keep from tearing off the thin layer of indifference that protected his own heart from the raw hurt that lay just beneath his surface of outward calm.

"Nobody has the right to tell me and my ma what to do!" Mick's emphatic sweep of his arms through the air right above his horse's head had the poor animal rearing back to avoid whatever swooped past its ears in the darkness.

"Have a care, lad. You'll not be wantin' to spook your mount." One look at the frantic boy, and Ryan swallowed the chuckle that nearly burst forth at Mick's awkward, but successful, attempt to control his horse.

"I didn't mean to spook him." As apologies went, it certainly sounded sincere.

"I know, but if you want to get on well with the rest of the ranch hands, you'll have to pay more attention to your horse." Ryan sidled his horse closer to Mick's. "A man depends on his horse out here. Without it, a man is as good as stranded. Maybe even dead."

Ryan wasn't sure which of his last words did the trick, but Mick opened up. "One of the places my ma worked was run by the biggest son of a bitch a body'd ever want to meet!"

Mick glanced his way, obviously waiting to be corrected for swearing.

Ryan decided to ignore it. "What did he do to you?"

Mick looked over his shoulder at the other men riding a few horse-lengths behind them, then back at Ryan. "He beat my ma."

"Bleeding, buggering eedjit!" Men who beat women were no better than cow shite.

Mick looked away and mumbled something more.

"I didn't hear you. What did you say?"

Mick turned back around, "It was right after she told him we

24

couldn't pay the rent and he told her—"

Mick's Adam's apple bobbed up and down, then he swallowed.

"Told her . . . ?" Ryan urged.

"They could work something out if she'd go with him to the back room of the Rusty Spur."

Ryan had heard enough. "Not all men are like that, Mick. I'd never lay a hand on someone weaker than me, whether it be a man, woman, child, or animal. I promise you."

The boy nodded, but it was the way he straightened his shoulders and lifted his head up that told Ryan the lad was beginning to tentatively trust him.

"I'll drive the wagon."

"I'll do it. I need you to hang on to my ma. She'd get hurt if you let her bump around in the wagon bed."

Ryan nodded. "You and your mother are welcome to stay at my ranch as long as you'd like."

Mick nodded and swiped his sleeve under his nose. "We'd best get that wagon."

# CHAPTER 2

The wagon lurched as the wheels slipped in and out of another rut in the sun-baked roadbed.

"Easy." Ryan heard the soft intake of breath of the woman he held and cursed under his own.

The slender wisp of woman moaned softly.

"I'm sorry, Mrs. O'Toole." Could she hear him? Would his words penetrate the fog of pain surrounding her and ease the worst of it?

Ryan pulled her close, hoping his gentle but firm hold would prevent any further jarring. By the saints, she was thin!

"Hang on, Ma!" Mick flicked the reins again, signaling the sturdy plow horse to keep moving.

In a bid to distract the boy, Ryan prompted, "Are you ready to tell me why you were with those rustlers last night?"

Mick's gray eyes widened, and he opened his mouth as if to speak. But one look at the frail woman Ryan held had the boy clamping his jaw shut.

*It's probably just as well. The poor lad's probably still wondering just how far to trust me.* "We can talk about it later. I made a promise to Marshal Turner last night that I intend to keep."

Mick didn't give any indication that he'd heard, but Ryan suspected the lad had.

The realization that he had two more mouths to feed hit him two miles south of his ranch. He couldn't have chosen a more difficult time to take in more strays. His sister Maggie was still missing, and only Marshal Turner's assurance that he was out looking for her kept Ryan from trying to track her down himself. Anything could have happened to her stagecoach, with delays at any one of the scheduled stops. He'd just have to be patient a while longer.

A soft puff of air blew across his throat. Startled by the feel of it, he looked down at the thin but lovely face. His sigh was loud; his thoughts distracted. Now here was a sight worth seeing. He shook his head. Fine time to notice her beauty, when the poor woman felt as if she weighed no more than a bird and looked as if she were wasting away.

A bleak thought struck him right between the eyes. Heaven help Mick if she were dying. *Dying* . . . the word wrapped itself around his heart and squeezed tight. The poor lass couldn't be as old as his sister, could she?

One way to find out, "How old are you?"

Mick didn't look away from the horse or the reins he held when he answered, "Thirteen come winter."

That would put Mick's mother somewhere around twenty-nine, if she got married and had Mick at seventeen or so. Maybe younger.

As the wagon made its way across the rough roads, ever closer to his ranch, Ryan thought about what life must have been like for the boy, protecting his mother from a young age.

"You said your pa left?"

Mick's sharp glance could have cut through steel. *Good for you. Don't let any man cow you.*

"Yeah."

"Do you remember much about him?"

Mick sat stone silent for so long, Ryan thought the boy wouldn't answer at all.

Giving the lad time, he focused on their surroundings, rather than on the silent young man at his side or the dangerously thin woman in his arms. Ryan stared up at the white puffs of clouds still off in the distance.

*Weather's moving in,* he could just imagine old man McMaster saying. A slice of pain slid through him. He'd give his right arm if it would bring the old curmudgeon back. Braving a glance down, he realized that some things were beyond his wishes or control. He owned the ranch now, just as McMaster had decreed as the old man lay dying. There wasn't a blessed thing he could have done to save his mentor, but as God was his witness, he'd do his damnedest to save this woman.

"I don't remember my pa."

Ryan looked over at the boy. Infinite sorrow flowed from the boy in waves. "Ah, well, sure an' that's a shame."

Caught up in the boy's emotions, Ryan told Mick about his father, slipping back into his childhood brogue as the memories returned. "My da was a big man. Hands and voice rough by turns, or gentle, whatever the situation warranted."

Mick nodded. If Ryan closed his eyes, he could still remember how it felt to stand at his da's side, his much smaller hand tucked securely in his father's, certain that the world would be safe so long as the man with a heart as big as Ireland stood tall and proud at his side.

When Mick stubbornly remained silent, Ryan added, "My da's gone too."

Mick's tongue loosened enough to share just a bit. "My ma says I look like Pa."

Ryan nodded, not wanting to interrupt the boy now that he was beginning to open up.

"He left before I was born. My ma says he just never came home." Mick's eyes were flint-hard when he turned toward Ryan. "But they were married. He must have gotten ambushed by outlaws or stampeded by cattle, or caught in a twister, or—"

Moved by the boy's story and fierce defense of a man he'd

never met, Ryan reached out a hand and laid it on the lad's shoulder. "You've no need to justify yourself or your father's existence to me. I believe you."

Satisfied with that small tidbit, Mick nodded and relaxed his hands on the reins enough that the horse looked over its shoulder as if to see just what Mick wanted him to do now.

"I think Finn needs you to grip the reins with just a bit firmer hand, lad," Ryan said with a nod toward the horse pulling their wagon.

Doing as Ryan bade him, Mick glanced first at his mother then focused all of his considerable attention to the rise in the road up ahead.

Guessing their conversation was over, Ryan told him, "My land begins just 'round the bend. By that oak tree."

Shifting Mrs. O'Toole in his arms, to better point out the tree, Ryan felt the slight swell of her hip brush against his lap. Damned if his body didn't stir itself just enough to be embarrassing. He'd better concentrate on something else before they got to the ranch house. It had certainly been a long while since any woman stirred his interest.

*Why now? Why this woman?*

Desperate to shake himself free of those dangerous thoughts, wracking his overtired brain for something to say or do to distract his growing physical awareness of the woman in his arms, he finally remembered Mick saying something about squirrel stew last night on the ride home. Hoping to get the boy to focus on something other than worry for his mother, while Ryan dug deep for the will to control his soon-to-be-obvious interest in the woman, he blurted out, "So you can cook squirrel stew?"

He hoped it would work, since the last thing he intended to do was scare the boy into thinking the man who had come to their rescue would take advantage of his very ill mother.

"Yeah," Mick finally answered. "I can cook Irish stew, too. But we haven't had mutton in a long time. Costs too much. Last year wasn't a good one for carrots, or anything else we planted. They just rotted off at the dirt. We thought we'd have such a fine crop—well at least enough for a summer's worth of good eatin'."

Mick paused, swiped a hand across his brow and nodded toward the steadily shining sun. "Too much rain put an end to our plans. We lost the potatoes too."

"Last year wreaked havoc on our garden too," Ryan offered, hoping to help the boy realize he was not the only one who had suffered from the weather. "But we had enough seed left over to plant again, once the blasted rains let up."

The knowledge that he had had to dig into the reserve of money he always set aside for his sister and their mother had kept him awake more than one night. But the knowledge that his men, and the townspeople who depended upon their vegetables, would starve without it went a long way toward easing his guilt.

"Not everyone is blessed with a big ranch and lots of money."

Ryan took in the clenched jaw and flinty eyes and realized the boy was burdened by that guilt as well. *Poor lad.* It wasn't enough that he was too young to have to provide for his mother, but knowing he hadn't had the money to pay for her doctor's bills and food must have nearly killed the boy.

"Well, I'd suggest you make the best of a good opportunity then, lad. I've a mind to sign you on as a ranch hand. But you've got to pull your weight."

Mick's eyes narrowed. "Just what do I have to do?"

Ryan smiled. "For starters, you can get rid of that chip you're haulin' around on your shoulder."

Mick's look was subdued, but he managed to nod his head in agreement.

"We always rotate chores around the ranch house. Tonight's Sean's turn to cook, but Sean burns more than he cooks." Ryan paused, "If you feel ready to tackle the cooking, we'd be mighty grateful for stew and biscuits . . . but we're fresh out of squirrel."

Mick's grin was lightning fast. "Got any beef?"

Ryan chuckled, thinking of the cattle he'd nearly lost to rustlers the night before. "We just might find some for you, lad."

Thinking of how many head of cattle he'd added since his former boss, Ian McMaster, bequeathed the ranch to him had his mind turning toward the rest of his mentor's last wishes. As he, Flynn, and Reilly had stood around the dying man's bed, Ryan vowed that he would never turn away anyone in need of a job, a meal, or a place to stay. McMaster had taken them all in; they owed it to his memory to do the same.

The vow had never been hard to keep, and four of his more talented ranch hands had wandered onto his land in need of feeding and doctoring. Ryan had gladly taken them in. The obligation had always been a pleasure; the responsibility had helped him to keep his connection with the tough old Scot alive.

Looking down into the nearly translucent, but porcelain-perfect, face of Mick's mother, he sighed. *Had he taken on more than he could handle this time?*

His thoughts turned back to McMaster and how the wily old Scot had tricked the truth out of him. The old man's threats to turn Flynn and Reilly out if Ryan didn't tell him who, what, and where he was running from had him smiling now, but he hadn't smiled at the time. He might have to do the same to Mick. He sensed there was more to the young boy's story, too. The lurch of the wagon brought his thoughts back to the present.

"She'll be all right, Mick." He hoped the boy believed him, although Ryan could not look the lad in the eye when he made that promise. The boy's mother was literally skin and bones, with not a spare ounce of fat on her slender frame.

"I'm sure we can figure out what ails your mother. If not, Doc—"

"No!" The strangled rasp was close to a whisper, but Ryan heard her anyway. He bent his head closer and asked, "No what?"

"Doctors."

"But, Mrs. O'Toole—"

"No."

He straightened back up at the same moment she opened her eyes. A shadow flashed in their velvety brown depths. He felt so helpless, unable to ease her pain. The soft light of the early morning tinted the pale blue sky with slashes of rosy pink, adding a hint of that same color to her pale, sunken cheeks. Ryan's gut clenched in fear. *Would he be able to save this woman? Would he be able to discover the strange sickness she suffered from in time?*

"Promise me." Though weak, the determination in her voice came through clear as glass.

"No doctors," he vowed. Would he burn in hell for making a promise he would have to break? If he or Reilly couldn't help Mick's mother, then he'd be fetching the doctor out to the ranch, come hell or high water!

The weight, though slight, of the woman in his arms seemed to meld and become a part of him the longer he held her, sending a wave of protectiveness toward the needy pair sweeping over him, threatening his sanity. First desire had threatened to swamp him, now protectiveness. The homeless pair certainly pulled at him. He relaxed slightly and wondered who had been putting food in the boy and his mother's mouths these past few weeks while she lay ill.

His head started to ache at the base of his skull as he thought of someone else he needed to protect but could not even find! *Damnation, where was Maggie?*

A hideous thought followed the last one, driving the breath from his body. *Would Big John and the posse out of Amarillo finally track him down?* Five years' time passing went a long way toward making Ryan feel safe and secure in his new life with his new identity. But for the sake of his sister, and now Mick and his mother, he'd best be on the lookout for trouble.

"They're here!"

Ryan heard Reilly's shout from the bottom of the lane, as Mick drove the wagon up past the dilapidated barn he hoped to someday soon have the time and money to rebuild, if his sister arrived in time.

The woman in his arms stirred then whispered, "Mick?"

"Yeah, Ma?"

"Don't let anyone fuss over me."

"You're in need of fussing over," Ryan stated flatly.

"I don't need—"

"Aye, you do. You need someone to take care of you. God obviously has a sense of humor, as he's dropped you and Mick into my lap. Even so, I intend to do my best for the both of you."

His heart clenched at the thought of taking care of another woman. He'd gone down that road five years ago. Well, this time he'd not put his trust or his heart in the woman's hands, no matter how badly he was tempted. Placing his fate in the hands of the woman he loved was a risk he couldn't take, a mistake he couldn't make.

"Jamie?"

He looked over at his foreman. "Aye, Reilly?"

Reilly's gaze met his. "No word yet from Turner."

The worry that his sister would not arrive in time was driving him crazy. He needed the papers he'd entrusted to her care to help prove he owned every one of the precious, blessed acres McMaster had deeded to him two weeks before the old man died.

If the bloody crooked banker hadn't destroyed the other copies, Ryan wouldn't have had to send for his sister, and she'd still be safe and sound back in New York instead of missing somewhere in eastern Colorado. God, he hoped she was missing and not—

"She'll turn up." Reilly looked so sure of it, Ryan swallowed the knot of fear and nodded.

"What have we here?"

Reilly's question helped snap Ryan's focus back on the immediate problem at hand. Today Ryan would focus on making Mick and his mother feel welcomed and cared for. Tomorrow he would have time to worry about Maggie's whereabouts.

# CHAPTER 3

Three days later, Ryan was about to burst from the combined worry of his still-missing sister and his two new charges.

"Flynn," Ryan began, biting back a curse as the worry tying his guts into knots became painful. "What has Mrs. O'Toole eaten today?"

The two men stood facing one another on opposite sides of the kitchen, sipping strong coffee in an effort to wake up.

The redheaded man's eyes looked bleak. "Not enough to feed a damned bird."

Reilly opened the back door and swept the hat from his head, smacking it against his thigh. Dust billowed out from both the hat and Reilly's denim-clad leg. "Are we talking about Mrs. O'Toole again?"

"Aye," Flynn answered with a nod toward Ryan. "Himself thinks he has to keep his word to the lass."

Reilly and Flynn exchanged a long look while Ryan swallowed a mouthful of hot coffee. "I don't give my word not intending to keep it."

"Didn't you now?" Flynn quietly asked before taking a healthy drink from his own chipped, enameled mug.

"No." Ryan set his cup on the table and reached for one of the empty ones, filling it with steaming brew from the pot. Sloshing coffee on his wrist as he handed it to Reilly, he swore "Bleeding—"

"—buggering eedjit," Reilly finished for him. "We've heard

the expression a hundred times over these past few days. Can ye not think of another, then?" Reilly smiled over the rim of the cup Ryan handed him.

Ryan scowled at his men. How could he put into words how he felt about breaking his word to the fragile woman lying upstairs, wasting away with each breath she took. He'd broken it more times than he could count in the last five years, and each time he did, he added another black spot on his already pockmarked soul.

She hadn't eaten nearly enough to satisfy him, although Mick proclaimed she'd eaten more today than in the past three. "She's warm, but I don't think she's feverish."

"No obvious sign of sores or lesions. What can the lass be suffering from?" Reilly demanded.

"You've got to bring the doctor in." Flynn challenged Ryan over the rim of his cup.

"I gave my word."

"Are ye prepared to let the lass simply fade away? She's not strong enough to last another week without food!"

Ryan knew Flynn was right, but he hated breaking his promise.

"Ye gave your word," Reilly said with a nod. "I understand ye'll not want to break it. But ye're an intelligent man, Jamie. Ye know we need to summon the doctor."

The sound of hoofbeats rapidly approaching saved Ryan from having to answer.

Raised voices stirred Bridget from a fitful slumber. "Maggie, me darlin'!" She strained her ears, trying to hear more.

"Go on down and see who it is, Mick."

"I know who it is."

"How? You haven't looked yet?"

"Mr. Ryan's been expecting his sister for over a week now."

"Please, Mick?" Bridget waited for him to do as she asked. He slowly got up from the rocking chair by the side of her bed, as if he were reluctant to leave her, then leaned down to press a kiss to her forehead, as she had done so many times when Mick had been sick.

"I'll be right back." He paused in the doorway and turned back. "Do you need anything? Are you hungry?"

Truth be told, she was starving—literally. But her stomach could no longer tolerate food. Covering up the deep-rooted worry, Bridget managed a fleeting smile, "Not a thing. Hurry back."

To distract herself from thinking of her stomach and the hunger that churned and roiled in it, she closed her eyes, promising herself just a short rest.

Bridget's eyes flew open, and she knew she'd slept longer than she'd planned. Brilliant sunlight poured in through the window, highlighting the dust motes dancing and swirling on the breeze.

Bits and pieces of remembered conversations flitted through her mind. Lord, she felt so groggy. Struggling to clear her head, she tried remembering what she could. She remembered Mick leaving to go hunting, then the next thing she remembered was being carried in strongly muscled arms, held carefully against a rock-hard chest. Who had carried her? How much time had passed? Straining to recall, she remembered a rather stern, black-haired man with the most beautiful, deep blue eyes. His concern, and that of his men, had warmed her heart, but it had been days since she remembered seeing him.

More tired than she ever remembered being, Bridget closed her eyes and drifted back off to sleep. Caught in a web of dreams, she fought against walls of flame and then against angry fists.

Awake again, she still felt fuzzy. Had the room gone warm, or had she? Brushing a hand across her brow, she felt the dry, brittle heat coming off her forehead and neck in waves.

Too weak and tired to call out for help, Bridget closed her eyes, drifting off again. Surely someone would come back to check on her, wouldn't they?

Something cool and wet eased the heat from her cheeks and forehead. Her eyes fluttered open and met those of a blue-eyed redhead she didn't recognize.

"There now, yer not to worry at all." The woman's soft, lilting voice crooned.

"Who are you?" The cooling cloths had eased some of the heat, for which Bridget was eternally grateful.

"Jamie's sister."

"Ahh, the missing Maggie." Bridget's smile was fleeting.

"Ma?" Mick called from just beyond the closed door.

"Here's your boy now." Maggie turned and motioned for Mick to bring the tray into the room.

"Have a sip of water, then we'll work on getting some broth into you."

Bridget looked from Maggie to her son and back. She was beyond help and knew it. Needing to tell someone, and not wanting Mick to hear, she motioned for him to come closer. "Would you see if there is any coffee or tea to drink?"

His gaze met hers, and she knew he wasn't fooled, but the boy was smart enough to know when to make himself scarce. She hoped he wasn't going to stand outside in the hallway and listen.

He nodded, brushing a quick kiss to her brow, then left to do her bidding.

"Ye've raised a strong and carin' son, Mrs. O'Toole."

Bridget smiled. "He's all I have."

"Ye should be proud." Maggie paused. "He's worried about ye. Can ye not bring yerself to have a sip of broth, then?"

Bridget was afraid to try. All her other attempts to eat had failed miserably. Her stomach muscles still protested from the last time she'd eaten and promptly thrown it up.

Eyes narrowed, Maggie demanded, "When was the last time ye ate yer fill?"

Bridget tried to look away, but Maggie's blue-eyed stare pinned her, as Maggie softly added, "And yer boy is a picture of health. Obviously well fed." The other woman nodded as if she truly understood. "Me own parents would have starved themselves to see me and me brother fed."

Bridget's gaze darted about the room before settling back on Maggie's. There was no use to deny the truth when Maggie had guessed it. "He's the image of his father . . ."

"Ye must have loved him something fierce."

A single tear slipped past Bridget's guard. "I did. But he's been gone a long, long time."

"Why don't ye try a bit of bread soaked in broth. It'll build up yer strength, then ye can tell me about him."

Bridget hesitated then crumbled against the pillow. "I can't."

"Can't eat, or can't tell me about Mick's father?"

Bridget felt the tears before her brain registered the fact that she was crying. She wiped the tears away. "I've tried, but I can't keep any food down."

Maggie's gaze flickered, then she rose to fetch a bit of bread from the tray. "Me grandparents suffered, the same as ye are."

Bridget blinked. "Truly?"

"Aye. Me parents lived through the worst of the famine. The trick is to take it slowly. Small meals five or six times a day . . . bread soaked in broth, sweet tea, and plenty of water.

"I'd like to try, but I can't . . ."

"Trust me. I know what I'm about."

Bridget gave up, no match for the other woman's forceful personality. She hesitated, then decided it might help to share the heavy burden, of knowing she was starving herself in order to feed her son, with someone who would truly understand. "Do you promise not to say anything to Mick or your brother?"

Maggie paused, thoughtfully tapping a finger to her full lips, then smiled. "I will, if ye promise to eat a least half this slice of bread with half of that broth."

Mounting frustration and growing fear nearly had Bridget bursting into tears again. Only the knowledge that her son could come back at any moment kept her from breaking down and sobbing like a baby. She nodded and told Maggie how she and Mick had come to such dire straits, needing someone to step in and help them.

Maggie patted her hand as she fed Bridget another bit of broth-soaked bread. When she seemed satisfied Bridget had eaten all her shrunken stomach could handle, Maggie gave her a few more sips of water, then helped her to lie back down. "Rest. I'll be back, and I'll send Mick up too."

"Maggie?"

"Aye?"

"I'll be eternally grateful to both you and your brother."

"Go on with ye now." Maggie fussed with the napkin, setting it back on the tray before lifting the tray to rest on her hip. "Try to close yer eyes and rest."

"I will," Bridget promised, letting her eyes drift closed. Strangely, her stomach no longer roiled. It felt full, but not queasy. Her last thought before drifting off to sleep was that she would live to see Mick's thirteenth birthday. She wasn't going to die.

Bridget woke to the insistent, but gentle, shaking. Her eyes fluttered open and focused on the face so familiar, she'd seen it a hundred times in her dreams. "Michael, you've come back!"

"No, Ma. It's me. Mick!"

The worry in her son's voice broke through the cobwebs her fevered brain had conjured up.

"Mick, I was just dreaming . . ."

He laid his hand on her shoulder. "It's all right. I understand."

Mick's gut clenched as worry tangled with fear. Every word he'd overheard earlier as he stood outside his mother's slightly open door ran through his brain, making it feel like he imagined a droplet of water did as it hit the surface of a hot cast-iron skillet. He wondered why his head didn't sputter, spit, and then just evaporate in a cloud of steam.

While he watched, his mother's eyes slowly closed before she fell back into what he worried was a fevered sleep. Hands in fists at his sides, he stood staring down at the woman who had loved him all of his life. The one who had tried to shelter him from harsh words and hateful gossip as they moved from town to town. She'd worked until her back bowed under the strain of standing over a washtub, scrubbing other people's clothes. Her hands were callused, not smooth like the ladies he'd seen at the Rusty Spur.

Funny how some of the richer ladies in town had always said the same things about his ma that they'd said about them fancy pieces of female who served drinks and did what he could only imagine in the upstairs rooms of the Rusty Spur. And he could imagine plenty!

He shook his head. His ma wasn't like them; she was a hard-working, devoted mother who'd starved herself to feed him. Guilt welled up from his toes to his knees, surging up to his chest. He'd only just realized what she'd done for him, and he couldn't forgive himself for not noticing sooner. He swayed before getting a grip on emotions he couldn't let take over. Careful not to disturb her, Mick pulled the cover up over her shoulder, tucking it under her chin. Sweeping the hair off her forehead, as she had done for him countless times as a child, he felt the heat pouring off her in waves. For a moment he didn't know what to do; fear for his mother had every drop of spit drying up in his mouth. If she needed him to call out for help just then, he knew he couldn't.

But while he couldn't speak, he could still move. He was out of the door like a shot, pounding down the stairs in search of help.

Ryan heard the back door slam open and looked up in time to see Mick burst through it like a bullet, before stumbling down the porch steps drunkenly.

"Flynn!" Ryan hit the bottom stairs in time to catch Mick. "Easy now, lad. Breathe in slow. That's it. Now, bend down. Concentrate. Breathe in slow and out slow."

Holding the boy's head between his knees, Ryan nodded as Flynn joined him. "Must have had quite a scare to lose your breath like that."

Mick's pale face was all Ryan needed to see to know what had scared him. "Flynn. Stay here while Mick gets his wind back." Mick's gaze pinned his, and Ryan assured the boy, "I'll take care of your mother."

Ryan didn't start to run until he heard the back door close with a thud. His long legs took the stairs three at a time. No more than five minutes had passed since Mick had stumbled out of the door when Ryan reached Bridget's side.

He could see that she had been covered up, but the blanket now lay in a heap on the floor. Her white cotton nightgown had worked its way up to mid-thigh, exposing long, lithe legs. A stronger man would have been able to ignore the punch of lust hitting Ryan in the gut as he walked toward the bed. Consumed with worry and responsibilities at the ranch, he had been too busy lately to ride on over to the Desert Rose. He had gone too long without a warm and willing woman, and his body let him know just how anxious it was to do something about it.

Stifling the curse burning the tip of his tongue, he stepped up to the side of the bed, grabbed the edge of her nightgown and pulled it down to her toes. Once she was covered, the sharp edge of lust dulled to a thick ache. The ache he could deal with. The white-hot need—well, he'd think about that later. Right now, Bridget and Mick both needed him. Mick was in Flynn's capable hands, leaving Ryan to tend to Bridget.

His sister had left a fresh linen cloth next to the washbasin. He dipped the soft cloth into the now-tepid water. Wringing out most of the water, he placed the cool, moist cloth on Bridget's forehead. Her soft moan made his stomach clench.

Berating himself for paying too much attention to the way his body reacted around the fragile woman, Ryan focused on trying to bring her fever down. He traced the line of her jaw and curve of her cheek with the cloth. Each time the cloth smoothed over her too-hot flesh, Bridget let out a small moan.

He hoped to God it wasn't pain she was feeling. Dipping the cloth into the water again, he brushed it over her cheeks and chin, patiently repeating the process until the cloth finally seemed to be as cool as the water. He'd drawn most of the heat from her face, but each time his fingertips brushed her neck, the heat still pulsed strongly there.

Giving in to the inevitable, he opened the top three buttons of her nightgown and pressed the cool cloth to the base of her throat. The soft intake of breath surprised him. It wasn't a moan this time. Maybe the cloth was too cool. Determined to help break her fever, as his sister had explained how to do earlier, he dipped the cloth again. A noise outside caught his attention. He looked over toward the window, then back, and nearly swallowed his tongue. His cloth-filled hand rested against Bridget's chest, but it wasn't the sight of his large, work-roughened hand lying against the alabaster of her skin that caused the reaction.

The chill of the cloth against the heat of her fevered body had the sleeping woman's breasts pearling against the sheer white of her gown. He shook his head and told himself to look away, but couldn't. The sight robbed him of speech.

"Eedjit! You're here to take care of the woman, not—"

"Not what?"

Ryan jolted, dropping the freshly dipped cloth. It landed with a squishy plop on the floor. "You're awake?"

"I am now." Bridget's eyes were bright, too bright, and glassy with fever.

"You need to drink more water. You're body's fighting to get better, but you have to help it along."

"Where's Maggie? She was here when I fell asleep."

Bridget sounded a bit lost, befuddled. Ryan suspected she felt as disoriented as he did, only for different reasons. "She's in town; she'll be back soon."

"Where's Mick?"

"Well, now, he's the reason I'm here." Ryan stooped to pick up the cloth. Turning his back on Bridget helped him to steer his thoughts away from her delectable body and onto safer ground. "He came tearing out of the house. Something must have frightened him. The lad could barely catch his breath."

"I wonder what it was?"

God love her, the woman actually stopped to consider what was wrong with her son, when it was obvious to Ryan that *she* was the problem.

"He's worried about you."

"That's silly. I'm fine—"

Ryan straightened to his full height. "You will be. But you aren't yet. You need to rest, eat, and drink more."

Bridget narrowed her eyes. "I can take care of myself."

Ryan ignored the annoyed tone of her voice, stomped to the side of the bed, and bit out, "You're doin' such a fine job of it now that yer starvin' yerself and ye don't even seem to realize it!"

"Maggie told you?"

*No,* he'd finally reasoned it out for himself. "Maggie didn't have to tell me. I've seen men starving before. I've just never known one to do it intentionally before."

The censure of his words hung in the air, like greasy smoke from a cook fire.

Bridget opened her mouth to speak, but he cut her off, not willing to hear what she had to say. "You'll do as you're told from now on. You'll eat what I say, when I say."

The daggers shooting out her eyes should have given him fair warning that she didn't take too kindly to being ordered about. *Too bad.*

"I take no orders from any one, even when they may be given with good intentions."

Ryan placed his hands on his hips, bending forward until his face was an inch from hers. He could feel the anger radiating from him and knew his temper was spiking, but the woman was being so difficult. "Ye'll do as I say, and like it—for Mick's sake."

Bridget crumpled at his words. He'd known the mention of her son would get her to agree to what he wanted, but he hadn't expected her to fold so quickly.

Ryan nearly felt sorry for her, until he looked back at her and saw the hollows in her cheeks where there should be flesh to spare. Anger spiked again. In order to tamp it down, he thought of how often he could get a rise out of his sister by playing on her sympathies. Likely Bridget O'Toole would be as easy to figure out. Hell, all he'd have to do was mention Mick's name, and she'd likely do whatever he wanted her to.

"You need to rest."

Bridget turned away and slumped down in the bed, dejection

evident in every line of her body. He sat down on the edge of the bed and reached out for her hand. It lay limp and lifeless in his. "I'm a good listener, if you want to talk about it."

Bridget turned back toward him, staring down at her hand resting is his. She swallowed audibly, then cleared her throat. "I've yet to thank you for your kindness to Mick and me."

Ryan started to push away, but she continued. "You may not want our thanks, but it's all we have to give in return. I haven't any money. But once I'm well again, I intend to make it up to you. I can cook, clean—"

His simmering temper shot straight to boil. Pushing up off the bed, he stalked to the door; fists clenched, and nearly put one of them through the wood panel. The overwhelming need to explain stopped him and had him turning back. "I don't need or want your thanks for doing what I was brought up to believe was expected. If someone I know is ill, I tend to them. If they need help building a new barn, I bring over a wagon loaded with planks of wood and my tools."

Ryan dropped his hands to his sides and stared up at the ceiling. *How can I make this thickheaded woman understand?*

"Your parents must be exceptional people, James."

Something warm flowed through him, loosening all the tight little knots of tension at the sound of his given name on her lips. His head whipped around and he pinned her with a look. "They were."

"Oh." Bridget's hand went to her heart. "I'm so sorry. You must miss them."

"It makes them seem closer when I do as they would have done." He walked back over to the bed. "I'm only trying to do the right thing. Mick and you need my help. Let me help you, Bridget. Let me help your boy."

Her eyes filled at his words. She tried to blink them away, but couldn't. Big, fat tears rolled down her cheeks. Her eyes reddened and her nose started to run. Their hands reached for the handkerchief on the bedside table at the same moment. For a heartbeat, neither one moved. Ryan's big hand clutching the linen cloth, while Bridget's much smaller one held on to his thumb.

Eyes swimming with tears, nose running, Bridget O'Toole felt her whole world grinding to a stop. Her heart lurched and her stomach fell all the way to her feet. Feelings for this man bombarded her as he handed her the handkerchief, holding it for her, ordering her to blow her nose.

She didn't want to feel anything for any man. She'd spent too many years loving the one who'd deserted her. Then the one time she trusted her heart again, the man had used his fists on her.

When Ryan ordered her to blow her nose again, her thoughts jerked back to the present. She couldn't afford to let her heart lead her down the wrong path again. She just wasn't up to the heartache that would surely follow.

Placing her trust in him would be difficult, but the man all but demanded that she do so while she recovered. Her mind raced, trying to figure everything out. Mick needed a place to stay, food, and tasks to keep his hands busy so he wouldn't get into trouble again. Heaven only knew how they ended up at James Ryan's ranch or what her boy had been hunting. Time would tell. She could always ask Maggie. Surely she'd know and would be willing to tell Bridget.

"If I accept your hospitality and help with my son, you must accept my terms in return."

When he bristled, she raced on. "When I feel recovered, you'll not stop me from pitching in where I think I am needed."

He rose to his feet and turned his back to her. Bridget wished she could see the expression on his face. Such a handsome face. Strong jaw, probably like granite, should anyone try to test it with a fist. She remembered how long her own had ached when . . . she shook her head, resolving not to think about that time in her life. It was over. *She'd survived. Mick had survived.*

They would move on when she was well. This time Mick might not want to go, but he would go. She couldn't think of life without her son. Wouldn't think of it.

Ryan turned back. "If I think you are overdoing it, you'll not wonder long. I will tell you."

Their gazes met and held, neither one giving an inch. She admired him for that. What he thought of her, she could only speculate. The sudden realization that he didn't frighten her speared through her, leaving her light-headed. Here stood a man well over six feet tall, raw-boned and muscled, with big broad shoulders and immense hands callused from working his land, but not once had she felt any tinge of fear when he was alone with her. Somehow she sensed he would rather break one of his own hands than so much as bruise one of hers. Comforted by that realization, and the further one that James Ryan seemed to care what happened to her son, Bridget settled back down against the pillows and closed her eyes.

At the sound of the door handle being turned, she opened one eye. He stood in the doorway, looking at her. Her other eye shot open as the heat from his gaze scorched her. Raw desire ripped through her, leaving her feeling weaker than the fever that had just broken.

Before she could speak, the look in his eyes changed. Like a shutter being closed, or a shade being drawn, the desire in his eyes was wiped out until only concern remained. He turned and walked out the door.

Her thoughts in turmoil, her heart beating madly, Bridget knew it would be a long time before she fell back to sleep. Reaching for the glass he had thoughtfully left within reach, she drank the cool water, all the while wondering how she'd ever cool the newly awakened desire for the man who opened his home and his heart to them. "A dip in the horse trough, most likely."

"A fine suggestion, but I don't think the horses like finding people in their drinkin' water."

"Maggie? I didn't see you there."

"Obviously," the other woman said with a grin.

"I thought you were in town?"

"I was. Now I'm back."

Bridget watched Maggie bustle into the bedroom with another tray in hand. "I suppose you're going to make me eat again."

"Count on it. We can either do this the easy way, or I can pinch yer nose closed and shove the bread down yer throat. Either way, ye'll eat."

Bridget sputtered and started to protest, but the look in Maggie's eyes stopped her. Pure animal stubbornness recognized its own kind. But right now, Maggie was on her feet and in fighting form, while Bridget lay on her back in bed, too exhausted to sit up half the time. For now, Maggie could tell her what to do. Bridget was smart enough to realize that she'd have to do it. Like it or not, Maggie wanted her to get well as badly as Maggie's brother did.

"You and your brother are two of a kind, you know."

"Aye. Both hardheaded as me da's old mule. I have a permanent lump on me shin where the blasted creature kicked me years ago."

Conversation was so easy with Maggie, Bridget didn't realize she'd eaten every bit of broth and bread until Maggie announced that she'd see if there was another bit left in the pan on the stovetop.

"No. Thank you, I'm full."

Maggie's eyes narrowed.

"Truly. And I ate two whole slices of bread tonight," Bridget pointed out.

"Well now, sure and I'd be fallin' on me face, if I'd only eaten that little." Patting her generous hip, Maggie laughed. "If only I could be as slender as ye be . . . but not for the same reasons."

Bridget marveled that someone with Maggie's voluptuous figure would want to be reed thin. "But you've such curves. Why would you want to be any different?"

Maggie laughed out loud. "Isn't it always the way? The good Lord gives us one thing, and we want another entirely."

Picking up the tray and resting it on her hip, Maggie bent over Bridget and smoothed the tips of her fingers across Bridget's brow. "Yer much cooler. 'Tis a good thing."

Bridget flushed, remembering how it felt when James had brushed his fingers across her brow.

Maggie's eyes narrowed. "Are ye feelin' poorly again?"

Bridget cleared her throat. "No . . . yes. I . . . I don't know."

The concern in Maggie's eyes went right to Bridget's heart. She had to make Maggie understand. It wasn't the fever from her illness that threatened to consume her; it was the fever of desire. How could she possibly confide in Maggie that Maggie's brother made Bridget's heart pound and her stomach flutter?

Never one to mince words, Bridget decided just to say it. But before she could say anything, Maggie smiled. "Well now that explains why me brother lit out of the house like his tail was on fire."

Bridget's mouth opened, then closed. *What could she possibly say now?*

Maggie smiled. "He's a fine lookin' man. Many's the lass back home who would've counted herself the lucky one, if me hardheaded brother ever asked one to wed. There was Moira

McGee, Shelia O'Brien. Oh, and how could I forget Katherine—"

"Maggie!" Bridget sputtered, embarrassed that she'd felt the spurt of jealousy at the mention of the women who'd loved James back home.

Maggie just laughed again, hoisted the tray back up, and promised to be back later.

Now mentally and physically exhausted, Bridget scooted down under the covers and snuggled against the feather pillows. How fortunate for her neither Moira, Shelia, nor Katherine were here at James's ranch. *She* was. She intended to stay until she was well, and then she planned on paying James back for all the kindness he'd shown them so far.

Whether he wanted her to or not, she'd be washing his clothes and cooking his meals before he realized she was at it. Bridget drifted off to sleep planning out how and when she could slip out of bed to wash a tubful of dirty shirts without James or one of his ranch hands being the wiser.

Contentment flowed through her as her breathing deepened and her head grew heavy. Maybe tomorrow she'd feel well enough to get up. If not tomorrow, definitely the day after.

# CHAPTER 4

The smoke blinded her. She couldn't find her way to the cabin door! God help her, she needed to get the baby, but she couldn't find his cradle.

Stumbling, sobbing, she thrashed her way to where she thought the cradle would be, as an ominous crackling sounded right behind her.

"Mick!"

Her cry was swallowed up by the rush of flames as it ate its way through the north wall of the cabin. She tamped down on her fear, put her head down, and dashed toward the flames.

"Bridget?"

Where was he? Why couldn't she find him? Dear God, help me find him!

*"Bridget!"*

The sound of her name being called finally broke through the nightmare, as did the teasing scent on the night wind. Leather, fresh-cut grass, and a hint of horse.

*James.*

The brush of callused fingertips across her brow pulled her the rest of the way free from the depths of darkness. Her eyes opened and slowly focused in the flickering candlelight. The breeze from the open window brought another wisp of scent past her nose. She breathed deeply, oddly soothed by it.

"There's a lass. Are you all right?"

Concern added an edge to his voice. Being pulled from his

bed in the middle of the night added a husky quality to it that pulled at her belly. Still groggy from the nightmare, she wondered about the desire she'd seen in his gaze earlier. Licking her dry lips, she nodded. She was all right, just confused. She only saw concern in his eyes. Did he no longer desire her, or did the fever have her seeing things that were not there?

"I heard you cry out. I thought something was wrong." He shifted from one foot to the other. The motion had her looking down at his feet, his *bare feet.*

She swallowed. Her tongue felt thick. It had been too many years to count since she'd seen a man without his boots or socks.

Her gaze slid up from his toes to his denim-clad knees and promptly got stuck as she stared at sun-browned skin one inch above the top button of his pants. Oh good Lord. He was shirtless! Thoughts of how his chest would look, how the muscles would form and meld into one another, had heat flushing her cheeks. *Did she dare to peek at his chest to see if it equaled her imagination?*

"Here now, are you feverish again?"

His concern was her undoing. She moaned out his name, unable to help herself.

He was at her side before she could stop him. Held against the strength of his chest, Bridget melted. It had been so very long. She hadn't leaned on anyone since Michael, hadn't wanted to. Especially after the way the townspeople treated her when she arrived in town with baby Mick in tow. No one believed that Michael O'Toole had gotten married, least of all to a nobody like Bridget Garahan. The words hurt then, and they still hurt now.

She shuddered.

James's arms tightened around her, then he began to stroke the back of her head with the tips of his fingers, easing the tension out of it. *Heaven*. His strong fingers were so clever. She couldn't help but relax against him as his fingers started working on her neck and shoulders. Warmth pooled low in her belly, spreading up her back, wrapping around to her heart. His touch was so gentle, his fingers so strong, yet they massaged her aching muscles with a deftness that showed he knew how to care for someone weaker than himself.

Although she ached for something more, his touch didn't ignite passion in her; it was all about healing and caring. Bridget's heart fluttered at his touch. It had been too many years to count since someone had actually taken care of her. She had been the rock Mick had leaned on for the last thirteen years. To have that load suddenly lifted from her shoulders, if only for a short while, eased the constant ache in her heart. For the moment she wasn't alone. She had James.

When Bridget melted against him, Ryan thought he'd go up in flames. Keeping his need for her in check was slowly killing him. He felt as if he were roasting alive on a spit, knowing he should only move his hands if they sought to comfort, not to excite. His hands should only ease tension from knotted muscles, not want to smooth across silky skin, eliciting tiny flames of desire as he stroked the path from Bridget's ankle up to the back of her knee.

He swallowed against the lump forming in his throat. God, he wanted to touch her. *All of her.* Her comfort was the last thought on his mind. His body ached, need too strong to ignore burning in his gut. But he had promised himself when he heard her cry out that he would only go into her room to see if she was all right. Not to trace the satiny skin of her face with the tips of his fingers . . . or run the tip of his tongue along the rim of her pretty mouth, before plunging deep, tasting the honeyed sweetness he was certain waited for his questing tongue.

Sucking in a much-needed breath of air, Ryan fought against

the urge to curse in Gaelic. The words formed in his mind, tripping down to this tongue, when he heard a sound from the other side of the room.

"What was that?"

"Hmmm?"

He loosened his hold and leaned her back against the pillow and rounded the bed. "Mick, lad, what are you doing sleeping on the floor when you've a perfectly good bed right next door?"

"I didn't know he was there," Bridget whispered, watching him start to squat down next to her son. "No," she said, when Ryan tried to move him, "let him be. He's tired."

Ryan nodded and straightened back up. *There was a cot on the third floor. He could set it up in here for tomorrow. The boy should be sleeping in a bed.*

Just then Mick mumbled something more in his sleep and turned over, kicking off the blanket he'd tossed on earlier. Ryan stared down at Mick, trying to decide if he should lower the boy's leg until it was flat on the floor again, or let him sleep with his leg bent all night.

"I'd leave him be." Bridget was sitting up on the bed, looking at her son with her heart in her eyes. He'd seen the same sort of look in his own mother's eyes, when she thought he wasn't paying attention.

Ryan's heart ached just a bit to be loved like that again. No questions asked, just loved for who you were, not what someone wanted you to be, or whom you thought you should be.

"He always sleeps like a log." Bridget smiled up at James. "Heaven help me, if I needed to move him during the night, I couldn't. He's grown so much this last year."

"You've taken better care of your son than you have of yourself."

Bridget bristled at his words, though she knew them to be true. "And what business is it of yours if I have?"

Ryan smoothed the covers over Mick as the boy turned back onto his side, facing the window. He slowly rose to his feet, his gaze never wavering as he spoke, "I made it my business the night I made the decision to save Mick from himself."

Confusion slid through her, chilling her. She rubbed her arms to warm them. "I don't understand."

Ryan sighed and ran a hand through his hair, making it stand up for a moment before falling back down against his skull. "I don't suppose you know where Mick ended up the night we met?"

A frisson of fear added to the chill she already felt. She started to shake. Ryan looked as if he wanted to wrap his arms around her again, but somehow she knew it wouldn't be to comfort her. Angry with herself for not being able to keep her thoughts off the rancher's beautiful face and rock-hard body, she asked abruptly, "Why don't you tell me how the two of you met?"

Mick stirred in his sleep again. This time he half sat up, opened his eyes, and then rubbed them. "Mr. Ryan. What are you doing in here?"

Ryan turned toward her boy and calmly answered, "Your mother had a nightmare. I came to make sure she was all right."

"Oh. She has those a lot."

Bridget was shocked. She didn't know she cried out at night. She thought her tortured dreams remained inside her head. Dear Lord, she tortured her boy with them as well? Guilt sluiced through her, and like hot oil, stuck to her, burning her.

"I . . . I do?"

"Sure you do, Ma." Mick scrubbed at his face, waking the rest of the way. "You're always calling me. So I come in to see what you want. But you never wake up. You just keep calling."

Bridget was almost too afraid to ask, but she bore down on her fear and whispered, "What do you do?"

Mick looked away, embarrassed. "Aww, I just sit there, hold

your hand, and tell you I'm right here." His gaze darted over toward Ryan, then he added, "Sooner or later you believe me and fall back to sleep."

Ryan crouched down beside her son once more. "You don't have to be embarrassed about caring for your mother."

When Mick nodded, Ryan went on to say, "I wish I had been there for my mother."

Bridget heard the regret in his voice and wanted to ask about his mother, but Ryan's next words stopped her cold.

"But I was off searching for my place in the world. I thought I'd found it, but I was mistaken."

"Where did you leave your mother?"

Bridget blessed Mick's curiosity. He'd asked what she wanted to.

"In New York City with me da and me sister."

Did he know how his voice changed when he spoke of his family and home? She doubted it. She'd have to ask him about that sometime, to see if he realized he slid into the musical lilt of his native homeland.

"Well, you didn't leave her all alone, then."

Ryan sat down on the floor next to Mick. "My da was ailing and me sister wasn't that sure of herself back then. She'd only just lost the man she was to marry."

"Maggie was married?"

"Nay, lass. He died the week before they were to wed . . . in her arms."

Pain and sorrow wound their way through Bridget, tangling up in her confused reaction to the black-haired rancher. He was kind to her son; he was kind to her. He treated his men well and offered Mick and her a place to stay when they hadn't a hope of sleeping on anything but the rock-hard ground outside. Why then did she detect a note of guilt in the man's voice over Maggie's husband-to-be's death? And why did he sound guilty about not staying in New York with his parents and sister?

Ready to ask the questions burning in her mind, she opened her mouth to speak, but Mick's next statement stopped her.

"We're grateful to you for taking us in, Mr. Ryan. I know my ma doesn't know why you did it, but I do. And I'll be in your debt forever."

Ryan ruffled her son's hair and got to his feet. "You two had best get some rest now. Morning's just a few hours away."

"I'll be down to make breakfast. It's my turn."

Ryan nodded at the boy. "Will you be making biscuits?"

Mick snorted, "I could get Flynn and Reilly to do all my chores for me so long as I promised them an unending supply of biscuits."

Ryan's laugh was low and rumbling. "That you could, lad. That you could."

His gaze swept the room, as if checking to see that all was in its place. Satisfied, he nodded, then looked over to where Bridget still sat on the bed. Her heart turned over in her breast. Refusing to acknowledge the emotion twisting through her for what it truly was, she met his gaze.

"Sleep sweet, Bridget O'Toole."

As quickly as that, her heart tumbled the rest of the way. She was his for the asking.

# CHAPTER 5

Ryan mentally kicked himself in the backside all the way to his room. An hour later, still wide awake, he gave up the fight, splashed water on his face, washed up, and dressed for the day. "No point in trying to sleep when there's no sleep in sight," he mumbled, stumbling into the kitchen.

"What's that yer grumblin'?" Reilly said from where he sat in the dark at the kitchen table.

"What are you doing up this early?"

"Couldn't sleep. Seems some people like to have tea parties, gabbin' in the middle of the night, keepin' hard-workin' men from their sleep."

Ryan grumbled, but apologized for waking Reilly. It was going to be a long day if the both of them were tired at the start of it. He'd learned early on with Reilly that once the gruff man had some coffee in him, he was a whole lot easier to handle.

The familiar motions of grinding the beans and adding them to the pot of water soothed the rough edges of his temper. He'd nearly acted on impulse upstairs, and that would have been a mistake. Ryan placed the pot on the stovetop, thankful that Reilly had started the fire in the cookstove before he sat down to brood at the kitchen table.

Sitting in the dark room while the coffee slowly heated to boiling soothed the raw edge off Ryan's temper . . . and put the final cap on his desire for the dark-haired woman sleeping upstairs.

"Why are you up?" Reilly finally demanded.

Ryan didn't want to talk about it, so he stalled by asking Reilly if he had gone out to gather eggs yet. Reilly's answer was short, rude, and physically impossible. Ryan grabbed a cup, filled it with coffee, and offered it to the other man.

"I'm still not puttin' me hand under a cranky chicken at this hour of the mornin', even for the likes of you, Jamie, me lad."

Before Ryan could think of a proper insult, Mick announced from the doorway, "I'll be making biscuits this morning. Scones, if you'd rather."

"The boy is a godsend, Jamie. A godsend!"

Reilly got up and walked out the back door, but not without stooping down to snag the basket they used for egg gathering.

"Well I'll be."

"He's just mad, feeling protective of your sister, 'cause of the way the marshal rode off without saying a proper goodbye to her, knowing how she feels about Marshal Turner."

"Maggie and the marshal?" Ryan couldn't quite get his thoughts around the idea of it.

"Didn't you see the way she looked at him the night he rode here with her?"

Ryan shook his head.

"Then I don't suppose you noticed the way he was looking at her."

"I'll kill him."

"Why?"

"Because . . . because he shouldn't be looking at me sister."

"But you just said you didn't see the way he was looking at her."

"Doesn't much matter. He shouldn't be looking at my Maggie."

"Why?" Mick sounded like he really wanted to know.

Ryan couldn't exactly put it into words, but it just wasn't

right, another man he liked and respected taking a liking to his sister. Not after what happened with Rory Muldoon. He closed his eyes and groaned. He hadn't ever asked Maggie if she'd gotten over Muldoon's death. God help him, he hadn't. Rory was his best friend from the time they both learned to walk. Leaving Ireland had been easier with Rory gone.

Since he didn't have the words to explain, he just said the first thing that came to mind. "If you had a sister, you'd understand."

"I think I'd be a good brother, if I ever had a chance to have a sister." Mick's voice sounded far away . . . thoughtful.

Ryan couldn't imagine life without his sister and his parents. His self-imposed estrangement these last five years had been by his choice. But before that he'd had a family. And it had made all the difference in the world.

"Well, sisters are a pack of trouble."

The sharp intake of breath coming from behind them was his only warning. "And brothers are like poking a sharp stick in yer eye!"

"Maggie. I didn't know you were there."

"Obviously."

"Are you up to making us breakfast?"

"I thought I heard Mick say he was making biscuits and scones?"

"Well, if you'd rather cook—" Mick slowly began.

"Why don't we work together this morning," Maggie offered.

Mick smiled and agreed. The morning passed—slowly, but it passed.

Right after the midday meal, Maggie and Mick were in the kitchen and heard a commotion coming from the barn. The sound of a familiar voice had Mick heading out the back door to stand on the porch. *Marshal Turner was back.* Mick was hesitant, but Maggie rushed out the back door, leaving him standing on the porch wondering if he should follow. Before he could, she was back, her eyes all red and misty. Mick wanted to ask her what happened, but she held herself so rigid, he knew by the way she stood she didn't want to talk about it.

Mick heard shouts from the direction of the barn, but he was more concerned with the woman who was here in the kitchen with him, trying not to cry. She reminded him of his mother . . .

"Maggie! Open the door!"

She ignored the command, and shoved hard on the door—and the marshal's hand.

Though the marshal shouted for her to let him in, she only eased up enough for him to slip his hand out, then continued to put her weight against the door, not budging. Mick added his weight to hers to keep the door closed, figuring that if she didn't want the marshal inside, then he would help her keep the man on the outside.

While Maggie and the marshal traded insults and threats, the door slowly pushed inward. In the end, they were helpless to keep it shut.

Suddenly the marshal was inside.

"Go get Flynn or Reilly!" Maggie urged.

Mick thought about stepping between them, but the way the marshal was looking at Maggie stopped him. He'd seen that look before—recently. James Ryan looked at his mother that way. He began to wonder if that meant what he hoped it did.

"Why didn't you tell me Seamus is your brother?" the marshal demanded.

"I didn't think I'd need to explain my family to the likes of you!" Maggie bit out. "Why should you care?"

Mick went down the hall and out the front door in search of the redheaded ranch hand. He hadn't seen Reilly since the man had stomped into the kitchen with a basketful of eggs. "Why does it matter what name Mr. Ryan goes by?" he wondered out loud. " 'Course even I know Maggie is James's sister." And he'd heard her call him Seamus enough times that he asked her why. She'd laughed and explained that James is the Americanization of Seamus. Mick was surprised a smart man like the marshal didn't know that.

"Flynn?" Mick called out, stepping onto the front porch as he spotted the redheaded ranch hand heading around back toward the barn.

"Who's Maggie arguing with?" Flynn wanted to know, changing direction and heading toward the porch.

". . . traveling west to be married . . ."

Mick grinned, "The marshal," and tried not to laugh at the ridiculous conversation they could hear bits and pieces of as the walked down the hallway.

". . . to me brother? Are ye daft?"

The sight in the kitchen was worth a chuckle: two people standing with their hands on their hips, swapping insults. Before he or Flynn could say anything, the marshal pulled Maggie into his arms and kissed her, just as Reilly burst into he kitchen.

"Jamie's gone into town to confront that crooked banker with his proof!"

The marshal set Maggie aside and lit out the back door. The set of his jaw made Mick feel a bit better. So long as the marshal was on his side, he wouldn't worry about making the man mad. But if he were that banker . . .

"He's got the deed now. There's no stopping him," Reilly said, following him outside.

"I thought you said the banker was trying to take the ranch away from him." Mick was worried about the man who'd taken them in. "Isn't it dangerous to just walk into the man's office?"

As they stood on the back porch watching Ryan's figure in the distance heading toward town, Reilly added, "Aye, lad, but the marshal here is just leaving, heading out that way as it were."

As the marshal turned his horse toward the lane, the sound of shots being fired galvanized the rest of the ranch hands into action.

"Go back inside, Mick!" Maggie shouted. "And for heaven's sake, lad, don't stand in front of the window!"

Mick nodded, too startled by the sound of gunshots to move at first. Then he got up his gumption and stole a peek out the window. He could see the marshal had his rifle in one hand and his Colt in the other as five armed men came riding up the lane, guns blazing.

Before Mick could think to enter into the fray, the battle was over. The armed men were trussed up like geese for Sunday dinner. And still Maggie and the marshal were arguing. Before the argument could escalate, Reilly calmly reminded them that Ryan had probably gotten to town by now.

The marshal and one of Ryan's men headed off into town. When they returned, Ryan had to help the marshal down off his horse.

Mick could tell by the way the marshal swayed that he'd been shot. It took Maggie a little longer. "Mick, fetch me sewing basket!"

Mick didn't wait for explanations. He knew the marshal had been badly hurt. Not that he wanted to stick around and watch while Maggie sewed him back up, but a small part of him did.

"Doc's here!"

Flynn's cry had Mick's heart settling down. At least the doctor should know how to stitch a man back together after his arm had been ripped apart by a bullet. Shouldn't he?

Ryan walked into the hallway and saw Mick standing there, watching Maggie. He pulled Mick by the arm, and led him out the front door.

"But I wasn't really listening . . ."

"It's all right, lad. I'd be listening too, if your mother hadn't told me not to."

"She did?" Eyes round with wonder, Mick waited for Ryan to say more.

"Aye. She said the marshal needed a moment alone to propose to my sister."

"How does my mother know that that is what he wants to do?"

Ryan shrugged, then laughed. "Far be it from me to argue with a woman, lad."

"Is it something I should know not to do?"

"Aye. Never argue with a woman. You'll never win."

As the two strolled out the door and down the steps, a cry of happiness echoed through the house. "Let's give them a little time alone," Ryan suggested.

By the time they rounded the side of the house and were headed around the back, Maggie and the marshal burst outside, grinning like two fools who had been in the sun too long and had had every ounce of sense baked out of their brains.

"I guess it's official then," Flynn said, coming to join them.

"About time," Reilly said with a nod.

"What?" Mick demanded. *What was official? What was about time?*

"We're getting married!" Maggie announced, her face like a beam of sunlight, her feet barely touching the ground.

Mick wondered what it would be like to see his mother that happy, with her face glowing and her feet dancing. *Worth every moment it would take to get her there.* He began to wonder if maybe he could push her in that direction, if he were very careful not to let her know what he was up to. Maybe . . . possibly . . . it could be done.

He knew which man he wanted to push his mother toward.

With a little help from Flynn and Reilly, he just might make it happen.

# CHAPTER 6

"You're lookin' well this mornin', lass."

Bridget looked over her shoulder and smiled. She felt wonderful. "You're not going to wheedle an extra scone out of me with flattery, Mr. Flynn."

"Scones!"

"Back off, Reilly, the lass is baking scones for meself," Flynn said with grim determination.

Bridget set the tray on top of the stove and whirled around, hands on hips. "If either of you thinks I'm still not strong enough to knock you both senseless if you try to snitch any scones, think again."

"Now why would you want to go and do a thing like that, lass?" Flynn wanted to know. The redheaded ranch hand scratched his head and waited for her to answer.

"She's feelin' put out is all," Reilly answered, taking a step closer to the stove.

"Mr. Reilly—"

"Now, lass," Reilly began, "we've told ye before, ye don't need the 'Mister' in front of our names."

"Reilly's right. Ye can call us 'Paddy' for all we care, just don't call us late for scones." Flynn flashed his boyish grin her way.

"You two men are the—"

"Dearest?" Flynn added.

"Most helpful?" Reilly offered.

"Laziest?" a deep voice suggested.

"James!" Bridget spun back around, her hand to her heart. Ryan's brows lowered as his clear blue eyes hardened, focusing on her. "What are you doing up?"

Bridget didn't know whether to smack him upside the head for being difficult, or be grateful for his concern. The last few weeks had been the slowest of her life, but she really felt she had turned the corner and was on her way to feeling like her old self again. She'd go so far as to say she felt fully recovered. She'd gained back some of the weight. Besides, even if she hadn't, she'd go absolutely stir crazy if she sat idle for another day!

She met his glare with a wry smile and snipped, "It should be obvious. Cooking."

The look on the man's face was telling; he didn't appreciate or approve of her working, or of her answer.

"Oh, let the lass alone." Flynn moved a step closer to her, as if to protect her from the lash of Ryan's temper. She was touched.

"Aye, she seems fit enough to me." Reilly slid behind Flynn.

Bridget noticed the movement, but didn't realize what the men intended to do until Reilly reached out and grabbed a hot scone off the tray. He tossed it back and forth between his hands, before breaking it in half and popping part of the scone into his mouth.

"Heaven!" Reilly declared with his mouth still half full.

"Bridget, the doctor specifically said—"

Brushing a strand of hair out of her eyes, giving him glare for glare, she replied tersely, "I know exactly what the doctor said, and I distinctly remember asking you not to bring the doctor here."

Ryan opened his mouth to speak, then clamped it shut.

The way he raked his hands through his hair was the first

clue he was upset. The way he closed his eyes and tilted his head up toward the ceiling confirmed it. *Probably counting again,* she mused.

"Well now, lass, Jamie here didn't exactly bring the doctor here to see you," Flynn said, moving to stand to the left of Ryan.

Reilly nodded, moving to stand on the other side of Ryan. " 'Twas the marshal who needed the bullet pried out of his arm, if ye'll remember."

The way the men flanked Ryan pulled just a bit on her heartstrings. More than one person at the ranch owed considerably more than their last meal to James Ryan. He'd taken each one in, or at least that was part of the story she'd heard. By all rights, she and Mick should be standing on either side of him right now. They owed their lives to him, too.

But all she seemed to do since she'd gotten out of her sickbed was upset the man. He was forever raking his hands impatiently through his hair and staring up at either the ceiling or the sky. After all he had done for Mick and her, the very last thing she wanted to do was upset him. But James simply didn't understand her need to pay him back. She couldn't continue to live off his beneficence, now that she was back on her feet. She'd gone down that road before: trusted when it seemed prudent, but in the end she'd placed her trust in the wrong man. Memories bombarded her and her throat tightened. Had she done so again?

She stole a look at the black-haired Irishman who'd opened up all the need inside of her again. It wasn't comfortable, and it wasn't a good idea. She struggled to clamp the lid back down on her emotions and rasped, "Coffee's ready."

Flynn nodded and stepped out the back door to ring the brass bell that hung on the back of the house. Men started arriving immediately, and she wondered if they had been hanging around anticipating the peal of the bell.

"Do I smell scones?"

"Is the breakfast ready then?"

Bridget suppressed her perverse need to walk over to James, wrap her arms around his waist, and lay her head against the strength of his chest, needing to feel the steady beating of his heart. She needed distance in order to tamp down the confusing emotions starting to bubble back up inside her. *So much for being able to control my feelings.* She sighed.

Focusing on serving the meal, she bustled about the kitchen. Setting the platter of crisply fried bacon and eggs in the middle of the long oak table, she checked to see that the freshly churned butter and still-warm bread and scones were there as well, and not on the sideboard.

Wiping her hands on her apron, she looked at the table filled with smiling faces and was struck by the notion that perhaps at last she and Mick had found a home. Could she risk embracing them as family? No one had made her feel inferior here, even when she'd been too ill to pull her own weight. Instead, they'd made her feel at home and set her son to working about the ranch, doing odd jobs here and there, all the while teaching him the value of hard work and earning his keep. More importantly, they taught Mick he was valued in spite of the fact that he'd known little more than how to muck out a horse stall.

Torn between the urge to trust and the fear of placing that trust in the wrong hands again, Bridget laid a hand on the back of the ladder-back chair. Before she could pull it out, James was there, motioning for her to let him. He pulled her chair out, waited until she sat, then helped her push it in.

"Ahh, always the gentleman, our Jamie." Flynn pointed the tines of his fork at James while he spoke out of the side of his full mouth.

"He knows how to behave in a lady's presence," Reilly agreed, slathering red currant jelly on a scone.

"So pay attention then, Mick, lad."

Bridget's heart warmed at the not-so-subtle lesson in manners. Her gaze flicked over to where James sat at the other end of the table. Their eyes met, and her heart tumbled in her breast. He was so lovely to look at with his ink-black hair and lake-blue eyes. The planes and angles of his face kept him from being too pretty. But it wasn't just his good looks and beautifully sculpted mouth that drew her gaze; it was his eyes and the sorrow mixed with the secrets swirling in their blue depths pulling at her, calling her.

"But she always makes me sit and eat before it gets cold. She's never ready to sit—"

"Now that you're older, Mick, you can insist that you will wait for her to sit down before doing so."

Bridget's fork clattered to the floor. Her fingers had gone limp at the suggestion that Mick should wait for her to be seated before eating. They hadn't eaten any meals together before coming to stay at the Ryan ranch. She'd been afraid Mick would find out the truth: that their money was gone. She tried to insist she wanted him to eat while the food was warm, when in fact, she hadn't been eating at all. Rather, she was giving her pitiful share of the food to her growing boy. He was always so hungry; he never seemed to notice that she wasn't eating with him.

"Are you all right?" Blue eyes level with hers surprised her. She hadn't heard James move. Yet here he was squatting down beside her chair, lifting her fork.

"Ye best blow on it, lass," Flynn offered. "The Murphy brothers didn't wipe their boots off when they came in from the corral. No tellin' what they tracked in!"

"We were in a hurry," the younger Murphy protested.

"Aye," the older one added, "and we caught the sweet scent of cream scones."

71

Grateful for the distraction, Bridget turned away from the intensity of James's gaze. "Next time, please wipe your feet."

Masterson handed Bridget his unused fork, while Brennan, who sat closest to the cutlery drawer, rose to get another.

She thanked them, watching James retreat to his chair out of the corner of her eye. Why hadn't she noticed how handsome he was the night she arrived? She struggled, trying and finally remembering bits and pieces of conversations in between bouts of fevered delirium. *Probably because you were out of your mind with fever,* her slightly rattled brain admonished.

She scooped up a forkful of egg and began to slowly chew. The yolk was not too hard, not too soft, just the way Michael . . . Bridget's breath caught. It had been a long time since she'd thought of how her husband liked his eggs prepared. She must be more rattled than she thought.

The men finished eating and were thanking her for the wonderful meal before she'd refocused on where she was and could take another bite. Thank goodness she could cook, and now that she was well on the road to recovery, shouldn't she be thinking about earning her keep? Now that Maggie had married and moved out, she could see the need for a housekeeper. She ought to discuss the possibility with James.

"I need to talk to your mother." James ruffled the hair on her son's head. "Why don't you help Reilly over at the barn?"

"That heap of rotting boards?"

"Michael Garahan O'Toole!" Bridget could feel her cheeks stain with embarrassment. "You'll apologize to Mr. Ryan for insulting his barn."

Mick's face flushed as he looked first at her, then at James. "I didn't mean . . . that is, I—"

"Well," James said with a grin, "it is a bit of a wreck. We're going to have a barn-raising in a few weeks. Maggie is organizing the townsfolk." He rubbed his chin. "Convinced them it was the least they could do after the way the town's founding father tried to swindle the ranch out from under me."

"I still think—"

"Go on, Mick." James interrupted him, and nodded toward the back door.

Bridget wondered what that was all about. Something had her son worried.

"It will be all right, lad. Go on with you."

Mick cast a worried look over his shoulder as he shoved open the back door.

"This sounds serious." Keeping busy would help soothe the unease sprinting up and down her spine. She started clearing the table, stacking dirty plates and wiping up crumbs with a dishcloth.

"It is." James took her by the arm and led her back to he chair. "I need you to sit down."

Her heart thudded in her chest. What now? Her mind raced while worry ate at her stomach. The air in the kitchen seemed to thicken, making it difficult to draw in a breath. "I'm sitting."

"Has Mick mentioned how you came to be here at the ranch?" he asked as he sat down across from her.

Bridget shook her head. "He said that when he met you, you offered to take us in until I regained my strength." Her eyes raised to meet his. "I'll never be able to thank you enough. Mick's so happy."

"He didn't tell you about the cattle?"

"What cattle?"

"So you don't know about Mick's run-in with the law?"

Bridget's head tingled when she tried to shake it at him. "Mick's never had trouble with the law before." The tingling spread, numbing the top of her head down to the tips of her fingers.

"He asked me not to say anything to you, because he was going to tell you himself." James scrubbed his hands over his face. "I thought you'd figured it out after that night. . . ."

Confused, Bridget asked, "What night?"

James raked his hands through his hair and continued, "When you had the nightmare and were worried about Mick." He paused, waiting.

Then she remembered! "You never did tell me why Mick needed to be saved from himself or what he'd been doing."

Ryan stared at Bridget for the longest time. There just wasn't an easy way to tell the boy's mother that the light of her life had been caught trying to rustle cattle from the Ryan ranch. He finally decided the truth would be the best approach.

*The truth!* His heart clenched and his gut churned. He had never told his mother, or his sister, the truth about why he'd left or why he never went home. He never would.

"Would you rather hear Mick's side of the story?" She'd probably understand and forgive Mick. Ryan wondered if once he confessed, he would be forgiven for his lies, or his past transgressions.

"No." She didn't hesitate, "I'd rather hear from you first, then Mick."

It was difficult to look into her warm brown eyes and tell her about Mick's falling in with a bunch of outlaws and trying to rustle cattle. He steadied himself against the growing feeling of unease sliding around inside of him. He had to do it.

"Just whose cattle did he try to steal?"

Ryan waited a heartbeat. "Mine."

Bridget shot up from her chair as if the rush-bottom seat was on fire. "*Your* cattle! He tried to steal from *you?*"

Ryan nodded and watched the vibrant play of emotions cross her face.

"Why? Did he say why?"

"I gather it had to do with the doctor bills you could no

longer pay." Ryan could sense the frustration seeping out from under the desperate hold Bridget had on her emotions, and knew it cost her dearly.

Slowly, she sat back down, dropping her head into her hands.

Ryan longed to put his arms around her and draw her close, but he'd been keeping his distance since the night he'd held her in his arms to ward off her nightmare. The night his need to comfort burst into a wildfire of need for more. But he had a feeling the widow O'Toole would not welcome any sympathy from him right about now. He wouldn't if their positions were reversed.

"Why on earth did you ever agree to take us in?" she cried. "My son tried to rob you!"

He shrugged and pushed back from the table. How could he explain why without admitting to his own run-in with the law?

"I need to understand. Please tell me."

Ryan paced in front of the back door. "Mick didn't look like an outlaw. Besides, he's still young enough to convince that a life of crime will only lead down a long and tortuous road to perdition, ending up at the wrong end of a long, knotted rope."

*As you nearly found out.*

Bridget rose and slowly walked over to where he stood. He sensed the change in her before he noticed the way she slumped her shoulders and stared at the floor. Reaching out a hand to her, he waited until she raised her eyes to meet his. She squared her shoulders and his admiration for her doubled. "I don't have the words to properly thank you for saving Mick's life."

He could feel the furrow forming between his brows; it was so deep, it made his head hurt. "And yours?" he asked.

"Mick's more important—"

"Oh, I don't think so." Ryan's voice was quiet, but firm. He let his gaze move along the line of her jaw, the curve of her cheek. Hadn't anyone in this woman's life valued her, or told her how special she was? "I don't think so at all."

Ryan marveled at the way patches of color stained her cheeks a soft pale peach. Drawn to her, caught up in the sorrow and mystery he glimpsed swirling in the depths of her velvety brown eyes, Ryan knew he was in danger of losing his mind. *Maybe his heart.* That possibility at this point in his life would be the same as losing his mind. Either way, he could wind up a dead man.

He had to get away from the dark-haired beauty before he forgot every reason he vowed never to get involved with another woman.

"I need . . . that is . . . I should clean up," Bridget stammered.

Ryan allowed himself one last, long lingering look while need hammered in his gut. At least this time, she had more clothes on. A vision in sheer white cotton tangled up his thoughts. What he *wanted* to say nearly became what he *should not* say. He sucked in a breath, pulling back from the need, burying it deep. In the end, he gave a quick nod and spun about on his boot heels.

Once he let the door close behind him and felt the familiar give of the back porch steps under his weight, he felt his self-control return, and his emotions settle to where they needed to be: contained in the tidy little box he kept in the far back corner of his heart.

Reilly's warning shout pulled him back to the present and had him sprinting toward the corral at full tilt. When he got to the fence, he realized Reilly had lost control of the stallion he was trying to break to saddle.

"Hang on!" Ryan shouted. "Don't let up on the reins, boy-o!"

He could see that Reilly had a death grip on the reins, but with a toss of the stallion's massive head, the man was lifted up in the air. He fell to earth with a hard *whump.*

Ryan grabbed the coiled rope off the fence post, slid his hands down to the knot, and began the slow rotating movement that would start the lasso in motion. As his wrist picked up momentum, easing into the rhythm, he slid his other hand down the rope and lifted the lasso over his head. Timing the revolutions, all the while keeping an eye on Reilly, he let the loop fly. It landed around the horse's neck first try. Ryan pulled hard and hung on. The black beast lifted his head, but couldn't shake the rope, or Ryan, loose.

"Reilly?" Ryan drew in a breath, ignoring the burning sensation in his gut. That last cup of coffee hadn't set right.

The burly Irishman was down on his hands and knees, but managed to lift his head and answer, "Aye."

Ryan watched his friend brace his hands on the ground and slowly push himself to his feet. Certain that Reilly was okay, he called out, "Back up."

Keeping his grip firm, he glanced over his shoulder to where Mick had been sitting, only to notice the lad was gone. "Mick?"

"Coming," the answering shout sounded from inside the old barn. Mick emerged with another coiled lasso. The boy could think on his feet, Ryan realized with a tinge of pride. "There's a lad. Think you can toss another loop around this ornery beast's neck?"

Mick nodded, then grinned. "I've been practicing some." In a smooth movement, the lasso flew through the air and landed right where Mick tossed it, around the stallion's neck.

Mick pulled the rope. The horse didn't like it.

"Loop your end around that fence post over there and tie it tight."

As soon as Mick had done what Ryan asked, Ryan placed a hand on the top rail of the fence and vaulted over it. Walking slowly toward the horse, all the while shortening the rope he held into a neat coil, Ryan spoke softly, soothingly, and without breaking stride. " 'Tis all right now. No one's goin' to hurt ye, laddie."

Slipping into his native tongue was as natural as breathing. The horse must have sensed something different in Ryan. Listening to the musical Gaelic, the animal quieted down enough to let Ryan stroke the side of his neck. He listened intently as Ryan praised him, telling him how handsome and smart he was.

"What's he saying, Reilly?"

"Well now, Mick, me lad," Reilly began, "he's tellin' the beast how grand he is."

"Why? The horse would have flattened you like one of my ma's flapjacks!"

Reilly nodded, and they waited in silence until Ryan settled the horse and walked over to where Mick and Reilly sat on the fence rail.

"Horses need to know who is in control, but never forget to be gentle with them," Ryan said to Mick. Then, turning back toward Reilly, he asked, "What happened?"

"I rushed things." Reilly scratched the dark whiskers on his chin. "I'll try again tomorrow."

"Good enough. Can you finish up here, or do you need me to comb him down for you?"

"I'll be fine." Reilly picked up the battered borrowed Stetson off of Mick's head and ruffled the boy's hair, then plunked the hat back down on the boy's head. "I've got Mick here to help me."

Ryan laid a hand on Mick's shoulder and looked down at the boy, noticing he'd done a bit of growing in the weeks since he first came to the ranch. Filled out some too, he thought with a smile.

"What?" Mick demanded when Ryan continued to stare at him.

"You did a great job." Ryan didn't want to dwell on how different the outcome might have been if they hadn't been able to get the stallion back under control so quickly. He shuddered, remembering shattered ribs and punctured innards, but pushed the grim memory aside. "I'm proud of you." He drew the boy in for a quick hug.

It was over before Mick could protest. Surprisingly, the lad blushed, looked down at the toes of his boots, and scuffed the dirt a bit before looking up at him.

"Aww, it wasn't a big deal," Mick protested.

Ryan didn't argue. In truth, he was concentrating on the changes Mick had gone through since he'd nearly sent the boy off to jail. Mick needed a man around to keep him on the right path, to make sure he wouldn't be talked into breaking the law again. The tremendous urge to be that man had Ryan's heart flipping over in his chest.

But he acknowledged it.

The overpowering need he felt where the boy's mother was concerned, now that was a problem. He could not fully accept it, nor was he ready to face it. One's perspective was far different in the dead of night, by the light of the moon. Then anything was possible. But the stark reality of day brought with it responsibilities of the present and memories of the past. He couldn't chance letting himself fall for another woman, even though she might be everything he'd ever wanted. Five years and a few thousand miles lay between Texas and Colorado, but there was a chance that Big John still had a posse out looking, trying to pick up Ryan's trail. He hoped to God the trail was stone cold by now.

Though he envied every loving look and gentle touch the pretty widow bestowed on her son, he could not afford to let his emotions be more than that. Ghosts from his past haunted him. More, they still had the power to destroy him and everything he had worked so hard to earn. He would store away the tender looks and loving touches so he could pull them out after Bridget and Mick were only a fading memory. He never doubted they'd leave. The question was: when?

# CHAPTER 7

Bridget's hand stilled at her throat, keeping her heart from jumping any further out of her breast. The danger Reilly just avoided would take a bit of time and concentration to forget. But it was the way James touched her son on the shoulder, quietly speaking to him and somehow eliciting a look of awe and pride from Mick, that she would hold on to and cherish.

Thoughts of the danger Mick could have been in if he'd been the one trying to saddle that big black beast were not lost on her. She knew there had to be a safer job for her son. One that would not place him in danger or threaten her weakening resolve to follow her heart.

She had worked long and hard to support the two of them. She had come to the painful realization that Michael would not be coming back. In her heart, she knew the only thing keeping Michael from her side, or from sending word to her, was that he was dead. There simply could not be any other explanation for the man's disappearance. The understanding had been a difficult, but necessary, step for her.

Slipping back inside the house, Bridget smoothed the hair out of her eyes. Tucking in a stray hairpin, she drew in one steadying breath, then another. Able to breathe without a hitch in her chest went a long way toward convincing herself she was back in control of the disquieting riot of emotions she had felt just a few short moments ago.

The kitchen was sparkling clean. A fresh pot of coffee was

brewing, and the wash water heating, by the time the back door opened.

"Ahh, Mrs. O'Toole!" Reilly seemed none the worse for wear as he stood in the open doorway wiping his feet on the bit of rug she'd left there for that purpose.

"Can I get you anything to drink, Mr. Reilly?" Bridget caught herself wringing her hands, then stopped.

"Mister?"

"Reilly then, if you must, but I hate calling anyone by their last name."

"Well then, ye can call me John." Reilly's broad grin nearly split his face.

"All right then. John. Can I pour you some coffee?"

"Thank ye, no. I just stopped in to tell ye what a fine lad ye've raised." The grin slid into a look of thoughtfulness. "We're comin' to depend on Mick around here."

Bridget didn't know whether to say thank you, or to run the other way screaming. She didn't want Mick to become too attached to James Ryan or his ranch hands. She had never meant to stay for more than a couple of weeks. Somehow, they had fallen into the routine of ranch life. Four weeks had come and gone, and she was well, growing stronger by the day. Up until James told her about Mick's brush with the law and the attempted rustling, she'd seriously considered staying. But now . . .

"Mrs. O'Toole?"

Dear God, if word got out about the attempted theft, gossip about them would start up all over again. She'd never be able to face it. Bridget knew she would have to tell Mick it was time to move on. But this time things were different. This time, she would not be looking for Mick's father. This time, when they moved on, she'd leave a big chunk of her heart behind.

"Bridget!"

"What?" Trying to remember what John had just said wasn't easy, but, she finally remembered. "Oh. Thank you, John. I depend on him, too."

She decided she couldn't afford to waste any more time thinking about how to approach the subject with her son. She would just do it. But she didn't want any interference or distractions. "Where's James?"

"Headed over toward the south pasture," Reilly offered. "There's a break in the fence and some rotten posts that need fixin'."

"Did Mick go with him?"

Reilly shook his head. "The lad is out by the corral, tryin' to sweet-talk a horse."

Bridget shuddered, remembering what that horse had tried to do.

"I'll be goin' back down to the corral," Reilly said, his voice dropping to barely a whisper. "I've left something unfinished."

As she watched him turn and walk out the door, Bridget could only guess what needed finishing. She hoped it wasn't another attempt to saddle the stallion. Shaking her head, she picked up the wicker basket she'd left in the corner of the room. It was time to think, and it would be easier if her hands were busy. If she and Mick were going to be leaving, she would make certain not to leave the ranch before finishing all the chores she'd set out to do.

She hoped James would still be in the south pasture for a few more hours. She knew she wasn't up to arguing with him, and he started arguing every time she lifted a finger. Reilly's assurance that he would be mending fences for a while eased her mind a fraction, but James never did what she expected of him. *Just a little while longer,* she pleaded silently, wringing the last of the freshly washed sheets with a deft twist of her wrists, and dropping the sheet into the wicker basket at her feet. Turning back to the wooden washtub, thinking to empty it, she was startled out of her deep thoughts by a voice.

"Don't lift that!"

Bridget spun around, a quick retort poised on her tongue, but the look of concern on her son's face had her biting back the words. She took a mental step back from the irritation bubbling up within her.

"And why not? I've finished the wash and need to dump out the water before I hang the sheets up to dry before—"

"Before James finds you slaving—" Mick began, but she interrupted him.

"Washing sheets is honest work," she said, choosing to ignore her son's use of their host's first name. "I'm feeling better, and I know my own strength."

Mick's eyes filled, then he blinked. "You nearly died!"

She had no reply for him. The same realization had struck her just as forcefully, a few weeks ago while she lay weak and feverish, unable to lift her head from the pillow. The excitement down at the corral, and Reilly's brush with near disaster, must have reminded Mick how tentative life could be.

Bridget knew she couldn't meet the accusation in her son's steady gaze. Besides, she had no intention of letting Mick see the truth of his words reflected in her eyes. Instead, she looked out over the land, so beautiful it made her eyes tear up. Looking closer to the ranch house, she admired the new fencing near the corral, then saw the run-down barn. It definitely needed a few well-placed boards and more than a handful of ten-penny nails.

Certain she had her thoughts and expression composed, she turned back toward Mick. A lock of dark brown hair fell into his eyes, and she nearly reached out to brush it out of the way, but something in his stance told her not to. She watched him blink, then straighten and square his shoulders. Thank goodness she'd not given in to temptation. He was no longer a little boy, and wouldn't appreciate any coddling touches from her.

Mick reached up, raking an impatient hand through his unruly hair, continuing to stare at her with his quiet gray eyes. A swift shaft of pain arced through her chest. A certain Irishman always raked a hand through his hair when he was troubled. Mick had somehow picked up the habit while they'd been living at the ranch.

Remembering her son's age, and his need to be reassured that all was still well within his world, she finally spoke. "But I didn't die."

Using the pause in conversation to her advantage, she forged ahead with what she knew would not be an easy topic. "Mick, I think it's time we moved back to town."

"But James said—"

Using the man's first name twice was no accident. All the ranch hands referred to their employer that way, but Mick wasn't a ranch hand. He needed to remember to respect his elders. Obviously, he needed to be reminded to address the man properly. "That's Mr. Ryan to the likes of you."

Mick's cheeks colored in response to her rebuke, but he didn't relax his aggressive stance. "Mr. Ryan said we could stay as long as we liked."

Standing toe to toe with her, more than ready to do whatever it took to convince her they needed to stay, put a dent in her plans and an ache in her softening heart. A heady mix of love and pride swelled within her. Her boy stood before her ready to argue. But was it because he truly felt it would be best for the both of them, or because he'd finally found a place where he fit in?

"But Mick—"

He stood even straighter, stiff as a board and just as inflexible. Her son. Her pride and joy. Just a few months shy of thirteen. He'd be thirteen by the time the first snow fell. *Look at him,* she thought. *So tall.* Summer had a way of helping young boys grow. *Must be the rain,* she mused. Gram always told her rainwater helped all things grow, including children. Looking up at him now, she believed it.

"Ma, please?"

Bridget didn't miss the note of longing tinging her son's words. If she could afford to be honest with herself, her heart urged her to stay, too. But some things could not be changed overnight. Even after a month living under the same roof of the kindest, most thoughtful man she'd ever met had not been enough to change her way of thinking. It had been ingrained in her over a dozen years: men could not be trusted. Although she'd like to think a certain rancher could be, she couldn't take the chance. She alone supported herself and her son. That way, no man could lay claim to what she was not willing to give.

In her time here at the ranch, she'd been lulled into forgetting all of her reasons for not trusting men. Her softening resolve would get her into trouble. Needing a distraction from her son's earnest face, and the dark thoughts troubling her, she draped the sheets across the clothesline one by one, all the while chiding herself for the way she felt. She'd learned life's lessons well. She'd best not forget them again.

Her husband's promise that nothing could tear him from her side had given her little comfort over the last dozen years he'd been gone. She'd spent those years supporting herself and her son with backbreaking work, traveling from town to town looking for her missing husband.

Assuming he was dead went a long way toward helping her reconcile herself to the fact that he wasn't coming back. Praying she was wrong kept the tiny flicker of hope alive in her breast. She shuddered, remembering the number of times her questions about her husband had led to speculation that he wasn't really her husband, that she'd gotten herself pregnant and was looking for the man responsible now that she'd had the baby.

After a while, the towns all seemed the same and the towns-folk's reaction to a young woman and a baby alone did too. Except for one time . . . Her mind drifted to thoughts of the second man she'd trusted. Richard Gray, the man who professed to love her and vowed to honor her promise to remain faithful to her absent husband and not press his suit. Instead, her refusal of his continued advances had enraged him to the point that he'd used his fists on her. Battered and bruised, she quickly learned that men who were bigger and stronger than she were not to be trusted.

Now she possessed better instincts about defending herself. Maybe she ought to thank Richard for that. No man had taken advantage of her since then, and as God was her witness, no man ever would again.

The ugly memory brought it all back: the emotional and physical pain, the horrible gossip that surrounded them at the time. Unable to deal with either, she and Mick had packed up and left under the cover of darkness, guided only by the stars. There would be no third time—or man. No matter how steady and safe, or warm and caring a man appeared to be, they all held secret desires and life plans that would hurt either her or Mick in the long run.

She stiffened her spine and her resolve. No man could be trusted.

". . . and I could work the ranch with Reilly and Flynn—"

"Mick, why won't you listen to reason? We can't stay."

"I'll listen when you start to make sense," he grumbled, turning away from her.

Tightness crept into her chest, constricting her breath, but she managed to say, "Mr. Ryan said we could stay while I regained my strength."

Mick's eyes narrowed and his jaw tightened. She reached a

hand out to him, but he turned his back on her and walked away.

Her heart lodged in her throat. He had never done that to her before. Something inside of her crumbled, making her want to call out to him and tell him they'd stay. They'd do whatever he wanted if he'd just turn around. This pain was far greater than the pain she'd felt when she realized Michael wasn't coming back.

Before she could open her mouth to speak, he mumbled, "You look puny to me."

Love for him rushed through her, and with it a feeling of lightness; he wouldn't leave her.

As long as she and Mick were together, they'd be all right. She walked over to where he stood, stiff and silent, and laid a hand on his back. She needed him to smile and knew just how to get him to. "I may be puny, but I know your weakness."

Her son drew in a sharp breath and tensed. "You wouldn't!"

"Wouldn't I?" Bridget slid her hand down to his side.

"But that's not fair, I can't help—"

"Life is not always fair, Mick."

He moved, trying to slide away from her, but she was shorter, lower to the ground, and moved like lightning. She had him begging for mercy in three minutes flat. "Give up?" she asked, tickling his ribs mercilessly.

"No. I never . . . can't—"

"I could go on all day," she drawled, working her nimble fingers up and down his sides, while he laughed, gasped, and struggled for breath.

"All right! You win! I give up!"

He let her pull him into her arms and hold him close. Bridget felt a lump of emotion building in her chest, spreading to her throat. She missed these daily hugs so much. But her boy was well on his way to becoming a man. From what she'd seen over the last few weeks, Mick had been attempting to act the part, unconsciously molding himself into James Ryan's image. Although that in itself was not a bad thing; it would only make it harder to leave, and they had not been asked to stay— permanently.

Even if they had been asked, how could she say yes, after what James told her this morning? It just didn't feel right working for the man her son tried to steal from. But she would repay him. She had to. But how could one repay a selfless act so far beyond the normal bounds of compassion and understanding?

She let go of Mick and picked up the basket where she'd set it down.

Mick's laughter died as quickly as it had bubbled up. "I've got to do the milking."

He turned and started to walk away. She could bear the weight of the cleanly laundered sheets, but was not sure she could handle the guilt weighing her down.

*How could she bear to see her son so unhappy?*

*How could she force him to leave the ranch?*

He'd slipped right into the routine, taking his turn cooking meals while she recuperated. His face lit up every time he rode out with the ranch hands, mending fences, finding stray cattle, lending a hand whenever, wherever, he could.

She thought of the way James had gone out of his way to help them and could imagine staying. "Why don't you go and see what Mr. Flynn is doing over by the grain silo?" Guilt softened the edge in her voice. "I'll take care of the milking this morning."

"But James—Mr. Ryan—said—"

"I'm well aware of all that Mr. Ryan has said and done for the last few weeks. You've yet to tire of filling me in on his words or his movements."

Mick toed the ground with his battered boot.

Bridget sighed, hating having made her son feel bad. "Go on with you," she relented.

The moment Mick looked up at her, she felt her defenses crumbling. Tears pooled in her eyes, but she frantically blinked them away. Mick always hated when she cried. Swallowing back the tears made her stomach churn. Although it was the right thing to do, leaving the ranch would be the hardest thing she'd had to do since she'd accepted the fact that Michael wasn't coming back.

For the first time in a long while someone appreciated the fact that the sheets were clean and the meals hot. Not that her son didn't notice. Well, all right, if she was honest with herself, Mick only noticed when the food was gone, not how it tasted. To her growing boy, everything tasted *fine*.

"But, Ma, Mr. Ryan said—"

"Hmmm?" For a moment she let herself picture life at the Ryan spread. Should they stay on, waiting for a more permanent offer? The house could use someone to keep it on a regular basis, instead of whenever any of the men had time or whenever they finally noticed the dirt, which they rarely did. Mick's smiling face and happy laughter filled her heart to bursting. Then another image, one of candlelight caressing broad shoulders and tousled black hair, took hold of her wavering thoughts, urging her to change her mind and stay. But could she live with herself if they stayed on? The guilt of how they'd come to be at the ranch would surely eat away at her heart and her pride.

One thing was certain: she owed James Ryan a debt for his kindness, for his care, and for his compassion for both Mick and herself. Maybe they could stay on until she'd worked off what she thought she owed him. Keeping house, cooking, and cleaning would free up the ranch hands for other chores. Lord knew there was enough to do at a ranch this size.

"We'll talk about it later."

Mick paused in the act of swinging his leg and ended up kicking the ground hard enough to churn up a clod of grass and dirt. He grinned, "I'm sorry I yelled at ya, Ma."

Watching him sprinting off toward the silo, Bridget sighed and inhaled deeply. The rich scent of fertile earth floated toward her on the faint breeze. Here at last was the one thing a woman could count on in life. The land would always be there. Vacillating between two decisions, unable to settle on one or the other, Bridget opened the kitchen door and placed the basket back in the corner on the floor. On her way past the stove, she lifted the lid on the coffee pot, checking the level inside. James's men usually stopped in the kitchen for a quick cup if they had a moment to spare between chores.

*Still full.*

It would hold them for the next little while. Smoothing a hand over her hair, tucking in a loose pin, Bridget straightened her apron then headed off to do the milking.

# CHAPTER 8

"So Reilly wasn't hurt?" Sean asked for the second time.

Ryan straightened and set aside the post-hole digger. Wiping his hand across his brow, he accepted the canteen the younger Murphy brother handed him. After a long drink of the still-cool water, he nodded. "Just his pride."

"Well, that could use a knick or two," Thomas said with a smile.

"Now Tom—" Sean began.

"You know it's true," his older brother interrupted.

"That's enough, lads, or we'll not finish setting the posts in place before Mrs. O'Toole rings the dinner bell."

Both brothers let out a long and satisfying sigh. "The widow O'Toole knows her way about the kitchen."

"Aye, such a light hand with piecrust and scones."

"Keep your minds on the job lads, or I'll bar you from the table."

"You wouldn't!" Sean gasped.

"Oh and why wouldn't he?" Thomas asked, rubbing the edge of his jaw. "The man's downright mean, when he feels he's got reason to be."

"Well we've not given him—"

"Keep your tongue behind your teeth and hand me that roll of barbed wire." Ryan swallowed the chuckle that bubbled up within him. He enjoyed Bridget's cooking every bit as much as the rest of his men. But it was the way he started craving the sight of her face across the table in the morning, and the slow sweet smiles she generously shared with all of them, that was slowly driving him to distraction. Maybe he should renew his offer for her to share his home.

Now that he thought about it, she hadn't said a word about it since the last time he had, some weeks ago. Placing yet another post into another hole, holding it in place while Sean shoveled the dirt in around it, Ryan allowed his thoughts to drift, and he remembered the first time he'd seen the Murphy brothers. They'd been bone-tired, three-day's hungry, and riding double on a what he'd thought at first look was a small underfed horse. A mule was what the beast turned out to be. He'd offered them jobs and a place to stay, and the brothers were still here, nearly two years later.

He decided that he definitely needed to make that offer to Bridget again. Everyone else to whom he'd offered his home to had stayed. It stood to reason she would too. Besides, Mick needed a place to test himself, to see if he could handle the hard work. Testing his mettle with outlaws was not the future path a young man should follow.

"Hold it still," he heard Murphy grumble.

He tried, but then started thinking about Mick's future again. If he had anything to say about it, and he'd like to think he did, Mick would be working alongside the Murphy brothers, Reilly, Flynn, and the rest of his ranch hands.

"Can ye not straighten it out?"

Ryan ignored the other man, thinking instead of Bridget. His thoughts naturally wandered back to a vision in white cotton, tossing and turning on the bed in his spare room, her dark hair sweeping across her shoulders and onto the pillow. His gut clenched as need swamped him. He'd gone too long without knowing the comforting touch of soft, smooth hands caressing his tired shoulders and aching back. Too long without feeling the fire burning deep within him, fire that only the right woman would be able to douse, when heat met heat and the twisting flames of passion burned high and bright until they burned themselves out. *But 'twas passion that had gotten him arrested in Amarillo.*

"I said, can't you hold it straighter?" Sean struggled to shovel dirt into the hole, while the post wavered and shifted yet again.

Startled, Ryan righted the post, but couldn't keep his thoughts from drifting back to the past, remembering how proud McMaster had been that first time he'd showed them the length and breadth of his land. The man had acres to spare, but had been more than willing to share his good fortune with strangers.

"I thought you were going to—" Sean began. Ryan looked up and noticed he'd let the post list a bit to the left again. He straightened it and remembered how down on their luck the Murphy brothers had been when they'd shown up. They'd been in need of a place to stay and were hungrier than Bridget must have been when she'd decided to sacrifice her health for the good of her son.

McMaster would want him to open his heart and home to Bridget and her son, just as Ryan had done for the Murphy brothers, and for Brennan, and Masterson . . . Why was he so worried about talking to the lass and how she would react to whatever he said? It had been easier to talk to the boy when he'd caught Mick trying to rustle his cattle, and that had been like trying to shoe a fractious horse. *Damned difficult.*

"That ought to do it," Thomas said, taking the snips from Ryan's limp hand, anchoring the last of the barbed wire into place, and cutting off the ends before handing them back to Ryan.

Ryan shook his head, still mumbling to himself, "She's far

too sensible to let a little thing like rustling a few cattle bother her. Isn't she?"

"Talking to himself again," Sean said, with a nod in Ryan's direction.

"That's how it all starts," Thomas added in a low voice.

But Ryan didn't hear them. He was too busy trying to decide how to broach the subject of Bridget and Mick staying with his hardheaded guest.

Leaning her head against the warm, coarse hide, Bridget continued to coax milk from the third cow. *One more to go,* she thought, looking over at the cow patiently waiting her turn to be milked. She wondered if the poor thing was anxious for Bridget to get to it and relieve the pressure of having to carry around too much milk.

Using the back of her hand, she brushed the hair out of her eyes. A pin slipped free and pinged against the side of the bucket. She ignored it, focusing on her task. Milk continued to squirt into the bucket in a steady stream. Though it had been a while since she'd last done the chore, she'd gotten the rhythm back down, managing not to rile the cows and soothing her own frazzled feelings at the same time. If only she could be certain she was doing the right thing where Mick was concerned.

But whom could she ask? Her parents had died when she was younger than Mick, and her grandmother not long after she met Michael O'Toole. *And her mother-in-law?* her too-tired brain prompted. A shudder rippled through her as she remembered the last time she'd seen Michael's mother, and the way the woman had stood in the doorway of her fancy Denver home, taffeta skirts quietly rustling with the agitated movements of her hands. Bridget could still remember the way the elder Mrs. O'Toole had frowned down at her and the baby. Shaking her head, she realized there had been no help from that quarter then, and there wouldn't be any forthcoming now.

If they stayed at the ranch, Mick would definitely have the best example of how a man should act. James's ranch hands had the best of intentions, too, she thought with a smile, though they were a bit rougher around the edges than James.

If she and Mick moved back to town, they'd have to face the rumors and innuendos that always followed a woman alone with a child in tow. They appeared down on their luck, and the townspeople, no matter which town, inevitably wondered why they were alone, never quite believing the truth. And the truth was all Bridget had left of her marriage.

Millicent Peabody's pinched face swam behind Bridget's closed eyes. Her stomach churned. What would she and Sarah Burnbaum have to say about Bridget and Mick living out here on the ranch, with no other woman for miles?

*"Moooo."*

The plaintive cry had Bridget running her hand gently across the cow's side, "Sorry," she soothed, "I didn't mean to bump you."

Rubbing her head where it had connected with the bony part of the cow's leg reminded Bridget of the importance of keeping her mind on the task at hand. She could worry about the town gossips later. Better still, she could ask James if he'd heard anything. *Then she would be able to make a decision.*

Satisfied that she'd resolved the situation to the best of her ability, she bent to retrieve the empty bucket, patted the cow, and settled down to begin milking the last one.

"Why don't you boys ride on over to the river and see how Masterson and Brennan are getting along, counting the herd?"

"See you back at supper!" Sean called out.

"Save us some biscuits!" his brother said on a laugh.

Ryan turned his horse around and headed back to the ranch.

Instead of thinking of questions he needed to ask Flynn about their grain supply, his thoughts kept returning to the lovely chestnut-haired widow who'd begun to make concentrating on his work a full-time chore.

He wanted to think about keeping Bridget and her son in his life, but could he with the ever-present worry that the law was still on his trail? Did Texas Rangers ever stop looking for murderers?

But he was innocent!

*Tell that to the hanging judge!* Big John's words still had the power to haunt him.

Ryan knew in that moment that he'd never be free.

# CHAPTER 9

After checking with Flynn, Ryan rode up to the ranch house, ready for a long, cool drink. The day had started out warm, with temperatures steadily climbing while they dug fence-post holes. After the ride home, he figured it was as hot as his mother promised him hell would be. He remembered she usually imparted sage bits of wisdom about the temperatures of hell when she'd caught him in some desperate act of childhood bravado.

God, he missed her! He'd just begun to grieve, only learning of her death a few weeks ago when his sister arrived on his doorstep.

After removing the saddle from his horse and rubbing him down, Ryan strode across the yard toward the well pump, not bothering to go into the kitchen for the water they kept in the bucket there. He worked the pump handle until water gushed out, then splashed water on his face and neck, cupping his hands beneath the cool stream, drinking his fill.

Satisfied with the morning's work, he headed over to the house, but got no farther than the back porch. Mentally ticking off the chores accomplished, he decided he'd earned a spare moment or two to survey his land. Propping a scarred, dusty boot on the weathered railing, he leaned forward, crossed his arms, and let them rest on his knee. A shorter man would never have been able to find the odd position comfortable, but to the raw-boned Irishman's six-foot-plus frame, it seemed as natural as breathing.

His gaze swept across the yard to the corrals and land beyond. One lone white puff of cloud floated by in the endless blue, the color so vivid it hurt his eyes to look up into it. In the distance, part of his cattle herd grazed contentedly. The soft lowing filled him with a sense of peace, while his heart swelled with pride.

The stakes he'd set in place, marking off where the new barn would be built, stood straight and tall, just waiting for the barn-raising. A dark thought disturbed the satisfaction he felt.

*He had almost lost it all.*

Ryan drew in a deep breath as a hint of honeysuckle blew past his nose. He glanced over to where the vine had latched onto the picket fence by the south side of the house, growing with a stubborn vengeance. The tenacious plant reminded him of his sister.

He and his men owed Maggie their lives for arriving in time from New York City with proof in her hand that Ryan owned the ranch. A lesser man would not have admitted to nearly giving up hope, but Ryan had traveled down harder roads before. He was more than willing to acknowledge that he had lived with fears of watching all he and his men had worked for, and spilled blood over, slipping through the tips of his tightly clenched fingers.

With the help of his sister and her new husband, the marshal, they had been able to stop the local land-grabbing banker from taking over Ryan's ranch and a handful of other ranches as well. The crooked banker would not profit once the railroad spur was laid. If the other ranchers wanted to sell their land so that the railroad had even ground for its roadbed that was their business. At least now the others had a choice. Neither the choice, nor their land, had been taken from them.

A flash of pale yellow amidst the lush green of the open field and rich browns of the earth caught his eye, distracting him. He looked toward the old barn and swallowed the growl of frustration searing his throat. The dark-haired woman crossing the open expanse of yard, a bucket brimming with milk in each hand, moved into his line of sight.

*Bloody hell, the widow O'Toole was too stubborn to be believed!* He stalked over to where she stood. "Where's Mick?" he ground out, intending to snatch the brimming buckets from her before she hurt herself. "It was his turn to do the milking."

Ryan watched as Bridget carefully set the buckets down, then raised a slightly shaking hand to her hair, tucking in a stray pin. Letting his eyes follow the movement, he noticed the knot she seemed so fond of fashioning in her hair slipping from its pins again. To his way of thinking, a woman ought to wear her hair loose, free to lift in the breeze. A few more gusts of wind, and her hair would be down around her shoulders.

"Good morning."

Her hesitant, slow smile stopped him in his tracks, and had him remembering moonlight illuminating a satin-smooth thigh. Mentally pulling the covers up over her long, lithe legs, as he had that night after she'd arrived at the ranch, helped him control the spurt of need rising up within him. He was painfully aware of her. Lifting his gaze from her tempting rose-tinted lips to her eyes, he noticed the snap of temper simmering in them.

In the last few weeks, as he became more aware of Bridget as a woman, not just an invalid sleeping in his guest room, he'd noticed the way the hue of her eyes changed from a soft warm brown to deep chocolate whenever she was annoyed.

Her eyes were darkening by the second.

*Good! They were even.* After hours spent digging holes, agonizing over whether or not he could afford to let her distract him, he was working himself up into a lather. "You're not to do any heavy work until the doctor says you are completely recovered."

From the look she leveled at him, he figured the tone of his words didn't have the effect he'd hoped. The woman dared to stand toe to toe with him, angling her head further back to glare up at him. If looks were any indication, he'd be meeting his maker in about two-minutes, tops. She sure as hell riled easily.

"I thought we'd settled that point earlier. I'm not sick, Jamie."

Her voice had gone soft, triggering a reaction in his brain, not unlike putting flame to a stick of dynamite. Damned if he didn't enjoy the way she slowly drew out his name, as if she were savoring the sound of it. Mentally, he shook free from the spell her voice cast about him. He'd already thought it through; he couldn't let another female work her wiles on him. Though intrigued by Bridget, entranced by her face and form, he couldn't afford to allow himself to go down that road again. The cold reality of the jail cell in Amarillo was a stark reminder of what happened when a man trusted a woman. Too many people depended on him now. He couldn't throw it all away for a sweet-smelling, warm-hearted, wisp of a woman.

"I may not look healthy to you, but I know my own strength. I've had to look out for myself and Mick all these years without any help."

"And a fine job ye've done of it lately." Her sharp intake of breath told him his words had struck her hard. He hadn't meant to be that blunt. But he did want her to see reason and understand why he could not let her overdo.

"I'm sure you didn't mean that the way it sounded," she said.

*Bloody buggering eedjit,* he mentally kicked himself, then closed his eyes and started to count. When he reached five, he opened one eye. It didn't help. He still had the urge to wring her slender neck. He closed his eye again and kept counting. By the time he reached fifteen, he no longer wanted to throttle her, but the havoc she wreaked within him still had him nearly giving in to the urge to yell at her.

He heard her breathing change and quicken. Resolving not to frighten the fragile widow, he swallowed his anger. God knows she'd led a hard life without a man to lean on. That she'd survived her own share of trials was something he knew instinctively. She could hold her own counsel too. Since she arrived at his home, he'd not been able to pry any of her past out of her.

He remembered the way she'd arrived at his ranch a few short weeks ago, so weak he'd been afraid she'd die. He had lived a hard life, worked hard to achieve all that he now owned. Life and death were an integral part of ranching, but somehow the thought of this vibrant woman never smiling again took the starch right out of him. Thoughts of her expressive dark eyes closing forever nearly broke what was left of his heart. He cared about what happened to her. She had obviously done the best she could with what little she had. One look at her son, and he could see where all of her energies and food had gone. The lad was the picture of health, but at a terrible cost to that of his mother.

A funny feeling beneath his breastbone had him pause in his counting. The feeling was not unlike the indigestion he suffered whenever it was Reilly's turn to cook. He rubbed absent-mindedly at the spot before deciding to ignore it, focusing instead on resuming his counting and controlling his temper.

*Twenty-five.*

He opened both eyes and prayed his anger was sufficiently under control. Damned if she hadn't been waiting for him to look at her.

"I need to speak with you." Bridget hesitated. "It's important."

Ryan sighed. If she mentioned paying him back for his hospitality again, he was going to lose the tenuous hold he now had on his growing annoyance.

Frustration added a razor-sharp edge to his voice, "I told you, I won't hear of you paying—"

She shook her head. "It's not that."

He drew in a breath. Counting hadn't helped. He was still mad. He waited, watching her face closely for a clue as to where this conversation was headed.

She cleared her throat. "Have you thought of hiring a house-keeper?"

Of all the things he could think of, he never thought she'd want to talk about hiring a housekeeper.

He watched as she grabbed fistfuls of her pale yellow cotton dress in each hand, all the while trying to decide what part of the woman's brain had ceased to function. The doctor had told her not to work, had said she was too weak. *He* had asked her not to work, didn't want her to work. How many different ways did a man have to come up with of saying the same thing?

*Were all women this thickheaded?*

*Only the ones worth caring about.* As Ian McMaster's gruff voice echoed in his head, he realized yet again how much he missed the old Scot. *Now more than ever.*

"You're not well enough—" he began, but one hard look from her and he fell silent, recognizing the need to try another tack.

The old Scotsman was right, and she was worth caring about. She was difficult, but if he could afford to care, she'd be the one. He turned his thoughts to a happier part of his past, and realized that, although he owed McMaster for the very land he stood on, he would willingly give it all back to have his mentor standing beside him, railing at him for letting this slip of a woman get the better of him.

Bridget unclenched her fists and smoothed the wrinkles from the sides of her dress. He watched the movement of her hands, mesmerized by them. They were so small, but so capable. God help him, was he losing his mind altogether?

This was not the first time he'd caught himself watching for small gestures particular to the woman who had become a part of his home and ranch; therefore becoming an essential part of his life. His brain warned his softening heart to harden, afraid the frozen organ was beginning to thaw.

As he stood there watching, she brushed a lock of hair out of her eyes. The movement reminded him of the way she stroked her son's cheek when she served the lad his meals. The way she ruffled her fingers through Mick's dark hair always had Ryan imagining how it would feel to have her slender fingers caressing his own scalp.

He could not stop staring at her. Though only God knew why she continued to captivate him. The woman irritated him no end, never listened to reason. Whenever she smiled, he felt his grip slipping. The way her lightning-fast grin flashed whenever Mick said something amusing pulled at him, drawing him inexorably toward her, though he tried to maintain a respectful distance.

He clamped his jaw down hard, grinding his teeth together, forcing his curving mouth to flatten into a line of disapproval. The woman was getting to him. There was no place in his life for a woman. He would never, ever, let a woman take hold of his heart. He shook his head, realizing she was speaking to him. Lord above, she'd make him daft!

"Mick and I are so grateful you took us in. Why won't you let me take on more chores in order to make it up to you?"

His gut clenched, churning, remembering the bony feel of her ribs as he'd held her undernourished body in his arms. "Do you have any idea how you looked when you arrived here four weeks ago?"

He watched as she clasped her hands in front of her and

stared down at them. What had her so nervous? Then it dawned on him: something Maggie had told him about Bridget's constant battle with gossip.

"I need to feel like I'm pulling my own weight." She set her mouth in a grim line. One that matched his own.

"Well now, that being the case, I'd say you more than used up your quota. Your weight can't possibly equal eight stone!"

Impossibly, her eyes darkened until he could no longer see the black centers. The look in her eyes reminded him of a certain fractious bay mare whose eyes would darken right before she kicked out with her back legs at whomever had the misfortune to be standing too close to her.

"You have done so much for Mick and me, even after he tried to steal from you! Can't you see I have no other way to pay you back for all you've done?"

He noticed the sheen of moisture pooling along her thick black lashes and mentally kicked himself for pushing her to the point of tears.

"Bridget, please," he began. "There is no need."

"Can't you see this is not about me?" she argued, furiously blinking away the evidence of tears.

"Well, I'd say—"

"And you'd be wrong," Bridget interrupted, placing her fisted hands on her slim hips.

He sucked in a deep breath and forced himself to calm his rising temper. Why did this one woman have the ability to get under his skin so quickly? The lass didn't mean to rile him, did she?

He pushed the Stetson further back on his head, all the while trying to figure out a way to get her to agree with him without her realizing she was being manipulated.

"Look at me, you daft man!"

He obeyed and looked his fill. Her cheeks had splotches of

pink on them, making her brown eyes seem brighter.

"Do I look ill to you?"

Lord help him, he looked, taking in the gentle curve of her cheekbones. They'd filled out a bit in the last few weeks. The sharpness of her features had softened and her color had certainly improved. His gaze swept from the top of her head to the toes of her high-buttoned shoes. She'd gained weight and now had curves he hadn't noticed at first. Well, hell. He was noticing now.

"If you don't want Mick and me to stay, that is another matter entirely," she continued. "I can always find work in town."

"I thought you couldn't find work in town," he retorted. "Wasn't that why you nearly died, starving yourself?"

A deep rosy flush swept up from the collar of her dress to the top of her forehead. Blast his temper. He never seemed to say the right thing where Bridget O'Toole was concerned.

"I was unable to find work." Her voice was even. She chose to ignore the fact that Ryan already knew what had happened to her and Mick.

"If you're worried about the old biddies gossiping about you living out here, don't worry."

She sighed, and her still-moist gaze swept back to him.

"They've been talking about you since the day we brought you here in my wagon."

Instead of soothing her worry, Ryan noticed the sharp jerky way her head snapped up at his words. The rosy blush drained from her forehead, cheeks, and chin, all the way to the lace-trimmed collar of her dress. The stark contrast of pale-as-milk skin and dark brown hair worried him. He recognized the anxious look. He'd seen it before; she looked desperately ill again.

Preparing to offer a steadying hand, Ryan stepped closer.

Bridget wet her suddenly dry lips, and struggled to stay

upright. She couldn't feel the top of her head, and she could swear her stomach felt as if the bottom had just dropped out of it.

*It was too late!* But then again, it seemed she was always too late to repair the damage her husband's leaving had done.

"Well now, and what did you say to them?" she countered, hoping at least this man who seemed so solid and upright had explained her desperate situation to the old harridans.

His look of confusion should have tipped her off. It certainly set her back up. She could feel her temper flare. *Just like a man!* She thought. He hadn't even tried to stem the gossip, probably just did what every other man usually did when faced with gossip: ignored it!

Or had he? Had he believed the gossips? Was that why he didn't say anything in her defense?

"Bridget, I never thought—"

"Aye, that you didn't Mr. Ryan."

The color seemed to leach from his eyes, leaving them a cold, lifeless, pale blue. Sweet heaven. Why couldn't she keep control of her biting tongue? Even well-placed blame would not solve her current troubles. She certainly should not fault him for acting the way any other man would.

She clenched her hands again and willed her churning stomach to be calm. "Has Sarah Burnbaum told you I'm not really a widow?" She didn't pause for fear he'd answer. "Has Millicent Peabody told you she doesn't believe I was ever married?" She watched his eyes widen while disbelief added lines of frustration between his thick black brows.

"Did the fine ladies of Emerson collectively wonder aloud just what type of service I'd be useful for way out here, away from their prying eyes and wagging tongues, with not another female around for miles?"

Bridget couldn't catch her breath. Her spiking fury simply

drained her. That the man she so admired could possibly remain silent, leading her to the conclusion that he had heard the gossip and believed it, drove the breath from her lungs. In that moment before he spoke, as a dark look tightened his jaw and furrowed his brow, she realized just how much she cared what he thought of her.

But she was far from worthy of his regard. An honest man like James Ryan, pillar of the community, deserved a woman without a tarnished reputation. Hers had been following her since she and Mick left Louviers, Colorado. She blinked back tears, hating the weakness they implied.

He took a step toward her, then another. They were a breath apart when he finally spoke. "Ahh, lass. Why would you think I'd ever judge you?"

The deep timbre of his voice eased a bit of tension from between her shoulder blades, but not the hurt slicing through to the marrow of her bones.

He reached out a hand to her.

"Everyone else has!" Bridget blurted out. Then sucked in her breath, wondering why she just didn't bit off the tip of her tongue. He didn't deserve the sharp edge of it. He wasn't the one with the murky past.

Though she wanted to clasp his hand between her own and draw on some of his strength, she couldn't—didn't—have the right. Not after the way the harsh words tumbled out of her mouth. Searching his face for a clue as to what he was thinking, she didn't have to wonder long. His eyes frosted over, like a shallow pond on a wintry day, chilling her. Though he hadn't moved, she could see him mentally stepping back from her.

He dropped the offered hand.

She had lost her chance. Making a last-ditch effort to smooth over the feelings she knew she'd tramped all over, she spoke softly. "You've a good heart."

He glared at her.

"You would never presume to judge anyone." And hadn't she done just that?

"Then why are you and Mick leaving?"

He honestly didn't have any idea. "What do you know about me?"

"You are a wonderful mother to a likeable lad." His eyes clouded for a moment, and a flash of what she recognized as pain flickered to life.

"What if Sarah is right?" she whispered. "What if the things Millicent has been saying are true?"

She watched the man before her stiffen, almost as if he were preparing to receive a blow.

He took her hand in his, nearly crushing it in his strong grasp, pulling her close to him. Bridget could feel the warmth radiating from his powerful form. She had to fight to ignore the feelings she had for him, and not give in to them as she'd wanted to from that first night he'd sought to ease her nightmares.

"It would not matter what anyone else said, or thought." His voice was firm with conviction. "I make my own decisions."

"Aye, and I'm sure all who know you bow to them." Bridget mentally kicked herself for failing to rein in her sharp tongue. She just couldn't seem to help herself.

His eyes widened, then narrowed. He seemed to be thinking deep thoughts again. She wished she knew what they were. James Ryan spent more time thinking than he did speaking. It was almost as irritating as his penchant for ordering her about!

"Marry me, Bridget O'Toole," he rasped, staring intently into her eyes.

For the life of her, she couldn't form a coherent thought in her head. It wasn't a question. It had been a statement. *An order.*

Marry him. *Was he daft, or did he truly care for her?*

When she didn't answer him right away, he shifted from one foot to the other. "Then no one would dare to question or speak ill of you again."

Her silent question had been answered abruptly. He didn't harbor feelings for her, other than his overpowering need to protect those he felt needed protecting. She'd been fooling herself, thinking she could stay. Worse, the fact that she'd fallen for more than deep-blue eyes and coal-black hair made her chest tight and her breath quicken. God help her, she would not cry!

Needing to get away from him before the tears started, she snapped, "I can't."

She had hoped to keep her heart out of the matter, but the shadows she glimpsed in his eyes had her questioning her need not to become involved with him. Steeling herself against the desire to throw her arms around him and say yes, she'd marry him, she wrapped her arms about herself. He deserved better than a widowed mother dragging her twelve-year-old son and tarnished reputation behind her. *Far better.*

"Thank you for the asking, Jamie."

"Bridget—"

"I owe you my life, such as it is. I'll never forget your kindness to Mick and me."

"Wait! You can't just—"

Before she could change her mind, and allow her resolve to weaken any further, she grabbed her skirts and lifted them just high enough to keep the hem from brushing along the ground. She was as close to loving James. No. She corrected herself. It was time to be honest and admit it. She was so far gone over him, she almost gave in to the need to turn around and tell James she'd changed her mind. But she couldn't complicate the poor man's life any more than she'd already done.

It was time she and Mick moved back to town, and that she

begin to rebuild her reputation and their future. Time to let James Ryan pick up his life where he had put it on the shelf a few weeks ago.

They had to leave.

Dear God, she wanted to stay!

# CHAPTER 10

"Why can't we stay?"

Mick's voice cracked, and Bridget's heart nearly broke at the sound of it. How could she begin to explain the choices she had made all those years ago, and how they still affected their lives today?

"Mr. Ryan said we could."

How could she tell her beautiful son anything without confessing the one truth she had never faced until today: his father had abandoned them. Wasn't it enough that Mick was old enough to understand the horrible rumors that followed them from town to town?

"He said I'm a natural at roping."

Her stomach began to churn as she thought of taking Mick away from the one man who had given her son confidence in himself.

*Would Mick recover?*

*Would he be scarred for life?*

Though the words nearly stuck in her throat, she managed to say, "You knew from the beginning it was only temporary, until I regained my strength and got better." She couldn't look at her son yet; if she did, her steely resolve would surely shatter to bits.

Focusing on the mountains in the distance, ignoring the road ahead, she silently asked herself if it wasn't better to sever the ties Mick and James were forging now, before the bond was so strong both would be devastated.

Stomach still roiling, throat tight, Bridget tried to ignore the uneasiness pervading her being. She was not sure she was doing the right thing by leaving, but she knew she could not stay.

Drawing in a breath through lungs that burned, she prayed James would understand and hoped someday Mick would forgive her. God help her, she knew she'd made the right decision. Hadn't she?

"But, Ma—"

"You have to trust that I know what is best, Mick."

The look he shot her hurt her heart, but she couldn't back down now. Besides, they were already in the wagon and she'd already embarrassed herself enough when she'd given James her answer. She shivered, remembering the coldness in his eyes.

From the way Mick slumped and the grim set to his unsmiling mouth, Bridget knew her words did not sit well with him. She could imagine how her answer sounded to a twelve-year-old boy being forced to leave the first real home he'd ever had, and the protection and friendship of a man he had come close to worshiping.

"Now then, Mrs. O'Toole, ye know Jamie wanted ye to stay," Reilly said, flicking the reins.

"I know he did, Mr. Reilly."

She knew it and would never forget the look in James's eyes. She could swear she felt James's gaze boring holes in her back as Reilly snapped the reins and headed down the road to town. But she didn't dare turn around to see if he was sorry or happy to see her go. Should it really bother James so much if they left? It would be two less mouths to feed. Well, three, really seeing as how Mick ate enough for two people. James constantly complained about any chore she did. Now he could complain when one of his ranch hands did the chores.

James truly seemed to be concerned with how they'd get along on their own. She huffed out a breath. Hadn't they gotten on fine without him all these years? A nagging thought chipped away at her defensive thoughts. They'd done better at the ranch with James, and Lord help her, she'd miss him something fierce come morning.

Could she tell Reilly what she had not been able to tell James? She shook her head, setting those dangerous thoughts aside. Bridget needed to get Mick settled back in town where she was in control of their lives, before he became too attached to the black-haired rancher, too comfortable living out at his ranch, before gossip about what a widow of questionable reputation could possibly be doing living at the ranch reached Mick's ears.

"Is there something else ye'd care to tell me?" Reilly prodded her.

Bridget cleared her throat and dared a glance at the slump-shouldered boy who looked as if he'd just lost his best friend. Though she'd gladly give her son the world to see him healthy and happy, she could never let her actions bring about the ruin of the finest man she had ever met. Honest, loyal, dependable— and so beautiful her heart squeezed every time she looked at him.

And that was the only grain of truth to her thinking: she was afraid of how it felt when she looked at James. Afraid of how easy it would be to let herself come to care for him if she'd stayed. She could probably work through the gossip and rumors, but she was absolutely scared spitless about her reaction to James.

But even if she had it to do all over again, she wouldn't stay. Vicious gossip swirling around the poor man and casting a dark cloud over his unblemished reputation would not be the way she wanted to repay him for his kindness.

James Ryan deserved more than that from her.

Concentrating on the scenery as the horse plodded toward town, Bridget was assaulted by a myriad of unanswered questions eating a burning hole in the pit of her stomach. Her head ached, and her heart hurt. She stole a glance at Reilly, whose massive hands held the reins loosely, guiding the horse with a slight tug on the leather traces. The need to explain to someone who would understand, who would listen and not interrupt as Mick was wont to do, burned through her.

Before she could speak, Reilly said, "Ye didn't have to get yer back up and leave us in a lurch," he huffed.

She nearly reached out to pat the man's hand. "I'm sorry. I'm just so used to taking care of Mick by myself." She cleared her throat. "It's hard to be beholden to anyone, now that I'm well again."

The half-truth nearly stuck in her throat. Up until the moment James informed her the town was already gossiping about her being at his ranch, she'd hadn't definitely decided to leave. But after learning that, added to the attempted rustling and possible ruining of James's good name and standing in the community, she knew they would have to.

Reilly nodded in reply and snapped the reins. The sturdy plow horse threw back his head as if agreeing it was time to pick up the pace. The wagon bounced in and out of the deep ruts, reminding her the road ahead would be just as difficult.

"So yer running away to work yourself sick again."

"No." She nearly groaned aloud.

Mick squirmed on the seat beside her. "Have a care, lad, or ye'll end up with splinters in yer backside," Reilly warned.

Mick sat still, then blurted out, "If you can't find a job in town, can we go back to the ranch?"

At least Mick sounded resigned to her decision. Heaven knew it would be so much harder if he fought against her. Although she'd begun eating again and gained some weight, emotionally she wasn't up to the possibility of doing battle with her son. Leaving James and his safe haven behind had been harder than she'd envisioned; she felt exhausted.

"We'll see," she said.

Screwing up her courage, straightening in the seat, and squaring her shoulders helped prepare her for her first glimpse of town in more than two months. The bend in the road skirted a stand of ancient, gnarled oak trees, and all at once the town lay sprawled before them. Squeezing Mick's hand once, then letting it go, helped to dispel the feeling of unease skidding up her spine.

The wagon wheels and trotting horse churned up a pale brown cloud of dust, enveloping them, announcing their progress into town.

The road ahead was busy. Two other wagons headed toward them, laden with barrels of food stores and sacks of grain. Reilly waved cheerfully to the other drivers. His greeting was returned with an equal amount of friendliness. Even the foreman of James's ranch was well known and liked. *One more reason to stick to her decision not to go back.*

The strong midday sun beat down uncomfortably on her worn straw bonnet. The high collar of her much-mended, but scrupulously clean, faded dress added to the building heat, making her feel lightheaded. She dug deep inside herself, finding the strength to ignore the heat and clear her head. Now was when she needed to be strong.

Reilly slowed the horse to a walk as they approached the mercantile, and Bridget had the uneasy feeling she was being watched. Out of the corner of her eye, she noticed the well-dressed older woman standing on the wooden boardwalk in front of the store, glaring at her!

"Dandy," she mumbled. "Sarah Burnbaum." Now word would spread like wildfire that the widow O'Toole was back in town. The woman stiffened, but did not turn away as the wagon slowed and Reilly tipped his hat to her.

"Pleasant day," he called out.

"Mr. Reilly." The older woman acknowledged the greeting, but pointedly ignored Bridget and her son.

"Good morning, Mrs. Burnbaum." Bridget's stomach flipped as her greeting went unanswered, but she managed what she hoped was an outward appearance of calm. The gray-haired president of the Committee for the Betterment of Emerson, whose main function was to find ways to keep the members' menfolk out of the town's three saloons and the nearby den of iniquity (at least that's how Bridget had heard Millie Peabody refer to The Ranch), narrowed her rapacious gaze at Bridget and lifted her hawk-like nose a fraction of an inch higher.

"Well, well. If it isn't the widow O'Toole."

Bridget squirmed under the scrutiny of the older woman. Though no other words were exchanged, Sarah Burnbaum had managed to deflate Bridget's flagging optimism.

As if Mick sensed his mother's mood shift, he greeted the difficult woman. "Good morning, Mrs. Burnbaum." Mick's smile was wide as he hopped down off the wagon. "May I carry that heavy basket for you?"

Before the woman could answer, Mick had the basket in one hand and her elbow in the other. Absolutely charmed, or totally at a loss for words, Mrs. Burnbaum let herself be led.

"I'll be droppin' yer mother off at Swenson's Boarding House."

"Aye, Mr. Reilly." Mick's reply was cheerful as he guided the reluctant, but moving, Mrs. Burnbaum down the uneven board-walk.

"Mr. Reilly . . . John, please stop." The urgency coiled inside of her had her entire body quaking with nerves. Her son was about to be eaten alive by one of the meanest women in all of Emerson. She took one last longing look over her shoulder, expecting to see Mick backing away from the woman in horror.

Bridget blinked, then rubbed her tired eyes, clearing her vision.

But the scene before her did not waver.

Her son had grown three inches in the last month, but it wasn't his height that had her heart swelling with pride before it slowly broke apart. Mick's posture was erect, his chin high. He walked with the newfound confidence of a young man who recognized his own self-worth.

Her eyes welled with unshed tears. One sneaked free; she could feel it trail down her cheek before she brushed it away. Mick was the one she saw with her eyes, but James was the man she saw with her heart. Every movement her son made confirmed what she hoped at first, then later feared, would happen. James Ryan had made an indelible impression on her son, and in doing so, had given Mick much more than a home. He had given Mick the gift of his time and attention, but still more. He had instilled a sense of worth in Mick that was beyond price. Something she had been unable to do.

Her son was becoming a man. Thank heavens James had saved Mick from his own worst enemy, himself. Her heart skipped a beat. *Then why was she taking him away from James?*

"We're nearly there."

"But I've changed—"

"Aye, ye have, Mrs. O'Toole." Reilly's voice was no longer smooth. She caught the rasp of emotion and turned to look at him.

His sad smile caught her attention and had her looking at the man, and truly seeing him for the first time. His dark hair curled into his eyes, but he didn't seem to be bothered by that fact. He brushed a fingertip up the bridge of his nose, effectively flicking the hair out of his eyes. Their deep, rich brown color was enhanced by the compassion she saw in his gaze. Bridget was shocked to notice that he cared, and very unnerved to discover

John Reilly was an attractive man. Why hadn't she noticed before?

"Yer a picture of health. No longer weak as a kitten, or pale as milk."

Bridget wished he didn't sound so concerned, and wouldn't look at her with such intensity. She'd had enough trouble with one thickheaded, black-haired Irishman; she didn't need to worry about another.

She sucked in a much-needed breath of air, and in an effort to compose herself, changed the subject. "You recognized the difference in Mick," she prodded. "Didn't you?" It wasn't a question. There was no doubt in her mind anyone who looked would see it.

"Aye." His sigh was heavy. "There is no finer man alive than Jamie Ryan."

Bridget could feel her emotions tangling. Threads of gratitude were becoming entwined with admiration. Not a bad thing, so long as that was all she allowed herself to feel.

Desperately hoping what she felt on the inside didn't show on the outside, a glimpse out of the corner of her eye dashed her hopes. Reilly's gaze narrowed. He truly was a very observant man. *Too observant.*

"Does Jamie know how you feel?"

Bridget shook her head. "Yes. No." *How could he when I'm not certain myself?*

After the way she acted back at the ranch, there should be no doubt in James's mind. She'd turned him down flat. No explanation, no softening of her rejection. Simply, *I can't.* Her second response was the real truth; James had no idea how she felt about him. He only knew she had ultimately rejected him, though he'd never hear the reasons why from between her tightly pressed lips.

Her stomach was back to roiling, remembering the hurt she'd

seen in the bold blue of his eyes. Why did her rejection seem to bother him so much? It wasn't as if he truly cared about her . . . did he?

She never wanted to hurt anyone the way she'd been hurt, but she had had no other choice. Besides, if she was going to prevent James from losing the respect of the other ranchers in the community, she had to sever the ties that bound them together from the moment he accepted responsibility for Mick and herself.

*If she was doing the right thing, why did it hurt so much?*

"Is there a problem?"

Ryan chose to ignore the concern he heard in Flynn's double-edged question. He knew what Flynn wanted him to say, but he'd be damned to eternal hellfire before he admitted he'd let another woman get under his skin. Why couldn't he forget the tentative looks she'd sent his way? Or the way she drew in her breath whenever he'd caught her looking at him? He should be concentrating on the way she constantly ignored his helpful suggestions, blithely going about her business as if she hadn't been at death's door a few weeks ago.

He'd been a fool. *Again.* He should have known better, after already losing his head over one woman. In spite of the vow he'd made to harden his heart against the lonely widow, he'd gone and done it again.

Bleeding, buggering eedjit! What ever possessed him to leave himself wide open for rejection like that, asking Bridget to marry him?

His skin itched, as if it didn't fit him anymore. Damn, but she'd gotten to him, with her big dark eyes and silky soft skin. She'd been so needy.

Just thinking of her had him kicking himself in the arse all over again. Why couldn't he get the image of her full, dusty-rose lips out of his addled brain?

His sister would have quite a laugh at his expense, of that he had no doubt. Thoughts of Maggie, and the last time he'd seen her, chased away the dark mood that had settled upon him the moment Reilly snapped the reins to drive Bridget and Mick back to town. The lightening of his mood didn't last, as the stark reality hit him right between the eyes.

He'd lost them. And they weren't coming back.

"Why don't ye ride into town and check on that grain shipment ye've been wonderin' about?"

He ignored Flynn's suggestion, in favor of asking himself if he'd ever really had them.

"I'd go meself, but the boss is a terrible tyrant lately. No sense of humor at all."

Ryan's head snapped around at the muffled laughter he heard in Flynn's voice. His guts felt like they'd been ripped out of him and someone was trying to stuff them back inside, and Flynn was laughing at him? His temper shot straight to boil. Before he could stop himself, he had Flynn by the throat, with the man's feet dangling in the breeze two feet off the ground.

Flynn's voice rasped out, "Is this how you coax yer men to work twenty hours a day for ye?"

Ice slid over the burn of humiliation lying in his twisted guts. He looked up into Flynn's face and saw only concern, not condemnation. *Never that from Flynn.* He unclenched his hands and flexed them, keeping them close to the redheaded man's shoulders on the outside chance he'd squeezed Flynn's neck too tightly for too long and would need to steady the man.

But Flynn was made of tough stuff. Hadn't he known that from the first? Wasn't that the reason he hadn't tried to stop Flynn from leaving the Texas ranch where they'd both hired on as cowhands, allowing Flynn to follow him down the long, hard road to Purgatory? The money had been good, the food better, and the owner an honest man . . . or so he'd thought. It still ate at him that he'd been wrong about that too.

Bridget's rejection had shaken his confidence, cutting him right down to the bone. He needed to ask Flynn, "Why didn't you stay on in Amarillo?"

Flynn tilted his head to the side and rubbed at the bright red lines Ryan's fingers had left on his neck. "Why do ye want to know now?"

Guilt added another layer of ice to the fear building in his stomach. "I've never needed to ask before."

*And it was that simple.* He'd been loyal to the men he'd picked up along his journey from New York City to Colorado. The path hadn't been straight, the work never easy, and somehow the years melded one into another.

Six years! Compared to the last thirty minutes he'd spent standing at the foot of the back porch steps, straining his eyes for a glimpse of the wagon he prayed would turn around, it seemed like yesterday. With each second that ticked by, he missed Bridget and Mick more. Every other minute he asked himself, *why?* And yet he waited, watching the road, positive he'd see the telltale wisps of ground-up dirt that a fast-moving wagon, heading up the lane to the ranch, would stir up on a dry-as-dust day like today. But he was only fooling himself.

"Ye saved me life."

Ryan shook his head, setting thoughts of Bridget and her son aside while he stared at Flynn. The man's red hair always made him think of Maggie, but it was the man's continued denial that his hair wasn't *that* red that made Ryan think of Flynn like a brother. Flynn and Maggie had a lot in common. Just last month on her wedding day, she was still denying her hair was red. He remembered her new husband trying to keep a straight face while she denied it yet again. Just one more reason to like the man she'd married.

"I didn't—"

"Ye didn't have to vault over the corral fence and wrestle that bull to the ground by his big ugly horns," Flynn continued as if Ryan hadn't spoken.

"Well, I—"

"And ye didn't have to paint the air blue with yer Gaelic curses until I'd shaken the cobwebs from me head enough to stumble to my feet."

"Well, English wasn't working."

Flynn clapped a hand to Ryan's shoulder. "A finer friend I've never had. Ye've let me travel with ye and never once tired of teaching me how to ride and rope until I no longer embarrassed meself."

"If ye'd let me get a word in—"

"Ah, so now the temper comes up and with it yer Irish!" Flynn smiled.

"Don't be sayin'—" Ryan stopped mid-sentence. He was doing it again. Every time he lost his temper, he'd revert back to his heavy Irish brogue, forgetting to speak carefully, without the musical inflection from his homeland. His heritage had been deeply ingrained, but on Ian McMaster's advice he'd kept it well hidden for the most part. He could either change his name and his life so he could continue to send money home to his family, or he could be true to his heritage and be tracked down like a dog and dragged off to jail inside of six months' time. Self-preservation, and the need to fill his belly, had been the reason he tried to suppress his temperament and his accent.

The Irishmen he'd encountered on his journey west reinforced the need for it. With so many of his people trying to find work, and an equal number of people unwilling to hire the Irish, Ryan had decided to change his name and his speech. Seamus Ryan Flaherty, immigrant, had become James Ryan, rancher.

He'd almost begun to believe the partial lie he used to cover up the real reason he'd changed his name. Amarillo and Rebecca Lynn Trainor were both a long way away. And so was the jail cell where he belonged.

"When are ye goin' to stop worryin' about the law catching up to ye?"

Ryan hated when Flynn knew what he was thinking. But the concern and worry in his friend's eyes warmed the ice sliding into his gut.

"I keep expecting to see Big John step out from behind the barn with his Colts aimed at my guts."

Flynn nodded. "I've had a few bad moments meself, worryin' over whether or not Smith or Shorty would ride up the lane."

Ryan gritted his teeth at the mention of Big John's ranch hands. "They didn't give me a chance to speak!"

Flynn nodded.

"Smith just hauled me out of bed and pinned my arms behind my back."

Flynn placed a hand to Ryan's shoulder. "There was never a chance for any of us to tell our side of it." The grim acceptance in Flynn's voice arrowed through Ryan with a finality that made him bleed on the inside. No one had believed him then. Nearly six years later, who would believe him now?

He looked at Flynn and forced a smile. "I don't want to talk about it anymore."

Flynn's level gaze met his. "Are ye sorry ye made an effort to save me neck?"

Ryan shook his head.

"Well then, ye can come inside and have a cup of me freshbrewed coffee and tell me why ye let the lass take herself and her boy off to town."

Ryan hesitated. Right now, he only knew one thing: there was a gaping hole in his life with Bridget and Mick gone, one he feared would never be filled.

"Are ye comin' then?" Flynn called out.

Ryan shook his head. "I think I'll ride into town after all."

# CHAPTER 11

Michael O'Toole straightened in the saddle, gazing at the land and its possibilities with practiced ease. His left shoulder ached where a Bowie knife's blade had bitten deep. The stitches pulled against the tender skin, but he couldn't afford to let it slow him down. Two of his men, Sam and Nick Paige, rode off to the left of him, arguing.

"Do you think the sheriff'll figure it out?" his right-hand man, Sam, demanded.

O'Toole shrugged, drew in a sharp breath against the hitch of pain that shot through to the bone, ignoring the question and the man.

"I still think—" Sam continued,

"I thought I saw smoke," Sam's brother Nick interrupted, needling him. In response, Sam whipped out one of his Colts and shot a piece off the brim of Nick's Stetson.

"Damn it, Sam!" Nick shouted, but before he could retaliate, O'Toole had his horse between the brothers.

"I'm getting mighty tired of having to step in between you boys to make sure you don't kill each other," he drawled, making eye contact with first one, then the other.

"Come on Mick, you know he don't mean nothin' by it," the younger Paige brother said by way of apologizing for his older brother.

O'Toole shook his head, and drew his gun. The Colt beneath Sam Paige's nose must have been unexpected. O'Toole could

126

tell it unnerved the man.

"I'm not going to put up with any more of your fighting, boys. Understand?"

The younger Paige brother nodded his head like a puppet on a string. The only time O'Toole had ever seen any real emotion in the man's eyes were the few times he'd had to threaten Sam to keep the both of them in line.

O'Toole didn't even bother to see if Sam was affected; he turned back toward his destination. "Let's see what kind of action we can find in this poor excuse for a town."

"I hear tell, there's a saloon owned by a woman, goes by the name of Pearl," Nick added.

"Pearl's place," Sam said with a sneer.

O'Toole let them talk, turning back to see if the rest of his gang had any objection to heading toward the saloon owned by a woman named after one of nature's jewels.

A simple nod and the gang headed toward the town of Emerson and Pearl.

With Flynn's question still ringing in his head, Ryan stood just outside the door to the sheriff's office. He hesitated long enough to hear the sheriff say he was leaving town early. Ryan opened the door to the sheriff's office as his brother-in-law was asking, "Are you certain you won't wait until the marshal arrives?" Ice formed in his gut as his worry for Bridget and Mick was temporarily forgotten in the wake of the trouble brewing in the sheriff's office.

He could all but feel Turner's anxiety. Ryan had seen disasters stem from less of a sticky situation than a sheriff retiring before his replacement arrived. He wondered what the sheriff was thinking.

"Marshal Justiss wired just last night," the sheriff said. "Should be here in a couple of days," the man added, rubbing his leg before reaching for the saddlebag he'd left on the floor

Ryan knew the injury still bothered the aging sheriff, but didn't think it was the main reason behind the man's early retirement. He remembered a similar conversation he'd had with his brother-in-law before Turner married Maggie. Once a lawman lost his edge, he was just days away from a bullet in the back.

Turner nodded, indicating he'd heard the man, but he didn't answer. Ryan wondered if Turner regretted retiring. He knew his brother-in-law had been a marshal for years, but then had given up his badge and life in the saddle, tracking down outlaws, to marry Maggie a few months ago. Then he thought of his sister, who seemed to walk around looking as if she'd swallowed sunshine, and he knew Turner had no regrets in that regard.

"How is Maggie?" the sheriff asked, putting a much-mended shirt into his saddlebag.

Turner didn't try to stop his lightning-fast grin, and Ryan envied his brother-in-law his happiness. Ryan had just lost his.

"I'll take that smug smile on your face to mean your pretty little wife is just fine."

Turner nodded and schooled his features, and Ryan laughed. "Don't let Turner use his marshal's face on you, Sheriff," Ryan said slowly. "He's just trying to change the subject and avoid telling us how he's going to explain to my sister why, after giving up his job as a United States marshal and marrying her, he suddenly has had a change of heart about leaving his job behind."

The sheriff nodded. "I'd like to be a fly on the wall for that one." He straightened up from his packed bag and stretched. "But my mind's made up. The marshal should be here tomorrow or the next day."

"I also know what can happen out on the trail," Turner said.

"More often than not, I got delayed by circumstances beyond my—"

"Just say it straight out, Marshal—"

"Retired marshal," Turner corrected.

"Oh, hell! No use talking to you once you've made up your mind, Turner."

"You always were a quick study."

"If you are so all-fired up about me leaving, why don't you come out of your blasted retirement and park your boots behind the desk here in my office until Justiss arrives?"

From the look on Turner's face, Ryan knew he had thought about it, but probably hadn't discussed it with Maggie yet. "I just might at that. Does the sheriff over in Milford know you're leaving?"

"Who do you think convinced me I was a statistic waiting to happen?"

Ryan looked at Turner, then the sheriff. But before he could add his two cents, Turner spoke up, "I don't blame you for retiring," Turner said slowly. "You're dedicated to the bone, and after clearing up the tangled web of lies and legal documents your local banker tampered with, I'd have made the same choice."

"Bullets have a way of convincing even the most dedicated public servants," Ryan added, turning toward Turner. "Isn't that the line of reasoning you used when you decided to retire?"

"Something like that," Turner said with brief smile. "I think I'll go talk to my wife."

"Well now, you be sure and do that, Marshal," the sheriff said, trying not to smile.

"I'm retired!" Turner snapped, pushing past Ryan and stalking out of the sheriff's office.

Bridget smoothed the flat iron over the linen tablecloth one more time. Setting the iron back on its stand, she checked the cloth for any missed wrinkles.

"Not a one."

Satisfied, she lifted the cloth and carefully folded it corner to corner, until it was a manageable size, and placed it on the top of the growing pile. Work helped her get through the day, and there seemed to be enough work at Swenson's to keep her busy for a long time.

She used the back of her wrist to brush the hair out of her face. The heat from the flat iron always made her hair corkscrew around her face. The springy curl fell back into her eyes, but she ignored it, already concentrating on the last of Sarah Burnbaum's laundry. The old harridan had decided Bridget was not fit company for her, but certainly fit enough to handle her wash. The irony of the situation was nearly laughable. She sighed and forced the rest of her uncharitable thoughts out of her mind. Only two dozen napkins left.

"Take a break, dear." Mrs. Swenson held out a glass of iced lemonade to her.

"Thank you." Bridget gratefully accepted the proffered glass. She didn't want to admit she was tired, but she knew from the week or so she and Mick had lived at Swenson's that not much slipped past the observant older woman. She always found the stray speck of dust Bridget never failed to leave behind while dusting the front parlor.

"You've worked straight through the last four hours. Did you stop for lunch?"

Bridget sighed and shook her head, then tilted it back and drained half the glass. The tart flavor danced upon her tongue on its way down her parched throat. Lemons had been a luxury she could never afford. Thankfully, Mrs. Swenson took the offer of room and board to heart and fed them well. In a town as small as Emerson, it was no secret Bridget had been ill, but she was still uncomfortable talking about it.

She finished her drink. "Thank you for the lemonade." She turned back to start on the pile of napkins, but the hand on her arm stopped her.

"I usually don't like to interfere with my boarders," the older woman began, "but seeing as you've held up your end of our bargain, picking up the slack in the cleaning and lending a hand with the laundry I take in, I'm about to make an exception to my own rule."

"I'd love to chat, but I've got to finish Mrs. Burnbaum's laundry before five o'clock."

"If you keel over, you won't get the order finished at all, will you?"

Bridget sighed again. The woman was right and obviously knew it. "All right. I'll take a short break."

Before she could set the iron back near the fire, the kindly rooming-house owner had put a bowl of thick beef stew on the kitchen table. As Bridget sat down, a small plate with warm bread, dotted with melting butter, appeared next to her elbow.

Inhaling the yeasty scent of freshly baked bread and newly churned butter, she sighed. The first bite disappeared before her taste buds realized it. Grateful for the break and the meal, she smiled. "I guess I was hungrier than I thought." The sudden need to blurt out her fear that she'd not be able to keep feeding Mick the same healthy meals they'd enjoyed at the Ryan spread nearly slid past her decision to keep her troubles to herself.

"From the looks of you, you've not been eating enough."

Mrs. Swenson took care of all her boarders, seeing that they were well fed, but she took extra care of Bridget and Mick. Why she did so was still a mystery. For some reason the older woman didn't believe the gossip surrounding them. Either that or the kindly Mrs. Swenson paid no mind to gossip.

"But I'm sure that trying to keep that boy of yours, with two hollow legs, fed takes a lot of time and effort."

Bridget felt a warmth flow through her. "He eats like he hasn't seen food for weeks."

Smiling and nodding, Mrs. Swenson filled their cups with hot tea, adding a generous dollop of honey and cream to both cups before sitting back down to discuss tomorrow's list of chores with Bridget.

A few minutes before five o'clock, Bridget set aside the pint-sized calico dress she'd stitched a hem into. Standing to stretch out the ache in her lower back, she tried to come up with an excuse for heading out the front door if she heard Sarah or Millie coming to the back door. The desire to be long gone before the Committee's leaders arrived was too strong to be put off.

The self-appointed head of the Committee for the Betterment of Emerson had recently spearheaded a campaign to run Pearl out of town on a rail. The only thing Pearl had ever done to anyone (as far as Bridget knew) was to serve the best chicken and dumplings this side of the Rockies. As owner of the notorious Chicken Ranch, affectionately called The Ranch by the local townsfolk—well, the menfolk—Pearl'd been shunned by the local women. As far as Bridget had heard, Pearl had never hurt anyone, nor had she done anything to deserve the attention of the Committee.

That hadn't stopped those hard-hearted ladies from making Pearl's life miserable, and in the end, completely ostracizing Pearl, who rarely came into town unless she needed supplies. Maggie had filled her in on how the Committee treated Pearl and others they did not approve of. Whatever convinced the women they had the right to approve or disapprove, Bridget couldn't say, but they reminded her of Michael's mother. She shuddered, pushing that memory away.

Poor Pearl. Bridget knew exactly how it felt to be on the receiving end of endless ill-humored jokes and countless rude stares of condemnation. She'd eaten bad fish once. The nasty stuff had made her stomach ache, just the same as it did whenever she'd heard gossip about herself and Mick. Over the years, she'd heard more than her fair share.

If Maggie's latest information was correct, Pearl needed their help. Coming to a decision, she asked Mrs. Swenson if she could borrow her wagon.

The older woman's brow was furrowed, her mouth grim. "You planning on driving out to The Ranch again?"

She nodded. Although she usually rode alone on her frequent trips out to see Pearl, she wondered if maybe Mrs. Swenson was waiting to be asked. After all, the woman hadn't yet denied Bridget the use of her wagon.

"Pearl needs help," Bridget blurted out. "Maggie said poor Mary burned her hand stoking the stove in the kitchen."

Mrs. Swenson nodded. "I heard Amy twisted her ankle hurrying down the stairs to feed the chickens."

Bridget's head snapped up at that. "I thought you didn't listen to gossip?"

Mrs. Swenson smiled. "Well, now, dear, there's gossip and there's some things that need to be passed on so a body can stay informed about what goes on in their own backyard."

Bridget nodded. Some people understood the difference between friendly nosy neighbors and downright mean, rumor-spreading harpies. Her heart clutched thinking of the other little one Maggie had told her Pearl had recently taken in.

"Have you heard about little Emma?"

Mrs. Swenson nodded. "Some men should be shot before they can sire any offspring."

Bridget's throat closed as she remembered what Maggie told her about the poor child. Disbelief had her heading out to see if she could help Pearl and the little mite. Her stomach clenched, but seeing is a whole lot more disturbing than simply hearing unpleasant things. The bruises spoke for themselves. She suddenly needed to know more about Pearl and why she was the only woman in town willing to help these poor runaways.

"What do you know about Pearl?"

"I've heard lots of things."

Bridget's gaze sharpened. "Well, I hope you don't believe everything you've heard."

Mrs. Swenson looked at her and was silent for a moment. "I'd have to be a halfwit to believe everything the women in this town spout as gospel truth."

Bridget unclenched her hands. When had she fisted them? "I hate gossip." And it was true. Bridget did. Unfortunately, sometimes it was the only way a body learned anything.

The older woman nodded.

"She's a wonder in the kitchen. There isn't any way of cooking chicken that she hasn't perfected."

Another nod of agreement.

Bridget swallowed and plunged into what disturbed her the most. "Have you heard she serves more than buttermilk biscuits, chicken and dumplings? And I'm not talking about cherry or apple pie."

"Whiskey?"

Bridget shook her head, sadness seeping into her stomach.

Mrs. Swenson sighed and slowly stood. "The trouble with gossip is that it grows. The first person who tells it sticks pretty much to the truth, but the one who hears and passes it on might add a bit to make the telling more interesting."

Bridget's stomach started to settle a bit. She blurted out, "Have you heard she has an upstairs room for entertaining?"

Mrs. Swenson's back went poker straight, stiff with whatever she was thinking. Bridget didn't have to wonder long what that might be. "Hmph. I knew it was only a matter of time before Sarah and Millicent went too far."

"Then they made it all up?" Bridget shuddered, remembering Richard Gray and the Rusty Spur's back room.

"I've met Pearl," Mrs. Swenson said. "She's an honest woman."

"If she did have a room and was forced by circumstances to—"

Before Bridget could finish, Mrs. Swenson interrupted. "Everyone has run up against trouble a time or two in their lives. If they haven't, they aren't really living. People are human. Humans make mistakes."

Bridget's skin iced over. She hoped Pearl had not been forced to entertain men in that upstairs room. Good Lord, she'd nearly been forced herself. If she hadn't—

Before her past could catch up to her, Bridget felt herself being dragged to her feet and wrapped in a fierce hug. "Don't drag the past up now. You need to concentrate on the present. You've a strong son who's teetering on the edge of manhood. Such a scary time. He's at the crossroads. He'll either take the right fork or the left one. You need to be there for him to help him choose the right path."

"Mrs. Swenson—" Bridget stumbled over her tangled thoughts, trying to come up with the right words. All she could find were the simplest. "Thank you."

"A body can't have too many friends, Bridget." Mrs. Swenson's smile was beautiful, touching something deep inside of Bridget. It'd been so long since another female had offered friendship, she was still unused to it. She'd nearly missed it altogether, and passed it up. She'd almost done that with Maggie's offer. too. Then again Maggie was a sharp one, and not about to let Bridget get off so easily. Bridget smiled thinking of her redheaded friend.

"I'm planning on heading out to see if I can help Pearl and her girls. Would you like to ride with me?"

The older woman dried the dish in her hand and set it down on the far end of the pine table, away from the laundry basket. She wiped her hands on one of the pristine white aprons she always wore before crossing her arms beneath her ample bosom.

"Let me get some things together. I've some salve that would help with Mary's burn."

"Anything we can do to help will be appreciated."

At the other woman's silence, Bridget stumbled on. "She's a special friend of Maggie Turner's. Any friend of Maggie's—"

"I been making up my own mind about people for nigh on thirty years. Besides I've got eyes in my head." Mrs. Swenson frowned. "Now tell me what else you've heard that you think I haven't."

Bridget swallowed past the lump forming in her throat. "I was just wondering if you knew whether Pearl's husband was still alive or not."

"Well now, seems to me I heard they rode into town about fifteen years ago and bought the place, but before he could turn it into much more than a glorified watering hole for itinerant cowboys moving from one spread to another, he died."

Bridget nodded. "Is that why the womenfolk around here and over in Milford convince their husbands not to have anything to do with her and The Ranch?"

Mrs. Swenson's mouth flattened into a grim line. "Well, that would be part of it. But the fact that the womenfolk around here couldn't keep their men away from The Ranch was the straw that broke the camel's back. When he died, word got out, and before Pearl knew what had happened, gossip that her well had gone bad spread. She couldn't get spit for the land after that."

"That's what Maggie told me. That it was Sarah Burnbaum and Millicent Peabody who single-handedly tried to close down

The Ranch and run Pearl out of town. Apparently they're still trying."

"But they haven't succeeded yet," Mrs. Swenson said with a slow sweet smile.

"No," Bridget agreed with a small smile of her own. "They haven't."

"The women in both towns have the right to an opinion as to where their menfolk spend their evenings," Mrs. Swenson added.

"Maggie's husband spends them at home." Bridget couldn't stop the smile that blossomed from within her, just thinking about her newly married friends. "But what no one seems to understand is that the girls who work for Pearl cook, clean, and tend the ranch. That's all they do. Why are people always willing to believe the worst?"

"It's the nature of the beast. Why don't you believe it?"

Well, that was a switch: someone asking why she chose to believe the best when only the worst stared her in the face. Rather than spill her guts and share what she hadn't in ten years, Bridget shrugged. Mrs. Swenson didn't pry.

"As far as I hear tell, she runs a boarding house, same as me, only she takes in young girls down on their luck—"

"But they don't sell their bodies for pleasure!" Bridget's stomach was back to clenching, her throat burning as the meal she'd eaten worked its way back up.

Mrs. Swenson placed her hands on Bridget's shoulders and settled her into the chair. Meeting Bridget's gaze, she quietly spoke. "No, dear they don't. No matter what others believe about Pearl, she's an honest woman. Even when she had no more than dirt to eat, she didn't sell herself to buy food. She's proud and she's strong."

"Then why didn't you stand up for her when the Committee tried to run her out of town?"

"I did."

"I don't understand." And she didn't. Confusion rumbled around in her brain until her head hurt.

"I told you. Everyone who's lived has made mistakes now and again."

Bridget wondered what mistakes Mrs. Swenson had made, but she wasn't brave enough to ask. She'd let it alone for now.

"Pearl didn't turn her back on those poor, tired, dirty, and bedraggled girls. Each one had a tale of hard luck that would just break your heart."

"How do you know?"

"Who do you think helped keep food on the table when Pearl was on the verge of starvation?"

"Then why do Sarah and Millie swear no one in town stood beside Pearl?"

"Because it makes for a much better story."

Bridget stood and wrapped her arms around her kindly landlady. "You're stronger than I thought you were. I'll be ready to leave for The Ranch as soon as I get a few things from my room."

"Inga Swenson!" Sarah Burnbaum flung open the door and marched into the kitchen uninvited and unannounced, shaking her head so violently her flower-bedecked bonnet bobbed wildly, threatening to fly off her head. "Don't you dare set foot in that establishment!" The head of the Committee for the Betterment of Emerson stood with her hands on her more-than-generous hips, her mouth set in a grim line of determination.

For a moment, Bridget wished she'd escaped before Sarah had arrived, but then she realized this was her chance to strike a blow for Pearl and the homeless girls who helped work her ranch.

"Last I heard, folks in the Colorado Territory could come and go as they pleased."

Mrs. Swenson smiled.

Sarah glowered. The hate-filled look she sent Bridget's way would have cowed her a few weeks ago, but she was stronger than the day Sarah had stomped all over her new-found confidence right after leaving James and his ranch. Being able to take care of Mick and herself, and having someone who appreciated her help, went a long way toward rebuilding the sense of worth Bridget had buried inside herself.

A certain black-haired Irishman had shown her that she was special, so special that he'd proposed—

She shook her head. She couldn't think about that now.

"Young woman," Sarah said, "do you dare to contradict me?" Before Bridget could say yes, the old bat continued, "You dare to shake your head at me?"

Sarah's face turned a hideous shade of mottled red as she drew in short, choppy breaths. It made Bridget feel bolder. "I have a name. It's Bridget, and if you'd rather not be on such familiar terms, Mrs. O'Toole will do."

"Well, I never!" Sarah sputtered.

"Exactly the reason why I've invited Mrs. Swenson to help instead of you. Pearl is a member of our community in need, and it's our Christian duty to see that she gets that help."

"I'll never set foot in that den of iniquity!" The heavily stomped foot punctuated the woman's declaration.

Both Bridget and Mrs. Swenson ignored her outburst. "I'll be ready to leave in a moment, Bridget."

"I'll just take Mrs. Burnbaum's laundry out to her carriage."

"Anyone who consorts with that fallen woman will be publicly ostracized!" Sarah jabbed her pointer finger high above her head, nearly tipping over the oil lamp hanging above the kitchen table.

"I've already received that same gracious welcome from the fine ladies of Emerson." Bridget kept her tone even, although her throat hurt from her overwhelming desire to shout at the dense woman.

"And justly so."

"And you would know all about justice, Sarah?" Mrs. Swenson's quiet prompting had the other woman falling silent.

Bridget looked from one woman to the other. Whatever Mrs. Swenson knew about Sarah Burnbaum had the power to silence her. Bridget would have to find out what it was another time. Right now she needed to get out to The Ranch. "I'll just put this outside."

"I'll carry it myself." Much to their surprise, Mrs. Burnbaum hefted the basket and swept from the room. Pausing on the top of the front step, she called back over her shoulder, "I won't be needing your laundry services again, Miss O'Toole!"

Bridget started to correct her, that it was *Mrs.* O'Toole, and that the laundry service belonged to Mrs. Swenson, but the aggravating woman was already inside her carriage, pulling away.

"It's just as well you don't have anything to do with that one." Mrs. Swenson pulled her shawl off the peg on the wall and drew it about her shoulders. "Let's see what we can do for our neighbor."

"I have a few things upstairs—"

"Do you need help getting them?"

Bridget shook her head, then dashed upstairs. By the time she'd gathered everything together, Mrs. Swenson and Mick were waiting by the already hitched wagon. Her son stood quieting the dark brown plow horse the older woman was so fond of. He'd obviously heard part of their conversation. Bridget shuddered; it had certainly been loud enough.

"Are you all right, Ma?"

Without looking at him, she reached over and patted his hand, wordlessly assuring him she was.

"Where to, ladies?"

Bridget turned to stare at Mick. For a moment she could have sworn it was James Ryan sitting beside her, asking where she wanted to go. Shaking her head to dispel the remnants of his voice, she answered, "Pearl's place."

Mick clicked his tongue against his teeth and snapped the reins, urging the big horse forward.

# Chapter 12

Marshal Ben Justiss reached inside his shirtfront pocket and pulled out the well-worn bit of paper he'd been carrying for nearly two years.

The face hadn't changed.

He hadn't expected it to, but at times he surely wished it had. He might have caught up to Michael O'Toole long before now if it had.

Wanted posters were not always accurate, and at times they could be frustrating if one had not seen the depicted outlaw in the flesh. Justiss swiped his hand across his forehead, mixing the sweat with the fine layer of dust his horse had kicked up, leaving a smear of dirt behind. Squinting up at the position of the sun in the bright blue sky, he figured it was heading on toward mid-afternoon.

He'd make the town of Emerson by tomorrow evening, if his luck held out and the wind didn't shift, bringing in the weather change he sensed was coming. He couldn't rightly say why he could always tell when the rain was headed his way; he simply accepted the fact that he could.

"What do you say, boy?" He gave his horse's strong neck two quick pats before squeezing his knees against the animal's sides. His mount responded as expected, with the lift of his equine head and snort of agreement. Justiss had to smile at the reaction; even his horse thought he had spent too much time thinking when it was time to be moving.

"Always thought you were too smart to be hitched to a plow." The affection in his voice echoed what he felt for his best friend. The heavily muscled blood bay was strong enough to have been a draft horse, and would have been, too, if Justiss hadn't seen the way the animal could flat-out run. The horse had heart; lots of it, and would run until he dropped if Justiss asked it of him. The horse rarely disagreed with him, and had saved his life. Twice. Red had a dizzying move that enabled him to outflank even the fastest of horses. Any man who harbored thoughts of consigning Red to a life drudging behind a plow should be shot first, and then asked why.

Damned if Red didn't nod his head up and down in the agreement. Sometimes the way the horse seemed to understand what he was saying to him jarred Justiss to the bone. But he never questioned Red's ability.

As he followed the sun, due west, the breeze shifted and blew harder. "Rain'll be coming." *Too bad it wouldn't hold off another day. He hated bedding down on soggy ground.*

He focused on the trail ahead, knowing in his bones that this time he would find O'Toole before the outlaw discovered he was being followed. Two years was the time limit he'd given himself to bring O'Toole in. One year and six months had seen the end of his patience. His anger was slow to build, but once he had a good head of steam going, it took a while for his temper to cool.

Justiss was nearly out of time, and out of patience. He sorely missed the comforts of home, the smile of a pretty woman (even if she was related to him), and the taste of a home-cooked meal. *Especially buttermilk biscuits.* He surely missed his sister's biscuits, but the need to bring O'Toole in forced aside all other thoughts.

Ryan's knock was answered immediately. The door swung open,

and before he could take the hat from his head, his arms were filled with a laughing woman.

"Jamie! Well, if ye've come for dinner, yer late." His sister hugged him tight to her. "If I had known you'd stop by, I'd have waited the meal."

Maggie's gentle reminder of the length of time between visits wasn't lost on him. "I've been busy."

"Oh, aye." She smacked his chest half-heartedly before pushing away from him, holding him at arms' length for a moment. The way she intently studied his face unnerved him. There was no use trying to school his features; his sister would see what she wished to see.

"I don't expect you to feed me every time you see me, Maggie."

Ryan hoped she would be sidetracked by his brusque words, but he didn't expect it. He was not surprised when she replied, "It gives me pleasure to watch ye enjoy what I've cooked."

Her furrowed brow was the tip-off that she was upset with him. Bloody hell, she'd probably be able to guess what he was thinking no matter how straight a face he adopted.

"There's no finer cook alive," he added, hoping to distract her from her train of thought.

Maggie sucked in a breath. "When did they leave?"

The hair on the back of his neck bristled. By the saints! How did she do it? *Could she read his mind? And why couldn't he keep her from doing it?*

"Who?" he asked, intensely gratified to see a moment of confusion mar her smooth complexion. Perverse of him, but he couldn't help himself. His sister was too often right, and on too many uncomfortable occasions, she knew what he was thinking.

"Bridget and Mick," Maggie huffed out. "Did ye think I wouldn't hear that they'd left your ranch and moved into Swenson's?"

"James!" his brother-in-law called out as he walked into the kitchen. "Did you bring Bridget and Mick?"

Pain flashed through him like a bolt of lightning, sharp, hot, and quick. He hadn't the time to try to hide his feelings from the only family he had left. He was a proud man, but not so proud that he would push aside the unconditional love his sister showered on him, or the friendship he and Turner shared.

God help him; he needed them both.

The stark need to be with his family had him leaving the ranch with chores unfinished and no word to anyone about where he was headed or when he'd be back. Anyone who knew him would have attested to the fact that something was very wrong. He never shirked his duties. *Ever.* He simply didn't act this way.

But in the last few days, his whole world had turned upside down and inside out. Feelings he thought were forever burned from his heart had taken him by surprise. That battered organ still had the capacity to feel. *To need. To want. To love.*

It scared him to the soles of his well-worn boots that he had no control over his feelings for the widow O'Toole. Had he been aware he was developing an affection for her, he would have blocked the feelings before it was too late. Hadn't he done so successfully for the last five years?

But he never even saw it coming and was in up to his neck before he recognized the signs of a man going under for the third and final time.

Unaware that he was being steered toward the big oak table, he started when he felt strong hands grip him by the shoulders and push him down into a chair. The silky soft cheek pressed against his broke the daze he was in. He reached up and gently tugged on the wavy strand of red brushing across his chin.

Maggie smiled. Her watery eyes were the clearest of blues. Everything she felt was reflected in their depths.

"I'm fine, Margaret Mary." He was careful to control his voice, careful not to let it crack over the jagged emotions running riot in his gut. *She was the image of their grandmother.*

Turner's fierce look had him trying not to smile. The mere fact that his sister's new husband was ready to knock some sense into him for daring to upset her was laughable. It would take a stronger man than himself or Joshua Turner to budge his sister once her mind was made up. At least he and Turner agreed that she was worth protecting and keeping happy.

He couldn't have found a better man for Maggie if he'd chosen the man himself. A sudden image of his boyhood friend Rory Muldoon with his arms about a much younger Maggie surprised him. He'd chosen Rory for Maggie. Praise the Lord she'd not let his death stop her from opening her heart again. *Did she ever think of Rory?*

Hoping to diffuse his brother-in-law's growing impatience and ease the look of sadness on his sister's face he asked, "What smells of heaven?"

"Your sister has a way with apples and cinnamon."

Turner laid a hand on Maggie's shoulder and squeezed it gently. The soft smile curving her generous mouth was swift and joyous.

Ryan wondered if he reached out a hand, would he be able to feel the invisible bond of love he knew connected the couple? It was palpable. Their love was strong and unselfish enough to include him. As his sister squeezed his hand, a jolt of self-disgust ripped through him. He didn't deserve their love. He didn't deserve anyone's. Accused of breaking the law, and still running away from the cold jail cell that waited for him back in Texas, nearly six years of helping other immigrants like himself cope with the strange customs of a strange land hadn't balanced the scales of justice. *He was still a wanted man.*

Maggie set a generous slice of warm apple pie on the table in front of him. Automatically, he lifted the fork to his lips and slipped the cinnamon-and-sugar-spiced flaky confection into his mouth.

He chewed and swallowed without tasting a thing. How could he continue to keep the truth from his sister, when she'd bravely ridden all the way from New York City to Colorado to help him save the ranch?

He was a bloody, buggerin' eedjit! During the weeks she'd been missing and he'd feared the worst, her stagecoach had been attacked by Indians and she'd been kidnapped. When she'd arrived on his doorstep, she'd been battered and weak, but not defeated. Still she had not turned back. She never let her fear get in the way of accomplishing her goal of delivering the legal papers he'd sent to her for safe keeping, the ones he needed to keep a crooked banker from foreclosing on his ranch. She'd risked so much to help him. How could he continue to keep the truth of his past from her now?

*Because she wouldn't understand, and Ryan couldn't take the chance she wouldn't believe him.* But he was innocent! If Big John and his beautiful two-faced daughter were standing before them right now with the so-called evidence, would anyone believe he'd not committed cold-blooded murder?

He set the barely touched cup of coffee next to the piece of half-eaten pie and pushed back from the table. "That was delicious as always, Maggie."

"But ye didn't finish—"

Her husband's hand on her arm effectively stopped her.

Ryan wished he didn't know that she worried about him. He didn't want her to, but knowing Maggie, he couldn't stop her, even if he wanted to.

"I'll be by again soon."

"For Sunday supper then?" Maggie asked.

"I don't know . . ."

"You're welcome any time."

Ryan shook hands with his brother-in-law, grateful for the honest offer, but careful to avoid his too inquisitive gaze.

"Thanks." He had no desire to get into the details of his past with the former lawman. A little while later, he wondered if he could trust Turner. With each mile he rode, his gut formed another twisted knot of tension, as he remembered the Big J Ranch. Images of the dank jail cell got all tangled up with the blond-haired, blue-eyed angel who had helped to put him behind bars. He would never forget how it felt to be hauled from his bunk in the middle of the night. Not one person believed that he hadn't broken into the wealthy rancher's new safe, and that he hadn't committed murder. But the arrow to the heart was hearing Rebecca Lynn swear he had.

McMaster believed him and had understood the reasons Flynn and Reilly had broken Ryan out of jail. McMaster had family in Scotland and sent money home regularly, too. But McMaster agreed with Ryan that he could never go back to his former identity, much less the state of Texas. Over a bottle of single-malt whiskey, the four of them had come up with a plausible story as to where Ryan had been born and what kind of family he had.

Ryan hated lying, but he couldn't earn money to send home to his mother and sister in New York City if he was behind bars. The need to help them outweighed the consequences he would suffer if he were caught.

So he immersed himself in learning to run McMaster's spread. The old man's knowledge was endless, his patience limitless. His final gift to Ryan, the ranch, could never be repaid, but Ryan would continue to honor the vow he'd given McMaster to help those in need.

He shook his head sadly. He'd never be able to tell Maggie. She believed in honesty above all things, and he'd already lied to her about why he changed his name. Yes, he'd faced some difficult times as an Irish immigrant, but that alone would never have made him give up his proud name. Protecting his mother and sister, making sure they could not be connected to the Seamus Flaherty wanted for murder in Texas, was the real reason.

He knew if he tried to explain everything to Maggie now, she'd feel obliged to tell her husband, the former U.S. marshal. Before his head hit the pillow that evening, Ryan would find himself handcuffed, headed off to jail to spend the night behind bars.

He clenched his jaw tight, grinding his back teeth. It was too late to tell the truth now. Besides, his secret could keep him company when he finally succeeded in pushing his friends and family away.

Michael O'Toole watched the flames of their campfire flicker, then flare up where the roasting rabbit juices splashed onto the hot coals. They'd arrive in Emerson soon. The plans were falling into place. Gossip was the local law was retiring. With luck, they'd have a few days before a replacement or a marshal would show up.

All they needed was some time to relax and unwind before the job. From all they'd heard along the way, Pearl's place, The Ranch, should just about fit the bill.

# Chapter 13

"Bridget!"

The musical voice was echoed by a chorus of feminine laughter. Half a dozen pretty young women burst out of the door and headed toward the wagon.

Thankfully, Mick had already set the brake. Otherwise, the horse would certainly have been confused by the way Mick handled the reins. The death grip he had on the leather traces would have the horse struggling between stopping and taking off like a plug out of a shotgun.

Bridget patted his hand and smiled at the girls hanging on to the side of the wagon, waiting to be introduced to the slack-jawed, freckle-faced, blushing boy.

She fought to hold back delighted laughter as she watched her son's eyes nearly pop out of his head when their wagon was surrounded by the excited group of lovely females.

"Good afternoon, ladies." Bridget felt their answering smiles warm her all the way down to her toes. At least here she could count on the welcome being from the heart, and not from a misplaced sense of civility.

"Aw now, Miss Bridget, you know we're just regular folk. Not real ladies," one chestnut-haired girl answered.

" 'Sides, we don't know anything 'bout being ladies, except what Miss Pearl's taught us," a tall, willowy blonde added.

"Well, that's why I'm here." Bridget's smile bloomed.

"I thought you were going to help teach us to cook!" two

others wailed, their distress loudly evident.

Mick snapped out of his stupor and jumped down off the wagon. His hand was warm, his grip sure, as he handed Mrs. Swenson down out of the wagon, then his mother. Bridget turned and smiled at the girls. "I've brought one of the best cooks Emerson has to offer to help teach."

She watched the way the girls eyed the tall, sturdily built woman standing next to her with more than a hint of hesitation. If she didn't know better, she'd almost think they were suspicious of Mrs. Swenson. Hoping to make them feel more at ease, she smiled and added, "Mrs. Swenson owns Swenson's Boarding House and makes beef stew so tasty, you don't need ketchup to hide the flavor. It stands on its own."

Six pair of eyes rounded in wonder, but before anyone could comment, Mick found his voice. "Then there's her biscuits."

Bridget turned, intending to say something, when he continued, "It's nearly a crime to sop up the gravy with her buttermilk biscuits." His sigh was huge and exaggerated. "She could make a fortune if she'd sell them."

Bridget's gaze flew to where Mrs. Swenson stood, still silent, but the small smile playing about her lips eased the tension Bridget felt. It would be all right. With the help of her friend, they'd get Pearl through this latest run-in with the Committee.

Before she could speak, Pearl walked out the back door.

"Bridget! I'm so glad you came."

Pearl's voice was too cheerful, her eyes too bright. Bridget had an idea it had to do with the newest addition to The Ranch's residents, little Emma. Maggie had filled her in on the latest news concerning Emma, but rather than ask outright, she decided to wait until she could get Pearl alone for a moment.

"I've brought help. You remember Mrs. Swenson?"

Pearl nodded and smiled.

"She's been kind enough to put us up over at her boarding

house." Bridget knew from the sympathetic look on Pearl's face that she understood what Bridget hadn't said. No one else in town had been willing to let Bridget and Mick stay with them.

Pearl walked down the steps and over to where Mrs. Swenson stood.

"If you're not comfortable here, please don't feel obliged to stay. You've already done far more than anyone else to help me."

Mrs. Swenson huffed out a breath. "If you think I'm going to let that old busybody Sarah Burnbaum influence what I think, you've got another think coming! Besides, I'd rather eat dirt than let the self-appointed president of that darned Committee tell me what to say or whom to say it to!"

Relief swept through Bridget. "Well, if that's all settled, shall we get to work?"

She turned back to the wagon and started hauling out the first of three sturdy wicker baskets she'd stashed there earlier.

Mick took the heaviest ones and let her carry the last one. She was struck once again by his gentlemanly manners. They hadn't been this polished or noticeable before his stay at the Ryan ranch. Was he maturing, or was it someone else's influence? Now that they were living on their own again, she began to notice more and more how much her son had changed, and how greatly his words and deeds resembled James Ryan's.

A brief image of the tall rancher flitted through her mind. Only this time, he wasn't quite so tall. In fact, he was down on one knee, holding her hand and asking her to marry him. "I can't," she whispered.

"Sure you can, Ma," Mick insisted. "You've a way with needle and thread."

Shaking her head to clear it, thoughts of the man who'd surely saved their lives scattered on the gentle breeze. "I'm sorry, I wasn't paying attention."

"But—"

Pearl smiled and patted her arm. "Sometimes I let my thoughts take me on a nice little side trip too, honey. No shame in dreamin'."

Bridget allowed herself to be guided up the back porch steps and into the kitchen. Though she smiled at the group of young women gathered there, her heart was not really in it. Her heart was miles away, held tightly in the hands of a certain black-haired Irishman, one who'd turned her life upside down with his declaration to protect her reputation.

*Why James? Why now?*

No man had cared to protect her before, except for Richard Gray, but Richard never understood her need for friendship. She hadn't been ready to let another man fill Michael's shoes. When she finally told Richard how she felt, his reaction had been violent. She shuddered, remembering the feel of his fists on her face, and his feet in her ribs.

Bridget drew in a deep breath and gathered her scattered wits. No use thinking about the past, or James. He didn't need the likes of her hanging around the ranch, causing more talk than there already was. She set her basket down on the table and lifted the first bit of calico fabric up for all to see.

"I've some spare fabric and bits and pieces of lace I've crocheted for trimming. Who wants to be the first to be fitted for a new dress?"

At the sound of someone clearing his throat, Bridget looked up and saw the look of panic on her son's face. He was surrounded by females. Taking pity on him, she called out, "Mick, if you're finished flirting with the girls, would you see to the horse?"

The look of relief he flashed her as he bolted for the door was sweet.

Mrs. Swenson smiled. "You've a fine son there. He'll be striking out on his own before you realize he's finished growing into a man."

Panic swept through Bridget, stealing her breath. Dear Lord, she hadn't thought that far into their future. What would she do without Mick? How could she go on, if she was all alone? *Who'd feed him? Who'd watch over him while he slept?*

The room started getting fuzzy about the edges. It had always been the two of them, since the night she'd thought to end her life and instead miraculously discovered she carried a new one inside her.

"Take a nice deep breath now. Easy." Someone rubbed her hand up and down Bridget's back, easing the knots of tension.

She did as she was told and drew in one breath, then another. Gradually the room came into focus again and her tension eased a bit.

"Drink this." Pearl's order was softened with a quick grin. "It'll put the starch right back into your spine."

Bridget's hand was not quite steady as she took hold of the small square glass. She forced herself to calm down, telling herself Mick would have to leave home sometime in order to make his own life. She'd been foolish not to think ahead to the day when she'd have to say goodbye and let him go make his way in the world, leaving her alone.

The mouthful of whiskey left a fiery trail of warmth from her tongue all the way down to her stomach. Pearl was right. It was enough to put the starch back. "Thank you."

"Shall we start with biscuits?" Mrs. Swenson's question was answered with a flurry of movement.

The girls soon paired up and set to work mixing dough, while Bridget and Pearl got to work taking measurements for the first of six new dresses.

In between fittings, Pearl leaned close to Bridget and spoke softly. "Emma spoke for the first time last night."

Bridget saw concern mar her friend's nearly perfect features. She wanted to soothe away Pearl's frown. "Do you want me to see if I can get her to tell me what happened?"

Pearl paused, the scissors open and resting against the fabric she'd been cutting. "I'd appreciate it. Try to get her to talk to you. So far, all we know is that her step-daddy is somehow involved in the beating."

Cringing at the thought of any man laying hands on a five-year-old girl in anger, Bridget nodded and rose. "I'll see what I can find out." Reaching into the bottom of the basket, she found what she was looking for and tucked the tiny gift she'd made into her apron pocket.

"Bridget—"

She turned back around to find the owner of The Ranch wringing her hands in agitation. She sensed there was more bothering Pearl than the little one upstairs. Bridget reached out to her. "What is it, Pearl?"

"Luann."

"Is she another homeless girl?"

"No." Pearl shook her head, seeming to need the time to gather her composure. "My real name's Luann. My husband thought I needed a fancy name to attract attention when we first opened the business. I just don't use it anymore. It doesn't seem to fit."

Bridget knew the other woman's husband was dead, but she didn't know too much else about him. "And did you need the name?" she asked quietly.

"I suppose. That first year, I'd cooked and served more chicken and dumplings than I'd thought possible, and dodged more grasping hands than I ever want to see again!"

Bridget did not miss the frown marring Pearl's pretty face. "Was that all he wanted you to do, attract attention?"

Pearl shook her head. "But I refused to entertain any of the

155

customers like he wanted me to."

Disgust surged through Bridget at the thought of a husband asking his own wife to flirt and do Lord knew what else just to bring in business. "I never thought you had."

Bridget's assurance seemed to chase some of the sorrow from Pearl's eyes.

"It means more to me than you know, having you and Maggie believe me."

Bridget would have said the same thing to Pearl, but Pearl had turned back to the task of cutting fabric. The rhythmic sound of scissors snipping cleanly through material followed her upstairs.

It helped knowing she was not alone in the world. There were others who'd suffered from the slings and arrows of gossipmongers. Bridget now had three staunch female friends who by turns needed her help and who were more than willing to help Bridget whenever they could. The bonds of friendship were cemented by the fact that polite society, or those who mistakenly thought they were polite, scorned them.

Bridget paused in the doorway. The tiny figure slumped against the pillow wrung a soft sound of distress from her before she could stop herself.

The child's head whipped around fast enough to have Bridget's head swimming. The terror in little Emma's eyes tore a gaping hole right through Bridget's heart. The yellowing bruises on the little girl's thin face and neck stood out against her pasty complexion. She immediately recognized the signs of near starvation. The poor little thing wasn't eating enough. Bridget should know.

What she didn't know was why.

She walked purposefully into the room. Bridget kept her voice pitched low; she didn't want to frighten Emma. "I'm Bridget. Remember me?"

The little girl's eyes lost that stark fearful look, but the wariness that replaced it didn't ease the tension in the room. But at least Bridget knew the child wasn't afraid of her.

When Emma nodded slowly, Bridget sighed with relief. "Wonderful. I've brought you something."

The look of wonder transforming the child's face had tears pooling in Bridget's eyes. The doll she'd hastily sewn for Emma, after meeting her just a few days ago, had yellow yarn for hair and embroidered blue eyes, and looked just like Emma.

Emma reached out a hand to Bridget, a shy smile lighting her face. Instead of putting the doll in Emma's tiny hands, Bridget clasped hers around the doll and sat on the edge of the bed. The confusion on the child's face was short-lived. "If you want to hold her, you'll have to sip some broth and eat a bite or two of bread."

Emma's eyes tracked back and forth between the yellow-haired rag doll in Bridget's left hand to the tray she had obviously been ignoring on the table.

In a raspy voice, the little one finally asked, "Can I hold her while I eat?"

A tear escaped as Bridget held the doll out to Emma.

Emma saw the tear and whispered, "Don't cry, or the bad man will beat you."

Bridget's breath snagged in her chest, but she ignored it, handing the dolly to Emma and plastering a pleasant look on her face before helping Emma eat. Dear God, the brute beat her for crying? If she had her way, he would pay. The man would definitely pay.

Later that night Bridget lay awake, her mind tormenting her with images she wished she could forget: the sight of little Emma's bruises, and the fear of condemnation in Pearl's eyes when she'd shared the horrible things her husband expected her to do. But mostly she remembered the sorrow in her son's eyes as they drove away from the Ryan ranch.

She rolled onto her side, and her thoughts whirled back to the past and the first time she realized Michael was not coming back. Shrugging that impossibly sad thought aside, she tried to clear her mind and relax. She nearly succeeded. Sighing deeply, she closed her eyes and images of James Ryan bombarded her. *James talking to her son. James sitting, talking to her over cooling cups of coffee.* The most disturbing one of all was the image of James looking at her as if she were the most beautiful woman he'd ever laid eyes on.

She swallowed the lump of emotion she knew would only lead to a serious bout of tears. Sniffing loudly, she rolled over onto her right side and stared out the window. A pale shaft of moonlight illuminated the windowsill with silvery beams. Another memory filled her. Moonlight mixing with candlelight, and the gentle touch of callused fingertips along the length of her jaw, the edge of her collarbone. Restless, she tossed the blanket aside and walked over to the window.

Looking down, she noticed a figure standing in the yard below. Before she could cry out, the soft light of the moon seemed to outline his form. Tall, broad-shouldered, and oh-so-familiar. Her heart lurched with longing. When she saw his body stiffen, she knew he'd noticed her in the window. Neither one of them moved for a heartbeat, then the man who had so gallantly offered her marriage turned on his heel and strode to the hitching post to untie his horse.

Why couldn't she have met James before Michael? The answer was so swift and obviously simple. She wouldn't have had Mick.

Watching the man she cared for far too much ride away, Bridget knew she'd reached a turning point her life. Her heart had finally healed and she was ready to love again. But for the first time in over twelve years, she was afraid her heart was in danger of breaking over a man she had no business thinking about.

The one emotion that had the power to scare the breath right out of her, the one she tried so hard not to feel, swept through her. Despite everything that had happened in the past, never mind her reputation and knowing her feelings could not possibly be returned, her heart ignored her head and leapt ahead. Dizzy with the sudden realization that she had absolutely no control over her heart, she realized she'd fallen completely and totally in love with the one man whom she could destroy simply by being herself.

# CHAPTER 14

Ryan rode like the devil was nipping at his heels, pushing his mount relentlessly until he finally noticed the animal had been breathing heavily for too long. He immediately changed his seat in the saddle and lightened up on the reins. The horse slowed to a trot.

What ever possessed him to ride into Emerson just to stare up at her bedroom window? Wiping a hand across his face in frustration, he knocked the brim of his Stetson up until it slid back off his forehead. He knew she had seen him, but not at first. He'd had the pure pleasure of staring up at her exquisite face illuminated by the soft, pale moonlight.

"Bugger it!"

He should have been home catching up on his much-needed sleep. The last few miles between Emerson and his ranch stretched before him and exhaustion began to ease its way inside of him. The barn-raising was set for a few hours from now. He'd no business being out and about, let alone spying on the lovely widow O'Toole. He urged his mount up the lane to his ranch. "Gawking at her, like a lad just out of short pants!"

He dismounted, looked down at his long legs and shook his head. Taking the saddle from his horse, he began to rub the animal down. Though bone-tired, he'd never ignore the needs of anyone, whether human or four-footed. He'd gone hungry and thirsty too many times and had to keep working long after his body needed him to stop for a breather. If he learned anything from McMaster, it was to value his ranch hands and keep them fed and happy.

Thoughts of eating inevitably had his mind curling around a slender brown-eyed widow. She looked like a dream and cooked like an angel. He didn't want to think about Bridget, and had tried to stop, but if the last few hours were any indication, he wasn't going to succeed.

All his efforts had been for naught; he'd been powerless against his fractured heart's painful reawakening. He rubbed a hand over his chest, trying to ease the dull ache throbbing there. God help him, he never wanted to feel those feelings again. He'd nearly sacrificed the rest of his life in the name of love five years before. The trap had almost swallowed him whole. He'd been a blind eedjit and had vowed to never set himself up to be used by a woman again.

His horse turned and looked over its shoulder at him when Ryan started currying a spot he knew the animal liked.

"Feel's good, doesn't it?" Running a hand over the spot he just combed, he smiled when the huge equine head nodded up and down in agreement.

"Can't you sleep?"

Reilly's gruff, sleep-filled voice echoed through the dilapidated old barn. For a moment, Ryan stood, transfixed by the fact that sound could possibly bounce off planked walls with more than an inch of air and moonlight coming in through them.

*Moonlight, gentle curves, ethereal beauty, illuminated by silvery beams.*

Ryan caught his thoughts drifting toward her again, and shook his head. It would do him no good to follow that particular line of thinking.

Reilly mistook Ryan's movement for agreement and shuffled

into the barn. "I've got more than enough planks set aside for the walls."

Ryan finished up currying his mount, then checked the feedbag. It still had grain left in it. "There's a lad." He patted the horse's neck. "Finish up, and we'll bed you down for the night."

"What's left of it." Other than his comment, Reilly didn't seem perturbed by Ryan's lack of response; he just kept talking. " 'Tis the beams that are givin' me a bit o' worry. I think we've enough, but they may have a bit o' green to them."

"The logs seemed dry enough when we checked them yesterday." Ryan wondered if he hadn't looked closely enough. Reilly's concern should be looked into; the man never worried unnecessarily.

"Aye, that they did."

"Well, then, what's the problem?"

Reilly hesitated, looked right at him, then away. Something was definitely bothering the man. "I thought to catch ye up on what's been happenin' around the ranch." Reilly's eyes were narrowed, his brow furrowed intently.

"I had things to do." Ryan was tired, irritable, and had to be up and about in three hours in order to ensure everything would be ready when the good people of Emerson and beyond arrived for the barn-raising.

One look at Reilly's clenched jaw, and Ryan knew the other man wouldn't leave until he said his piece. Reilly's words confirmed it. "If yer tired, 'tis yer own fault. Harin' off earlier, and then again in the middle of the night, like a hound was snappin' at yer heels."

A slow burn started filling Ryan's gut. "Leave it alone." Ryan was losing his temper, but didn't want to. He clamped his mouth shut. Volatile tempers were just part of the pleasure of working with fellow Irishmen. They all shared that one thing in common, as well as others. Each and every one of the men he'd taken in over the years had tempers to match his own, with engaging personalities that made him ache for the green homeland he'd left far, far behind. Though troubles had followed him all the way from County Clare to New York and on to Texas, he didn't feel so alone as long as Reilly and Flynn were working alongside him. For that he owed the both men more than he could repay.

When he remained silent, Reilly spoke up, "Ye did what ye set out to do. The lad and his mother had a place to stay while she got her strength back."

Ryan grunted.

"Aye, she's fit and fine now. The picture of health. Such a lovely, slender frame—not that another stone on her frame wouldn't sit just as well."

"Reilly . . ." Ryan warned. He didn't want to think about Bridget or her willow-slim body right now.

"Well," Reilly huffed, "I'm just sayin' a man wouldn't mind a woman with a bit more to hang on to when he—"

"*Enough*," Ryan snapped, stomping off toward the house. He'd be hard pressed to sleep at all, but he wouldn't let his friend know he'd gotten the better of him. Without looking back over his should, Ryan called out, "Get some sleep, Reilly. You're going to be needing it come morning!"

"Coffee." He could smell it: hot, black, and sweet as sin, just the way he liked it. Ryan scrubbed his hands over his face. When that didn't knock the sleep from his eyes, he raked his fingers through his hair until his scalp started to tingle.

"All right then," he mumbled. Maybe his brain was finally awake.

Following the heady scent from the back porch, where he'd dropped into his favorite rocking chair a few hours earlier and fallen asleep, he stumbled into the kitchen. Barely awake and far from feeling pleasant, he snatched the offered cup and downed half of it before noticing whose hand the cup had been in.

"Well, then." Maggie's soft voice snagged his full attention. With half a cup of coffee in him, he was more or less awake. "Isn't it grand? Me brother's such a sunny personality first thing in the mornin'."

"Maggie?"

Ryan's body stiffened as someone called out to her, followed by the sound of heavy footfalls and muffled voices coming down the hallway toward the kitchen.

"In here." Ryan's sister stood with her hands braced on her hips, her pointed little chin tilted up, as if poised to receive a clip on it.

Though he was often temped to lash out with his foul temper, he'd never struck anyone in anger. Defense, maybe, but never anger. His words . . . well, he'd not go down that rocky road right now. His sister was demanding his full attention, and it was all he could do to focus his bleary eyes and aching head.

"What are you doing here?"

"Aren't you hosting a barn-raising in a few hours?" his brother-in-law asked, stepping into the kitchen. Maggie looked over her shoulder at him. While Ryan watched, all tension drained from her. Turner placed his hands on Maggie's shoulders and drew her back to lean against the front of him.

Maggie sighed and closed her eyes.

"You shouldn't be letting yourself get all riled," Turner admonished.

"I thought you two had been married for over a month." Ryan couldn't believe Turner had actually lived with his sister for all that time and not witnessed his sister's mercurial temper.

"Aye," Maggie answered. "That we have." Smiling at Ryan, she turned into her husband's arms, letting him hold her close.

The temperature in the room seemed to rise, while all the tension in his rigid body eased away. To be held like that, loved like that . . . The couple radiated happiness.

He shook his head; it was so much more than that. Love, a living, breathing, tangible emotion that he'd at one time ached to lavish on a certain rancher's daughter, but she'd not loved him in return.

" 'Tis yer redheaded sister!" Flynn called out, bursting into the room with one of the ranch hands hard at his heels. "Have ye come to save us from Sean's cookin'?" Flynn nodded at the ranch hand and stared at Maggie, waiting.

Before Ryan could open his mouth to remind Flynn not to tease her, Maggie turned back around and grabbed hold of her husband's hand. "I don't have red hair, Flynn," she said with the toss of her red head. "You do. Besides, I cannot let ye rile me."

The breath whooshed out of Ryan's lungs. *Something was wrong with Maggie.* He could tell from the way his sister had calmly answered the taunt that in the past had usually managed to get her back up.

Bloody hell, was she ill? Had someone hurt her?

He could think of only one man to blame. "Turner!"

Instead of the worried reaction he expected, his brother-in-law smiled at him, all the while pointedly watching the way Ryan clenched and unclenched his fists. Damn the man for knowing he was angry.

"Ryan?"

"What have ye done to me sister?" Ryan nearly bit his tongue off. Bugger it, he hated the way his temper brought out his brogue. He'd tried so hard to lose the lilting way he spoke. At the time, it had been a matter of life and death. It still was.

"Now, Seamus." Maggie used the Gaelic form of Ryan's name. "Why don't ye finish yer coffee? The scones'll be comin' out of the oven in a moment."

"Scones?" Masterson stood in the doorway to the kitchen with his head tilted up, and his nose theatrically sniffing at the air. "Do I truly smell just-baked scones?" The big man whipped his head around and pinned his gaze on Maggie. "I knew you'd come back and save us from your brother's cooking! We haven't had a decent scone since Mrs. O'Toole . . ."

The mention of her name had Ryan's blood boiling. He was ready to throttle the man, but one look at his sister had the dangerous need subsiding. *What was wrong with Maggie?*

He turned his attention back to Turner and demanded, "I asked you a question."

He took a menacing step closer to the man who'd helped him save his ranch. Damn, if it wasn't for Turner . . . He swiftly set that thought aside and concentrated on his sister. Her well being was paramount. "What's wrong with me sister?"

His brother-in-law seemed unmoved by Ryan's rising anger. He brushed a fingertip down the line of Maggie's jaw and touched it to the tip of her nose. "I think Maggie has something to tell you."

"Seamus, why don't ye have a seat?" She drew her brother over to an empty chair. Head pounding, body weary, and mind confused, he let himself be led.

Her face was too pale. Dear Lord, don't let her be seriously ill. He couldn't face that.

"Joshua and I are going to start on that passel." She flushed a delicate pink.

"Yer fixin' a passel?" Reilly asked, his perplexed expression comical.

"What's a passel?" Flynn demanded.

"I didn't know it was broken," Masterson added, a decidedly wicked gleam in his eyes.

*What does he know?* Ryan wondered, watching the way

Masterson spun Maggie into his arms hugging her.

Flynn and Reilly watched with identical blank looks on their faces. Ryan could all but imagine the way their like minds were furiously working to figure out the Gaelic equivalent to the word. He wasn't sure he knew what a passel was himself, until his brother-in-law's hand slid from Maggie's waist to rest protectively on her stomach. Then it hit him, right between the eyes. Before Rory died, Maggie had wanted a houseful of kids.

A passel must mean a lot! "A baby?"

He stood up and walked slowly over to where Masterson had left his sister standing. "Are ye certain?" He didn't quite know whether to hug her close and spin her around, or bundle her up in a blanket and demand she stay in bed for the next nine months.

One look at his sister's glowing face, and he knew he was going to be an uncle. "How? When?"

Turner's burst of laughter filled the room. "Well now, I'm sure I don't need to tell you the how. As to the when, late winter—we think."

While Ryan watched, Turner drew Maggie against his side and settled her there.

"Are ye goin' to let those scones burn?" Reilly's question broke through Ryan's scattered thoughts. *A baby.* His little sister and her husband were going to have a wee one.

"I'll take care of it." Flynn picked up the towel draped across the edge of the dry sink and doubled it over. Opening the oven door, he reached in and grabbed the tray. He lifted it closer to his nose and breathed deeply. "Perfect!"

Ryan managed to get his emotions back under control, and his speech as well. "Maggie, are you feeling well?"

Turner frowned. "Wakes up sick as a dog every morning." Turner's statement was met with silence.

"I'm fine," Maggie insisted. "Just a bit of an unsettled

stomach when I wake." Smiling at her brother, she started lifting the scones off of the tray onto wire racks to cool.

"If you're pregnant, why are you here hours before the rest of the women?"

"Do ye think I'd trust any one of them in yer kitchen?" she demanded. "How do I know they'll feed the likes of ye properly?"

"But you should be resting—" Ryan started to protest.

"If Bridget were still here—" Maggie bit down on her lip to stop the flow of words.

*Probably bit her tongue as well.* Ryan watched the way his sister scrunched up her face. Though now that the words had been spoken, the need he hadn't succeeded in suppressing surfaced. He wished Bridget and Mick were here, too.

It hadn't been a full two weeks, and he missed her like crazy. There were fistfuls of dead wildflowers in bone-dry mason jars throughout his house. No one else thought to replace the flowers, or the water in the jars, since Bridget had gone.

The curtains she'd stitched with her slender fingers still hung in the kitchen, but their softness looked out of place in a house filled only with men. The room was suddenly too hot. He started to unbutton the cuff of his sleeve to roll it up, when the button popped off. He watched it fly across the table to land with a plop in the pitcher of cream someone, probably Maggie, had placed there in anticipation of breakfast.

"Well," he said, swallowing the lump of emotion he did not care to acknowledge or name.

"I'm starving," Flynn announced in the uncomfortable silence. *Clever man,* Ryan silently admitted.

"Ye poor man." Maggie sympathetically handed him a warm scone, then picked up a spoon to fish the button out of the cream.

"Yer an angel," he whispered fervently, popping half the scone into his mouth. Flynn chewed, stopped, then let out a heartfelt sigh. "Light as a feather, with just a touch of sweetness to tease the taste buds." He sighed again, " 'Tis a shame ye married the marshal," he said with a gleam coming into his eyes, "when ye could have married me."

Flynn's teasing broke the tension that settled on the group at the mention of Bridget's absence. No one had suggested they not discuss her and Mick's leaving, but the group had seemed to come to the same conclusion: that it was wiser not to bring up the touchy subject just yet.

"Now then," Maggie began, laying thick strips of bacon in the huge, cast-iron skillet. "Why don't ye fill me in on who is comin' and what food they'll be bringin'."

All through breakfast and everyone's second cup of coffee, Ryan remained silent, letting either Reilly or Flynn answer his sister's questions. He let everyone think he was paying attention to their plans for the solid post-and-beam construction of his new barn, when in fact, his mind was conjuring up the image of a chestnut-haired beauty with warm brown eyes dressed in a thin cotton nightgown bathed in moonlight.

# CHAPTER 15

Bridget adjusted the collar of her much-mended gingham dress again. Nerves had her throat tightening to the point that she couldn't swallow the cool water she so desperately craved. Her mouth was dry as dust. When she promised Maggie she'd help at the barn-raising, she never thought to miss James or his ranch so much that her head ached and her heart hurt. But God help her, she missed him. She and Mick had been accepted and treated as part of James's extended family. Not one person at the ranch had made her feel as if she worthless because of her background. Coming back here was so hard.

In the time she and Mick'd been living in town, she'd been on the receiving end of cold shoulders, glares of contempt, and out-and-out hatred. And all because of one woman's crusade to keep her own milk toast of a man from stepping foot inside The Ranch.

While Bridget had become used to the rudeness, the loneliness was another story. Thank goodness she could count on Maggie, Pearl, and now Mrs. Swenson. There were times when a woman needed the instinctive understanding only another woman could offer.

"The men on the south side of the new barn need more lemonade."

Sarah's voice grated across Bridget's frazzled nerves. The woman's brusque announcement was not directed at any one person in particular, but the way Bridget's name was conspicuously left out told her *she* was the one expected to fetch the lemonade for the men.

"Millie, dear," she heard Sarah say in a much softer tone, "would you kindly go on over to the house and ask Mrs. Turner for more lemons."

What a difference it must make to be socially acceptable, Bridget mused.

Millie nodded and turned toward the ranch house, but not before sending a glacial glare Bridget's way. *Well, that was subtle.* Was that the tenth or eleventh glare the co-chair of the Committee had fired her way? She supposed it really didn't matter. After all, she had come because she promised to help Maggie. Well, to be honest, it was not the only reason. If she happened to catch a glimpse of James, while he used those brawny arms of his to lift a hammer and pound nails, or heft another of those immense beams into place, her day would not seem as bleak as it truly was. The brooding Irishman was pure pleasure to look at. If that was all she'd ever have, then she intended to look her fill. Looking never hurt a body.

"Ma!" She heard Mick call out to her as she made her way over to the barn. Taking a moment to admire the workmanship, she smiled up at her son. He was steadying the ladder James stood on, while the object of her musings set another bit of the structure into place.

He turned abruptly and stared down at her, the ladder bowing under the weight of his large frame. "When did you get here?"

"Hours ago."

The deep timbre of his voice flowed over her sleep-deprived muscles. Her arms ached from fetching and carrying large trays of food back and forth from the ranch house to the tables set up under the oak trees in the side yard. Now that she thought about it, not too many other women had been sent to fetch and carry. No wonder she was so tired! Just another not-too-subtle way the Committee had of reminding her she was not their social equal.

As he stared down at the glass she offered up to him, she bobbled the tray balanced in her other hand. "Have a care, or you'll drop that tray."

A flush bloomed on her cheeks, hot enough that she knew he could see it too. "I'll not drop it."

"Mick!" he called out. "Brace the ladder for me."

Bridget watched her son react to James's words and brace himself against the bottom of the ladder, while James backed down the length of it.

Why was it he seemed so much bigger when he was standing right in front of her? She tilted her head back and decided he was at least a head and half taller than her husband had been, and twice as broad through the chest and shoulders. Working a ranch depended upon brute strength, and from the looks of things, James Ryan had it to spare.

An uncontrollable shiver wracked her slight frame, as she thought about being held in those strong arms again. Though it had been a few weeks, Bridget could still remember how her stomach fluttered when he held her against his broad chest. Her heart stuttered in her breast when she recalled waking to find his face a breath away from hers. His touch had been beyond gentle, soothing her when she wakened from a nightmare.

She watched, mesmerized by the way his throat worked. As the tangy lemonade slowly disappeared, the fluttering in her stomach intensified. When he came up for air, he swiped the back of his arm across his forehead, smearing a line of dirt, mingling it with his sweat. He caught her staring at him and flashed a grin. The lopsided tilt of it wormed its way right into her heart. Drawing in a steadying breath, she took a mental step back from the charm oozing out of the man's pores. Looking over her shoulders, she checked to make certain none of the other ladies were watching her. She couldn't afford to be seen fawning over James Ryan while the prim-faced, starch-drawered Committee members watched, ready to pounce on any wrong move she made.

"Have you spoken to Maggie yet?"

Bridget smiled. "I have, and the proud father-to-be, too."

James's smile mirrored her own. "They deserve to be happy."

Bridget thought she heard a trace of wistfulness in his voice. Did he want children of his own? The skin on the back of her neck tingled. Sarah must be at it again. She imagined the woman's hard-eyed stare drilling a dozen tiny holes into her back.

"I'd best be getting back—" Loud voices distracted her train of thought. A ruckus must be in the making.

"And I'm sayin' yer nailin' the wrong side of the board to the framin'!" a voice said hotly.

"Is that Mr. Flynn?" She wasn't sure how to react to the heated argument brewing between one of the Burnbaum's young know-it-all sons and Flynn.

"Aye." Ryan turned on his heel and stalked over to where the ranch hand stood, hands fisted at his sides, face flushed, and his red hair standing on end. Flynn must have raked his hands through it repeatedly to get it to stand up like that.

"Maybe I'd better—"

"Heads up!" a deep male voice barked out.

Before she could react to the shouted command, or the ominous shifting and creaking overhead, James swept both her and Mick out of harm's way. A heartbeat later, she looked down through the billowing cloud of sawdust at the rough-hewn beam inches away from their feet.

Bridget brushed the hair out of her eyes with shaking hands. Mick stood hunched over staring down at the huge piece of wood, as if expecting it to get up and walk about on its own.

"Samuel!"

The tone of James's voice brooked no arguments, or delays in responding.

"Mr. Ryan. I thought I had it . . . that is—"

Bridget watched the eldest of the Burnbaum brothers. The young man stood in front of James, red-faced and stammering, a far cry from the overconfident young man who'd been arguing with Flynn.

She felt a bit sorry for the boy, even thought he'd nearly created a disaster. He couldn't have been more than a few years older than her own son. So tall and broad through the chest and shoulders for a young man, while still so much a boy in head and heart.

Ryan waited for the boy to finish trying to speak before clearing his throat. "Do you understand the need for working as a team now?"

"Mr. Ryan, I'm so sorr—"

"What's all the ruckus, Ryan?"

Bridget nearly swallowed her tongue when the boy's father strode over. The man was nearly the same height as James, though a bit thinner. But it was his demeanor that had her sidestepping away from him and closer to the doorway and freedom. She'd heard him verbally slice his sons to ribbons once before, and she braced herself, not sure if she should interfere.

"Everyone is fine now." She could hear the soothing sound of James's voice.

Mr. Burnbaum didn't listen. "Samuel!"

"Yes, father?"

"Did you have anything to do with this?"

Bridget hesitated at the doorway and looked over her shoulder. Jake Burnbaum had his son by the shirtfront and was attempting to shake the answer from him. Her need not to become involved was outweighed by the need to stand up for the poor young man being publicly humiliated by his father.

She turned back, "I'm certain that whatever part Samuel had in all of this was purely coincidental." She hoped that would be the end of it, but she didn't think it would be.

"This doesn't concern you."

"Your son made a mistake," Bridget continued. "Can't you—"

"This doesn't concern you. Stay out of it!"

Her simmering temper shot to full boil, "It most certainly is my business. 'Twas my skull and my son's that your boy nearly bashed in with that oak beam!"

Her words had the older man turning abruptly and stalking over to where she stood, just outside the gathered group of men. His jaw was clenched, and his brows knitted together. Bridget was swept back in time. He reminded her of Richard. Fear curdled in her stomach.

Nausea snapped her back to the present. She wanted to step back from his obvious anger, unsure if she would become a target for his temper as she'd been for Richard's. One look at the dejected boy standing to the left of them, and she knew she couldn't let anyone hurt or threaten him. Samuel needed her.

"You'll want to rein in that mad of yours, Burnbaum." James's voice was deadly soft.

His voice echoed in the stillness that followed his command.

"My temper and my son are my business," the other man spat out. "Stay out of it!"

As if expecting it, James dodged the first punch, coming back with a quick jab, followed by a wicked right cross.

The older man stood for a moment, dazed, before crumbling into a heap on the barn's earthen floor.

"Flynn—take him outside and cool him off."

"Me pleasure," Flynn answered, bending down to lift the

fallen man by hooking his hands under Burnbaum's armpits.

Bridget still couldn't find her voice as she watched Burnbaum being dragged outside. James gently placed a hand to her elbow and led her back over to the ranch house.

"Why don't you go up to the house and see how Maggie is. I've a feeling she's doing too much when she should be resting."

Bridget looked up into his impossibly blue eyes, surprised by the turmoil in them. He wasn't angry, exactly. But, then again, he wasn't sad. She perceived a mix of the two emotions in the clear blue depths.

"Thank you."

He misstepped and Bridget heard him mumbling under his breath about someone having the brains God gave a goat.

"I'm glad you didn't let Mr. Burnbaum handle things."

"Burnbaum doesn't spend enough time with his sons. He wouldn't know when the poor kid's struggling with following orders, simply not up to the task, or when he's just ignoring orders deliberately."

"But you did." Her heart softened, opening just a bit more to this man who suddenly seemed so lonely. "You didn't have to take the time or care about someone else's son."

Their eyes met, and she knew she owed him at least that much where her own son was concerned. "After what Mick did, stealing from you like that—"

"He never actually stole from me."

She trembled and wasn't sure her voice would work properly, but she owed him a special thanks for what he'd done for Mick. "You're doing it again. You didn't have to take him in, and you didn't have to take on his desperately ill mother either."

"Were you doing that well on your own?" His eyes shot daggers at her.

For the life of her she couldn't understand why he was getting riled. "It takes a special person"—she stumbled over the words—"man . . . to care about others. Especially when everyone else has decided they aren't worth worrying over."

She couldn't look at the compassion in his eyes without wanting to wrap her arms around his waist, lay her head on his chest, and just hold on. Tight. God, she needed to hold him. Fussing with her skirts helped her to regain the composure she'd lost when he turned the full power of his gaze on her.

"My da always gave me the chance to learn, to make my own mistakes. On the one or two occasions where someone would have been hurt by a mistake I'd made, he'd step in just in time to prevent it. Then he'd let me know where I'd gone wrong in no uncertain terms."

She watched his gaze slide over to take in the father and son a short distance away, then swing back to her. "But the rest of the time, he had the patience of a saint."

She'd never met James's father, but she could imagine he was a very special man, too. She fell into step beside him as they made their way over to the house.

"You were lucky to have a father to look up to." Bridget couldn't help the tug of wishful thinking that pulled at her. Mick had only recently had someone to look up to, someone to emulate. Her stomach tightened again as she wondered if she'd made a huge mistake by taking Mick away from that someone.

"Maggie," James called out, stepping onto the bottom porch step.

"Are ye bleedin' then, brother mine?"

Bridget couldn't help but smile at Maggie's words, "Does she always talk to you like that?"

"Demanding that I'd better have a good reason for disturbing her while she was hard at work in my own kitchen?" The nod of agreement and look on James's face had laughter bubbling up inside her.

"I'd say the answer was yes." Bridget envied the close relationship James and Maggie had. She didn't have any brothers or sisters. Watching the way he and his sister interacted made her realize how important family must be when a child was growing up. *Mick had missed so much.*

He pulled her up the steps and into the kitchen, where Maggie was removing a tin of heavenly smelling butter cake from the oven.

Maggie frowned at the both of them, but spoke to her brother. "You'll be wantin' to wipe yer boots and wash yer hands before ye can come into the kitchen, boy-o."

Ryan backed up, wiped his feet, then leaned forward to brush the hair out of his sister's eyes.

Watching their closeness had envy curling with something close to despair inside of Bridget. She'd never had the chance to offer Mick that closeness. Michael had never even known they'd had a son together. She hoped he was looking down on them, watching over them. Content for the moment, she set aside her growing sorrow about not being able to provide Mick with a younger brother or sister to play with and fight with.

"Bridget." Maggie sounded concerned. "Have a care. Ye look all done in."

"I'm fine," she lied.

"She looks like she might keel over," Maggie insisted. "Take her into the parlor and make her lie down."

Bridget shook her head, nearly laughing out loud. "We came up here to make sure you were the one resting, Maggie."

At Maggie's narrow-eyed glare, Ryan added, "Bridget's fine. We just had a bit of a close call down at the barn."

Ryan's careful evasion of the near accident and emotional turmoil didn't surprise Bridget. She knew he didn't want to upset his sister in her delicate condition.

She did her best to compose her features so Maggie wouldn't

guess just how upset she still was. No one had been hurt—well, except for Burnbaum, but he'd deserved it. The rush of air that had followed the beam's decent had told her just how close she'd been to a nasty accident. But thanks to James, she and Mick had escaped unscathed. She turned to look at him, wondering for the first time if he'd been grazed by the beam.

Maggie stood staring at the two of them as if she were their mother and they had been caught filching fresh-baked berry tarts. Bridget knew they both owed it to the woman and her condition to be honest with her.

"There was a mishap at the barn," Bridget said slowly, "but your brother handled it. No one got hurt."

Bridget filled Maggie in on what happened, and as was her habit with her son, brushed a soothing hand across James's back. He flinched, then stiffened.

Bridget was shocked, but Maggie didn't seem to be. Her blue eyes narrowed on her brother. "Oh, aye. No one was harmed a bit."

The two women looked at one another, then at James. "Have a seat, boy-o."

When he simply stood there, they took matters into their own hands. "Always the difficult one," Maggie muttered as she moved to the left and Bridget to the right. They reached up and gently pushed down on a shoulder until he was sitting.

"There now, let's have a look." Maggie lifted the tail of his shirt out of the back of his jeans.

"Here now, Maggie darlin'," Flynn said, coming in through the back door. "Ye've got yer hands on the wrong man."

"Flynn—" Ryan began, only to suck in a sharp breath when Bridget touched his back again.

"Me brother seems to have run into the wrong end of a bit of wood, Flynn."

The other man nodded his head in agreement. "That he has, lass."

"Oh, James!" Bridget couldn't keep the shocked sympathy from her voice. His back had to hurt dreadfully. The bottom of his shoulder blade was scraped raw and bruised a nasty shade of blackish purple.

Maggie moved quickly, snatching her healing basket off the sideboard, and began preparing a poultice to keep the wound from bruising further. While she did, Bridget dipped a clean, soft bit of cloth in warm soapy water and carefully cleansed the area.

Turner stepped through the back and demanded, "Is your injury so great you need two of the prettiest women in all of Emerson to tend you?"

Bridget was about to say something, but noticed the twinkle in Maggie's husband's eyes. She also noted the way they narrowed on Maggie before settling on James, who squirmed in his seat. "They didn't give me a choice. They just starting prodding and poking until I had to give in."

"Oh, aye." Flynn laughed. "His eyes crossed when the lovely Mrs. O'Toole started tending him."

"Flynn—" Ryan warned, but the Irishman laughed right in his face, "Ye should have seen yer face, Jamie boy."

Maggie swept past Flynn with the poultice, silencing the man with a hard look. "Now, ye can just sit there for a bit while the comfrey root does its work," she instructed her patient.

"Maggie—" He took her hand. "Thank you, but I don't have the time to sit. I need to get back to the barn-raising."

"It'll do ye no good to argue. 'Tis me turn to win," Maggie announced.

"I believe it is." Turner chuckled. "Why, just this morning, she lost the argument we had about who would get to be on to—"

Maggie flew across the kitchen and clapped her hand across her husband's mouth. "That'll be enough from the likes of you!"

Bridget had a feeling she knew what the man had been about to say, but agreed some things were best said in private.

Maggie took him by the elbow and steered him toward the back door, "Ye can just make certain that those poor Burnbaum boys keep out of trouble until their papa can uncross his eyes enough to drive their wagon home."

"Here's your hat." Turner started to mumble before Maggie pulled him back for a satisfying kiss. They broke away, with Maggie blushing and her husband whistling.

"Flynn," Turner called, holding the door open, "give me a hand, won't you?"

"And miss this?" Flynn demanded.

Maggie's even look had the redheaded man moving.

"How do you do that?" Bridget demanded.

"Do what?"

"Get any man to do your bidding."

Maggie shrugged, then wiped her hands on her apron, before turning back to the stove to grab the steaming teapot, "From watching me mother."

"Let me," Bridget offered. "You're looking tired." She poured the hot water over the tea leaves. "How do you feel?"

Maggie eyed her brother before answering, "Wonderful."

"Margaret Mary," he said evenly.

" 'Tis not every day that a woman can be helpin' her brother feed the neighbors that've come to help him raise a new barn." Her blue eyes softened as she looked at her brother.

When Ryan smiled, Bridget felt her lips curving upward of their own volition. In spite of her smile, she felt strangely empty inside. She placed the steeped cup of tea in front of James. The sudden sense of loneliness added to the hollow feeling already spreading through her chest. She missed being here at the ranch, helping with chores, being a part of their extended family.

Dear Lord, she missed the comings and goings of the friendly ranch hands, and the generous compliments they always had for her cooking. But most of all, she missed James. She hadn't had a solid night of sleep since moving back to town.

"Margaret Mary—"

"Oh hush, Jamie," Maggie interrupted. "I feel fit as a fiddle, and cannot wait to hold me babe in me arms. I'd not do anything to risk having a healthy little one."

Understanding filled Bridget, and her heart went out to Maggie, remembering just how miraculous the connection had been between herself and Mick when he was born. The years hadn't diminished the feeling. She still felt tied to him. When he was troubled, she was troubled. When Mick hurt, she hurt.

As if testing her belief, a twinge of pain arrowed up her back, and Bridget rushed over to the window to look out. She couldn't see Mick, and unease spread through her. Stepping out on the back porch, she turned when Mick called out to her and waved as he passed by on his way from the pile of logs to where the men were waiting.

*Mick wasn't hurt.* Then why the phantom pain? She waved and walked back inside.

The look of intensity in James's beautiful eyes matched what she was trying so hard to ignore. Ever since James had stepped in to protect the Burnbaum boy from his own father, she'd felt the connection to James, an invisible bond that linked her heart to his. From the first, she'd felt it whenever he spoke to Mick, but she'd buried the feelings, knowing she'd never be able to act on them.

The sudden realization that the pain in her back meant the connection to James was still strong and true shot through her.

Perhaps they were connected by more than just what they felt for her boy.

"Are ye headed back outside then?"

"Just checking on Mick." Turning her back to the door, she added, "Let me finish rolling out those crusts for you, Maggie. Then you can have a bit of a lie down."

When Maggie glanced over her shoulder at the cast-iron pot on the stovetop, Bridget offered, "I'll keep an eye on the stew."

Ryan had been quiet for the longest time. She thought he'd been trying to get a handle on the pain he must be feeling. She turned to him now, intending to enlist his aid in getting his sister to take a short nap.

Before she could ask, he spoke. "I could carry you into the parlor and sit on ye until yer eyes closed, Margaret Mary."

Bridget nearly swallowed her tongue to keep from commenting on the look Maggie threw at her brother. It was without price and definitely promised retribution.

"But," Ryan continued, "I know ye'll lie down because it will be good for the baby, as well as yerself."

Bridget noticed the way James's brogue had become more pronounced. It had in the barn when Burnbaum had threatened trouble, too. Now it came up again when he was upset with Maggie. She wondered why most of the time he didn't have the musical lilt to his words. Did he try hard to cover it up? Was there was more to James Ryan than she'd originally believed? More than one mystery seemed to be a part of him. His disappearing brogue was one. The brutally efficient way he'd knocked Burnbaum down with just two punches, and the way he stepped in to help the young Burnbaum boy, were a couple of others.

Separately the actions didn't add up to what she thought she knew about James Ryan. There was definitely more to be discovered, if she were brave enough to admit she wanted to spend more time with him. *But what of the gossips? What of his reputation?*

Confused and unsure of what to do next, she thrust those unsettling questions aside for now. She turned toward Maggie. "Your brother is right. Think of the baby and lie down for his sake."

Maggie grinned. "All right then, but maybe I'll be lying down for *her* sake."

# CHAPTER 16

"Do ye think it's truly over?" Maggie stood on the back porch surveying the new structure. She seemed refreshed from her short nap.

"Yes, and I'm not sorry to see it done." Bridget rubbed at the ache in her lower back. It was a good ache. She'd been able to pull her own weight all day.

"How many smashed thumbs do ye think we bandaged today?"

"I wrapped five, but that's not counting fifteen mashed fingers." Bridget desperately needed to sit. Exhaustion coupled with little or no sleep last night was taking its toll on her. "What about Cyrus Jones's arm?"

" 'Tis wrenched, I'm thinkin'."

Bridget nodded. "I thought so, too, but I'm not as experienced with doctoring as you are, Maggie."

"Lucky for us she is." James's smile was a bit ragged about the edges.

Bridget wondered if his back was paining him again. "Do you need another poultice on your back?"

James waved her away. "I'll be fine. Just need to sit for a bit."

Maggie smiled over at him. " 'Tis a grand barn, Jamie."

Bridget happened to look over at Joshua and noticed that when his wife smiled, he smiled. His entire face seemed to light up when Maggie was smiling.

Her throat tightened and her breath snagged. Had Michael

ever looked at her like that? Like his entire existence depended upon her happiness? She shook her head; she'd never know whether he had or not. Her parents were long gone, and she had no one else to ask. There was no one to remind her of the loving looks Michael had sent her way, no one to chide her when she was too tired to carry on.

Maggie and Joshua were so wrapped up in each other, they didn't notice how upset Bridget was. She could feel the blood leaching from her face and neck down to her toes.

At least she and Mick had each other. An awful thought hit her. What if James Ryan hadn't happened along the night Mick tried his hand at being an outlaw? Good God, what if James hadn't taken them into his home and nursed her back to health?

If she'd died, what would have become of Mick?

Desperate thoughts hurt her head and made the room start to spin.

"Here now, Bridget." Flynn took her elbow and started to lead her back inside the ranch house.

"She's exhausted." Bridget heard Maggie's voice from far off. "Have you an extra bed upstairs, Jamie?"

Bed? Bridget's tired mind struggled with why she shouldn't just accept James's hospitality and lay her head down on his bed. *His bed!* Her head snapped up, miraculously clear as glass. She could not sleep under the same roof as James now! Not with the women in town making nasty comments all day long. If she stayed here tonight, things would just go from bad to worse.

Struggling with the combination of inner turmoil and just plain exhaustion, she answered, "Thank you, but no. We have to get back to Swenson's."

It wasn't a lie, more of a fib for a good reason. She took a step and felt her knees give way as a wave of fatigue swept up from her toes, robbing her tired limbs of every ounce of energy.

Her head felt fuzzy. She'd definitely pushed herself harder than she should've. But there had been work to do, and she couldn't let Maggie handle the burden all alone.

"Drink up." A steaming cup of tea was thrust into her hands. She looked down at it and wondered why the cup was blurry. Blinking, she couldn't remember when she'd sat down. Closing her eyes to rest, just for a moment, she felt a bit better.

"Jamie, if ye don't carry that woman upstairs before she whacks her head on yer kitchen table, I'll tell everyone about yer scar!"

"I've plenty of scars, Margaret Mary," he answered evenly.

Bridget tried to follow the conversation, but only caught the mention of James's scars. She'd seen the wicked-looking sickle-shaped one that slashed across his lower back, when she'd come upon him washing up at the well pump by the back of the house.

"Aye, that ye do, laddie," she heard Maggie agree, "but not all of them are visible with yer clothes on."

Bridget thought of her own scars and wondered if James would ever have the chance to notice them. At that dangerous thought, her eyes shot open, and she found herself staring into the deep blue of James's eyes. Funny, she hadn't heard him move.

"I can walk," she mumbled. "You'll do more damage to your back if you carry me."

He grumbled something under his breath that she didn't quite hear. Slipping an arm beneath her knees, and the other around her back, he gathered her close and lifted her into his arms. All thoughts of protesting died on her tongue. Pinpricks of heat seeped into her weary muscles, relaxing her. Leaning against his broad chest, with her head nestled in the crook of his arm, had her wondering if this was what heaven felt like.

If not, she'd have to rethink the wisdom of wanting to go there. Reveling in the feeling of being taken care of, feeling as close to cherished as she ever had, she closed her eyes, thinking to steal just a bit of time for herself. An hour. She yawned. Maybe two.

All of the worries she'd carried since sunup faded away as she melted into James's arms. Such broad, capable shoulders, she thought, letting the tiniest moans of pleasure escape. Sure he hadn't heard, she snuggled closer to his heat and finally let go, falling into a deep sleep.

Ryan wondered if a man could die from lack of pleasure as easily as he could from too much. He heard every sigh, every tiny little sound the woman in his arms made as he carried her upstairs. Instead of putting her in the guest room, as he had in the past, he put her in his bed.

He might regret it later, but he had to see her there. Ever since that night he'd seen her illuminated by the moon, he'd imagined her here in his bed. Her dark hair and darker eyes such a contrast to the pure white of the bed linens.

"Eedjit!" he muttered. If there was trouble brewing, it was bound to find him. Slipping Bridget onto his bed, he stood back and stared. Such a beautiful woman. How could he keep away from her? How would he live with himself if he didn't? She'd made her choice. She'd left the ranch. Left him. Turned him down flat. No explanations, just "no."

Tucking the sheet over her shoulder, he ran the tip of his finger along the line of her jaw. "Never could walk away from a woman in trouble. Either you're in trouble, or you are trouble, Bridget. Either way, I'm sticking until I can find out which."

"I didn't know you were married, O'Toole," Sam Paige muttered into his fourth glass of whiskey.

"Was," O'Toole mumbled. The Irish always went right to his

head faster than the cheap red-eye whiskey most places served. "She's dead."

He looked over at the owner of The Ranch and narrowed his eyes. Pearl was a looker all right. She had curves in all the right places and then some. The food she served was some of the best grub he'd had in months. But where were all the ladies she kept? After all, he was thinking a little feminine companionship would just about top off the evening.

"Where's the women?" he demanded, rising up out of his chair, making his way over to where she stood.

"What women?" Pearl's voice sounded strained.

"The ones you pay by the hour," Nick Paige added, his bloodshot eyes telling O'Toole his back-up man was in no shape to guard the door, let alone find it.

"I told you before," she said, "I don't run that kind of place."

"I saw women in the kitchen!" O'Toole took a step closer to the now-pale Pearl.

"I hire women to cook, clean, and take care of the livestock. You want food? I'll serve you." Her voice quivered slightly as it rose in volume, but she didn't back down. "You want whiskey, I'll serve you."

"What we want is willing women!" Sam Paige thundered, taking up a position right next to O'Toole and Paige's younger brother, effectively boxing Pearl against the back wall near the bar.

"Then I suggest you head on over to the Desert Rose. It's just three miles outside of Emerson. Shouldn't take you long to find it." Pearl turned away from the men, hiding her shudder. Just thinking about any one of these brutes coming near her girls made her feel sick. Her hands shook, but she managed to pull out a deck of playing cards and offered them to O'Toole and his men.

"Why not play a few rounds of poker? The drinks are on the house."

The shouts of agreement sliced through her already aching head. While the men settled down to play cards, she angled her head so she could see the door to the kitchen. As she'd hoped, it was not quite shut. She gave the signal, nodding her head once. The door closed without a sound.

Pearl breathed a sigh of relief, filled the last glass, and brought the tray over to the disreputable-looking lot of cowboys. *Face the truth,* she thought, *they're outlaws.* Hopefully, help would be on its way soon. She surely hoped the sheriff hadn't hung up his gun belt just yet. Pearl had a sinking feeling she'd need all of the help, and fire power, she could get, come closing time.

Sam leaned over and pitched his voice to barely a whisper. "You ever find that missing mine payroll?"

O'Toole shook his head. "I told you before. When I got back to the cabin, there was nothing left but a pile of ashes."

"A key wouldn't burn," Sam insisted.

"That fire was so hot, there wasn't anything left—" O'Toole stopped and drew in a breath. Even after all these years, he did regret that she'd died. He hadn't loved her, but she didn't deserve an end like that. "My wife suffered the same fate as the O'Toole family Bible. Nothing left but ashes."

"Why worry about a Bible?" Sam sounded amazed.

O'Toole clenched his jaw tightly, thinking of the safe deposit box key he'd sewn into the back cover flap of that Bible. Damn his luck, and the woman he'd thought of far too often for his sanity.

"Hey, are you gonna place yer bet, or what?" Nick demanded, his fist hitting the table hard enough to rattle the glasses and spill the just-poured whiskey.

"Dang, that's a waste of perfectly good red-eye!" one of O'Toole's men muttered.

"It's still on the table. Why don't you lick it up like the dog you are?" Sam cuffed the man who'd complained.

"There's no call to be getting surly," another man said slowly.

"Either place yer bet, or fold!" Nick spat out.

All bets were placed. Six pairs of eyes narrowed, and one by one, they laid their cards face up on the table.

"You can't have a royal flush!" Nick hissed. "You must be bottom-dealing again!"

"You're just sore 'cause I beat ya."

The sound of pistols being cocked echoed in the room. Chairs scraped against the floor as six men rose in unison.

"I swear, O'Toole, I didn't!"

O'Toole looked from one man to the next. Each one had his hand on the butt of a Colt. If he didn't have a bank job coming up in two days, he'd let them all shoot it out. But right now, there wasn't time enough to find more men to do the job, let alone go over the plans again until their moves were mapped out and the timing set down to the minute. He couldn't let them shoot each other . . . yet.

He looked over at the lovely Pearl and noticed the color had completely drained from her face. Good. Fear meant she'd be a more agreeable hostage. It was time to see just how many women Pearl had running the place, and just how willing they'd be.

# CHAPTER 17

Bridget woke when her dress got caught beneath her. Sleepily she lifted her head and noticed the sleeping gown lying across the end of the bed. With her eyes half closed, she slid off the bed and undressed, slipping the nightgown over her head. She was dead to the world by the time her head touched the feather pillow. Exhaustion forced sleep upon her, but she slept badly. Dreams of heat and flames had her racing about the tiny cabin in Louviers, only this time Mick was a young man, and she could not lift him protectively in her arms and carry him to safety. He was too heavy, and she couldn't wake him. She cried out in her sleep.

A strong steady hand brushed the hair off her forehead in rhythmic motions, soothing her.

"Aye, there's a lass. Wake up now. 'Tis just a dream. Yer boy's fine."

The softly uttered words drew her from the depths of troubled sleep. "James?" Bridget couldn't keep the surprise from her voice. In the soft candlelight, she recognized the stark planes of his handsome face. Her gaze slid lower and found what she'd hoped. He was shirtless, all that lovely muscle exposed. Belly-churning pleasure warred with the knowledge that he shouldn't be here, in her room.

"Aye?" he continued smoothing the hair back off her face.

"I . . . that is, we . . . what if . . ."

" 'Tis the middle of the night, and everyone's asleep." His

sigh was long and deep, as if he were drawing on a reserve of patience. "No one else heard you. Go back to sleep."

The ghost of a smile playing about his firmly sculpted lips caught her attention. She stared at them, wanting to reach out and trace their edge. The quiet of the house combined with the soft candle glow made her feel bolder. She reached out a tentative fingertip, watching, waiting for his permission to touch.

"Bridget," he whispered, closing his eyes.

Emboldened by the way his rasped out her name, she traced the top edge of his mouth, reveling in the way it arced up and the dip right smack in the middle of it.

She'd thought his lips would feel cool and soft, but she was wrong, they were firm and warm. As her questing fingers reached the apex of his lips and started their downward trip, he moaned out her name and crushed her to him.

Enraptured by the feel of his mouth on hers, she felt her grip on sanity begin to slip away from her. She arched her back and pressed her breasts against his chest. Heat met heat and melded them together. God in heaven, how had she survived so many years without the touch of a man? The cold, stark years since Michael left dissipated like early morning fog burned off by the sun.

"Bridget, wait. We can't—"

A wisp of cool air across her face brought Bridget sharply to her senses. She clenched her hands to keep from reaching out to touch him again. 'Twas bad enough she harbored the need, but acting on the need again, once he'd made his intentions clear, would place both of them in a compromising situation she was certain neither of them wanted.

*Should she apologize even it she wouldn't mean it?* "I'm sorry. I don't know what came over me?"

"You don't understand—"

Oh, but she did. Far too clearly. He didn't want her kissing him. Maybe he didn't want her at all. She'd misread all of the signs. What a pitiful fool. "I'm afraid I do understand."

"Do you?" James could not resist running the tip of his finger along the slight curve of her jaw, tapping the rounded point of her chin. Though still far too thin, Bridget O'Toole had velvety soft skin. Her cheek reminded him of his mother's roses back in Ireland. One of his earliest memories of home would always be running his fingertips across rose petals, releasing the flower's scent, though he'd learned the hard way not to grab the stem, risking having to suffer later while his mother pulled the thorns from his fingers.

The confusion darting in and out of Bridget's eyes stirred up a mix of emotions. In the light of day, he could convince himself he didn't need her but here at night, by the soft glow of a candle, the connection between them pulled him inexorably closer. Though her cries of distress would bring him to her room, it was her frailty that kept him at her bedside long after she drifted off to sleep. James continued to stroke the side of her face until she relaxed. Hoping he could soothe her and walk away; he'd done it before.

"James . . ."

It wasn't the way she said his name as much as the longing in her dark brown eyes. He felt the same longing. He'd gone too long without the tenderness of a woman's touch in the night. But he didn't just need any woman. Devil take it, he needed the widow O'Toole!

"Bridget . . ."

All of the reasons he should turn and walk away churned through his mind, making his head ache. He wanted her, not just in his bed, but in his life. But more than that, he wanted her gangly twelve-year-old, would-be cattle-rustler son in his life, too.

He shook his head, knowing he should leave. But Bridget was

tossing the covers aside and standing before him. He couldn't speak. The light from the candle he'd left on the bedside table shone through the soft linen of her nightgown, silhouetting her softly curved body. *Ripe breasts jutting against the thin fabric, begging for his touch.* His hands itched, and he flexed them. Unable to stop himself, he crossed back over to where she was standing and placed his hands where they needed to be, cupping her waist, pulling her close.

He breathed in the scent of sun-warmed wildflowers and was lost. He buried his head in the curve of her neck and breathed deeply. Of their own volition, his lips traced a path up her neck to the gentle curve of her jawline, kissing their way to the dent in her chin.

"Oh my Lord!" Bridget whispered, groaning as his lips found her mouth again and kissed the breath right out of her.

She melted against him, eager to feel the hot length of him pressing against her, fitting the muscled planes of his work-hardened body against her soft curves. For a moment, she wondered if she should give in to the overwhelming need to remove her nightgown and press herself against the hot hard chest that lured her from the first.

"James, tell me to stop."

He shook his head, as if trying to clear it. "Bridget, you don't want me—"

"God help me, I do. I've never been with anyone but my husband."

Unsure how he would react to the news, she looked down at her feet. Before she could draw in a steadying breath, she felt the tip of his finger on her chin, forcing it up until she looked him in the eye. "Don't expect me to walk away from you, not now that I know you've been waiting for me."

It was suddenly clear as glass. She had been waiting for him. *Half her life.*

C. H. Admirand

"Make love to me, James."

"Bridget, we shouldn't—"

Emboldened, she stood on the tips of her toes and pressed her lips to his neck, felt the rapid pulse beating there, and rejoiced: he wanted her. He was trying to hold back. She let her lips trail kisses down the side of his neck and onto his collarbone, dipping lower, licking, and kissing a path all the way to his heart.

Just as she was thinking of being bold, of dropping to her knees and kissing along the edge of his unbuttoned trousers, his hands gripped her shoulders and jerked her away from him.

Pain sliced through her. He didn't want her as badly as she wanted him. She turned her head away. "Bridget," he said, his voice ragged. "Tell me to stop."

Her gazed darted back to his, and she saw everything she was feeling reflected back at her from the depths of his beautiful blue eyes. "I don't want you to stop."

His hands were everywhere at once. Sliding up and down her spine, brushing over her breasts, making her nipples stand at attention, begging for more.

"Oh, please—"

But James didn't speak. He continued to caress every inch of her body. When she thought she'd simply melt into a puddle on the floor, he lifted her into his arms and carried her back to the bed. Laying her in the middle, he stared down at her as he undid his pants and stepped out of them.

He was glorious, naked and hers for the taking. Nerves skittered through her taut belly. Every fiber of her being called out to him to take that first step forward because she was afraid to. *What if this was a mistake? What if she woke in the morning and regretted making love with him?*

As if he sensed her fear, he knelt on the bed, never breaking eye contact, then placed his lips against her breast where her

196

heart beat, and her fear evaporated. Whatever he wanted, she'd gladly give him. *She loved him.* She should have realized it before, but she had been too busy trying to ignore the signs. No longer the wide-eyed fifteen-year-old who'd fallen so hard, so fast, for a sweet-talking pretty face, Bridget lifted her hand to James's face and brought him closer. Placing her lips against his, she kissed him softly, then breathed deeply and let everything she was feeling pour into the kiss.

"I've needed you for so long," James whispered against her lips, kissing her back, caressing her curves with a gentle touch.

"I was afraid to want you," she admitted, not caring if he thought her crazy.

"Ye've made me daft from the beginnin'."

The soft, lilting tones of his voice added fuel to the fire burning deep within her. "Make me daft, James. I want you."

Watching her, James grabbed the hem of her nightgown and waited for her to stop him. She didn't. He lifted the gown over her head and sat back on his heels and just looked at her.

His eyes caressed every inch of her body. The body she'd thought too thin.

She pulled him down against her, reveling in the feel of his strong chest against her soft breasts. Before she could urge him to do so, he'd gently nudged her legs apart and settled himself at the very core of her womanhood. Heat surged up from deep within her, as his erection hardened and grew.

"I don't know if you'll . . ."

"Shhh." He pressed his fingertips against her lips. "I want you too, Bridget O'Toole. From tonight on, you're mine."

She opened herself to him and watched as his eyes turned midnight blue, with passion. "Say it."

"I'm yours," she breathed, drawing in a breath as he slid home deep inside her.

Time had no meaning. It stood still as they loved one another, soft touches, hard thrusts, closer and closer, until she screamed out his name. *"James!"*

"Aye lass, I'm here, and I'm yours."

His words pushed her over the edge into oblivion. Her world shattered as he poured himself into her.

"I love you, James."

The candle sputtered and went out as he drew her close and confessed, "Not as much as I love ye, lass."

"Marshal!"

The insistent pounding on the back door woke Turner from a sound sleep. He smothered a curse as he stumbled out of bed, stubbing his toe against the bedpost.

"What time is it?"

Maggie's sleepy voice had him cursing again. The ride back from his brother-in-law's ranch had been long, but necessary. He wanted his wife to himself, and not rising up at dawn again to cook for the hired hands that worked the Ryan spread. If they had stayed there last night, she'd have the first batch of scones ready to put in the oven right about now.

The knock came again, louder this time. "Damnation!"

Turner pulled the door open and stared at the slight young woman standing on his doorstep, wringing her hands.

"Please, Marshal Turner," she cried, "you've got to come! They have guns! Poor Pearl! You have to help us!"

Turner tried to digest everything the young woman was telling him while struggling to clear the sleep from his brain. He wanted to remind her he was no longer an acting marshal, but her fear touched him, and he let that thought slide. "Why don't you come on inside and sit down. Then you can start from the beginning and tell me what happened."

She nodded and followed him inside.

Maggie was already at the stove, heating water to brew a pot of tea. "Ye poor wee thing," Maggie crooned. "Have a seat and catch yer breath, Mary. Then ye can tell us what happened."

"But Pearl—"

"If you don't calm down enough to tell us the whole story, I can't help you," Turner said, keeping his voice even. He didn't want to rattle the young woman more than she already was.

"Six scruffy-looking men came in to The Ranch wanting a meal."

"Do ye know any of their names?" Maggie asked.

Mary shook her head. "No."

"That's all right. Go on," Turner urged.

"They were eating and drinking Pearl's best whiskey, then they started calling for the women."

"What women?" Maggie demanded.

"The 'willing' ones," the girl whispered, staring down at the hands she'd folded in her lap.

"Of all the nerve! Pearl doesn't run that kind of place!" Maggie seethed.

Mary looked up at her with tears in her eyes. "She told them that. But they . . . they wouldn't believe her."

"What happened?" Turner demanded.

"Pearl got out the playing cards, hoping to get them interested in playing poker instead of—"

"We understand." Maggie pulled a chair up right next to the girl's. She took her hand and patted it. "Ye don't have to think about that now. Yer here, so tell us the rest of it."

"I think one of them was cheating. Or at least someone accused another of cheating, and then the chairs started scraping against the floor. They were shouting and guns were being cocked."

"Were any shots fired?"

Mary looked over at Turner. She seemed to settle down as she watched him strapping on his holster and tying it around his leg, then she nodded.

Maggie brushed a hand across the girl's brow. "Drink yer tea, and get comfortable. Yer not going back there tonight."

"But what about the others?"

"Joshua will see that a posse of men ride out to The Ranch with him. Don't ye worry," she soothed. "It will all work out just fine, ye'll see."

"Henry Peabody! If you set one foot in that den of iniquity, you'll burn in the fires of hell!"

"Now, Millie . . ."

Turner shook his head in amazement. This was the fourth stop on his way out to The Ranch, and so far, not one man was willing to cross his wife. And every wife so far had forbade her spouse to have anything to do with riding out to The Ranch to rescue Pearl and her girls.

"Why don't you go on back up to bed, Mrs. Peabody," he suggested.

"Don't you dare tell me what to do, Mr. Turner," she huffed. "I don't care if you *were* a U.S. marshal. You're retired now and have no jurisdiction over my husband or any other man in this town!"

"You're right as rain, Mrs. Peabody. But with the sheriff already gone, and the new marshal not yet arrived, I'm the closest thing to the law that you have."

Stalking over to his mount, he realized there was no point in arguing with the irritating woman. She'd set her jaw, straightened her shoulders, and glared at him. Turner bit his tongue and tipped his hat. "Ma'am."

Turner had hoped to have at least five men riding with him out to Pearl's. After two more refusals, he started to worry. He jammed his Stetson back on his head and swung up into the saddle. Time was running out, and he didn't have time to ride out to the Ryan spread to get help.

If the two men he'd roused down at the livery weren't able to get help from Ryan, the odds would be one man pitted against six . . . not the type of odds he favored. He hoped it would be the other way around and prayed he could count on Ryan and a few extra guns.

Making his way down Main Street, he realized that his last duty had come down to a shoot-out after all. He didn't have the heart to tell Maggie what he feared he was going to find out at Pearl's. It didn't matter who held Pearl and her girls hostage. Too many whiskeys never made the job of negotiating for a hostage's freedom any easier. He forced that grim thought away.

Right now there were five innocent young women and their protector, the only woman in town Christian enough to take them in during their time of need. They were all alone at the mercy of some gang of disreputable men. On the government's payroll or not, he had a job to do. Nothing would stand in his way.

A hundred feet ahead of him, a pair of horses and riders moved out of the shadows. "Did you find Ryan?"

"He'll meet us on the way."

"Let's ride."

"Are ye sure? You could have heard wrong."

Mary shook her head. "Positive."

Maggie could not seem to catch her breath. It wasn't the babe she carried that caused her panic. It was the name the poor girl had just remembered. God help them! She had to find her husband and warn him just what he was up against, but she had to tell Bridget first. By all that was holy, she hoped there were two men with the same name.

# Chapter 18

Marshal Justiss swigged the last of the coffee in his canteen and turned his horse to the east. He was just outside the town of Emerson. The trail was still warm. O'Toole was nearly in his sights.

"Faster!" A wagon rumbled up over the rise in the road. Some blasted female and her passenger were riding hell-bent for leather down the middle of the road. He knew the moment the redhead saw him.

"Merciful heavens!" He watched as she tried to rein in her horse.

He yanked on his own horse's reins, and moved out of the way. She nodded, by way of thanks he supposed, and snapped the reins again, coaxing even more speed from the huge draft horse.

Justiss had seen that look before. The woman who barreled on past him had not just seemed determined. Her grip on the reins and squared shoulders tipped him off. It was utter desperation that drove her forward, toward a goal he feared was beyond the woman's capabilities.

He decided to follow along behind and see if he could lend a hand. Knowing it would be a waste of good breath to shout after her, he wheeled his mount around and gave chase.

Maggie's eyes were focused on the back of the horse she coaxed more speed from, and on the road to her brother's ranch. She felt Mary tugging on her arm, but didn't dare look away from the road.

Time was of the essence.

Her vision tunneled until all she could see was the road before them and the horse. Maggie's brain registered the sound of another set of hoofbeats, but she ignored them, focusing on her mission. God help her, she had to find Bridget!

Rounding the bend in the road, she turned off and headed up the lane to Jamie's ranch. Let him be there, too, she prayed. They would need his help, if what she feared had come to be.

"Whoa!"

The deep male voice at her elbow startled her. She looked away from the ranch house and saw a brown leather vest with a silver star pinned to it. Her eyes flew up the man's broad chest to his clean-shaven chin and penetrating grass-green eyes.

"Yer the marshal we've been waitin' for?"

The man nodded as he took the reins from her and helped her down from the wagon.

"Yer late, Marshal Justiss!" Maggie turned away from him and shouted, "Bridget!"

The woman came hurrying over toward them. "Don't worry about your husband," she soothed, "James and his men rode out to meet him."

Maggie shook her head, " 'Tis you I'm more worried about. Tell her." She urged the young girl to tell her what happened out at Pearl's.

Bridget felt her stomach knot up as she listened to the tale. "Are you certain that's the name you heard?"

Bridget's stomach burned when Mary nodded her head. It didn't have to be *her* Michael. It could be another Michael O'Toole. 'Twas a common enough name. Wasn't it?

She looked up and saw the way the marshal was watching them. She wondered if he had heard their conversation.

A flush stole across Bridget's cheeks when she remembered

the way she'd given herself to James last night. She'd never made love until she was exhausted before. With Michael . . . good Lord in heaven above, could it be him? Could her husband be alive after all these years? The thought nearly drove the breath from her lungs. Why now?

Shooing everyone into the kitchen, Bridget steadied her hands, making sure to pour the hot coffee into the marshal's cup, not onto his hand. His bright green gaze reminded her of Maggie's husband. Both were lawmen, and both were prone to stretches of watchful silence.

A chill swept through her, leaving her shaking and covered with gooseflesh. Something was terribly wrong; she felt it all the way down to her toes.

"Thank you, ma'am."

Bridget watched as his eyes seemed to settle on one empty chair after another, as if he were mentally counting the number of able-bodied men he was prepared to deputize.

"Mr. Ryan and his men rode out a little while ago," Bridget offered.

Unsure of what the marshal was thinking, worried she would hear a truth she could not bear, Bridget sent up a silent prayer that the man the marshal was after was not the same man she had taken vows with. She shook her head and nearly laughed out loud. Of course, it couldn't be Michael. He was dead.

*Wasn't he?* She'd never have given herself to James otherwise . . . or would she?

Now that the niceties had been observed, she wanted to get Maggie alone to find out if there was more her friend was not telling her. But the marshal had other ideas.

"Mrs. Ryan—"

His direct gaze unnerved her. "I'm not Mrs. Ryan. I'm a widow."

His eyes pinned her with a hard look. "Do you keep house for Ryan?"

Bridget cleared her throat and decided the truth would be the easiest to remember. Her mind was so muddled right now; she would never be able to keep a string of fibs straight. "I did for a time."

"But not now." He finished the statement for her.

She met his penetrating look openly, daring the lawman to judge her. Everyone else had within moments of meeting her, why not Marshal Justiss?

"I noticed a new barn." His voice had softened a bit. The edge was gone, but his eyes were still wary.

Bridget nodded toward Maggie. "James Ryan is Mrs. Turner's brother. We had a barn-raising yesterday."

"And you came back to help?" he suggested.

She nodded, waiting for the recriminations to start. Though she was weary of them, she braced herself for yet another round.

"A lot of work goes on besides the actual construction of a new barn." Bridget watched the way he looked first at Maggie and then turned back to look at her. "I imagine you ladies had your hands full feeding everybody and taking care of mashed fingers."

Bridget sucked in a breath and held it, waiting for him to criticize the fact that she was still in the man's home; a man she was no relation to.

The marshal watched her, as if he knew what she waited for. *Could he read her mind?* Lack of air was making her dizzy. She let the breath out in a whoosh.

"You might want to take a sip of coffee. It's mighty good."

The compliment surprised her, but not as much as the man's easy acceptance of her presence at the Ryan ranch. Bridget could not remember the last time she had been so readily accepted. Actually, she could. James had accepted her during one of the lowest points in her life.

Maggie spoke up then. "I'm forgettin' me manners again." She turned toward Marshal Justiss. "Allow me to introduce you to one of me greatest friends, Bridget O'Toole."

The marshal's eyes narrowed to pinpoints of deadly green. "Widowed, you say?"

"Aye, she and her young son Mick were all alone in the world, until me brother came to their rescue."

Bridget had seen a similar look to the one in the marshal's eyes once before, and she had been on the receiving end of that man's wrath as well. She pushed her chair away from the table and stood up.

The marshal blinked and the look was gone. He took another swallow of coffee, set his cup down, and pushed his chair back as well.

Bridget took a step back and looked over at Maggie. *Bless her heart, she understood the look.*

"Shouldn't ye be on your way to help me husband and brother?" Maggie demanded.

Bridget wanted to hug her for trying to deflect the marshal's attention from her. But the man was like a greedy dog with a juicy bone.

"I'd like to ask you just a few questions before I head on over to The Ranch."

Bridget screwed up her courage and faced him. She had to crane her neck back to look him in the eye. He must be near in height to James. The anger she had glimpsed in his gaze receded a bit. Fighting the urge to take another step back from him, she nodded. "What would you like to know, Marshal?"

"When did your husband die?"

Bridget managed to clear the tightness from her throat and answer, "Nearly twelve years ago."

"Where did he die?"

"I . . . I'm not sure. That is—" Bridget stumbled over her answer. She was not sure where Michael had died.

"You weren't with him at the time?"

The marshal's tone, and his questions, raised her suspicions. He knew something that she did not. She would never have had the courage to speak up before, but a certain rancher had changed the way she felt about herself. She now had the courage to ask her own questions.

"Why do you ask, Marshal? Is there a specific reason for your questions about something that occurred more than a decade ago?"

"Would you step outside with me for moment, Mrs. O'Toole?"

"Ye don't have to speak to him alone, Bridget," Maggie warned.

Bridget hesitated, then looked up at the marshal's closed expression, struck by the realization that while he looked stern, she did not have anything to fear from the lawman. He was simply doing his job.

"It'll be all right, Maggie."

Bridget preceded him through the door he held open for her. Once outside, he grabbed her by the elbow and spun her around. "I don't have time to waste on civilities, Mrs. O'Toole."

Bridget felt a frisson of icy fear sprint up her spine.

"I have reason to believe the Michael O'Toole I followed here is responsible for the hostage situation out at The Ranch. But before I ride out there, I need to make sure of a few facts."

She stared down at his hand, still clenching her elbow. At her pointed look, he let go.

"O'Toole is a common name."

"I also have reason to believe that he is your husband."

"But my husband is dead!"

"And you buried him where?"

Dear Lord, she had no idea how to answer the marshal's question.

"But . . . but he never came back!" she whispered.

"How long did you wait?"

*A lifetime, she thought.* "A year."

"Only a year?" He was standing right in front of her again, and the toes of his trail-worn boots touched the tips of her serviceable boots.

"There was a fire . . ." Her voice trailed off. *Was Michael alive after all these years? Could it possibly be him?*

"You left after the fire," he said.

Bridget nodded. Her head began to pound.

"Why didn't you go home to your parents?" he asked.

Shocked by the possibility that Michael could still be alive, Bridget could not seem to find her voice. Oh, my God. After last night . . . how could this be happening?

Her brain felt as if she had been head-butted by an ornery billy goat, repeatedly. "My parents died in a carriage accident right before I married Michael." God help her, she couldn't think. Was it written on her face that she'd spent the night in James's bed, in his arms, loving him?

His eyes narrowed, and he opened his mouth as if to speak. He shook his head, and Bridget wondered if the man had answered his own silent question.

"So you are all alone, then," he suggested.

She shook her head, no. "I have Mick."

"Mick?"

"Aye, Marshal," her son answered. Relief speared through her. She watched her son as he walked up the path to the back porch. "She has me."

The marshal was a smart man. Bridget watched his face closely and knew the moment he put two and two together. She nodded. "I'd like to introduce you to my son, Michael O'Toole, Jr."

Mick wouldn't take the man's hand when the marshal offered it. He stepped around the marshal and put an arm around his mother. "Maggie was worried. I've just come from town. I was able to talk a few men into riding out to The Ranch with me."

"That won't be necessary—" Marshal Justiss began.

"You don't know anything about Pearl or her girls," Mick countered. "You don't know the lay of the land, like I do."

The marshal stared at Bridget's son.

Mick stared right back. While a bit unnerved by the glare the man was directing at her son, Bridget couldn't deny that she was proud of Mick. He was unafraid to speak up for what he believed was right.

"How many men have you got?" she asked, hoping to deflect the marshal's attention.

Mick turned and smiled at her. "Five."

"But . . . I thought Marshal Turner couldn't convince any of the town's menfolk to ride out with him?"

Maggie stepped through the back door with her arm around Mary. "Now that he's retired, he couldn't," she said softly.

"How did you change their minds?" Bridget prodded.

"He didn't," Marshal Justiss said, looking out at the yard behind Bridget.

"We're ready when you are, Mick!" a young voice called out.

Bridget turned around and saw the group of *men* her son had gathered together. They ranged in age from eleven to sixteen, but she had no doubt that they were capable of holding their own in a fight. She'd seen them working side-by-side with their fathers just yesterday. They were young, strong, and every last mother's son could shoot the head off a diamondback at twenty paces. Bridget nearly smiled as she remembered the day she had happened upon that particular shooting contest.

"Do be careful," she whispered, smoothing the hair back off of her son's forehead.

"You too, boys," she called out to the group of brave young men ready to ride out and avenge the honor of her friend Pearl and her homeless girls.

"Yes ma'am," the group called back.

"Have a care!" Maggie warned. "Watch yer backs and listen to Marshal Justiss!"

As one, the group nodded.

"Be safe," Mary called.

Mick turned back and placed a hand on the girl's slim shoulder. Bridget watched the look of tenderness fill her son's expression and soften the hard lines around his mouth. "We won't let anything happen to them, Mary," he promised. "You have my word on it."

She reached up and put a shaking hand to Mick's face. "Hurry back, Mick."

As the group rode off into the growing light, Bridget brushed a hand over the young woman's back and pulled her into a quick hug. "My Mick's a smart lad," she offered.

"And can hit a snake between the eyes at twenty paces," Maggie said with a grin.

"I'll get my healing basket," Bridget said, holding the door to the kitchen open. "With any luck, the men will all be back before noon and ready to have their scrapes tended to."

Her heart lurched, thinking of her son riding off into such a dangerous situation. But he wouldn't be alone, she thought; he was riding with Marshal Justiss. Maggie's husband, a former marshal, and James Ryan, the man she'd only just realized she'd trust Mick's life with, were already riding toward Pearl's. She just hoped they'd all arrive in time.

# CHAPTER 19

Ryan heard the sound of shots being fired as they approached The Ranch from the back.

He tried to block out a woman's high-pitched scream of terror, riding his horse right up onto the back porch and leaping off. He raised his Colt into the air.

"Wait for my signal," Turner whispered.

As they slipped off to their assigned places, James thought of Bridget and Mick and the life he wanted to offer them. A safe home and his protection and caring—

*"Now!"*

James burst through the back door, leveled his Colt and shot out the light. He heard Turner crash through the front door at the same time a window shattered off to his left. He had time to draw in a breath, while the outlaws stared at them in the dim light with their guns drawn, ready to fire.

Then all hell broke loose.

When the dust settled and the black powder cleared, a blessed quiet descended, giving Ryan time to take stock of the situation. His brother-in-law's left arm was bleeding just above the elbow, but he didn't seem bothered much by it. In fact, the man stood with both guns pointed at the battered group of men sprawled on the dining room floor.

"Who do we have here?" Ryan asked, pulling out one of the spare bits of rope he'd thrust into his vest pocket earlier. He walked over to lend a hand tying the prisoners up.

The largest man in the group glared up at him. Although he couldn't place the man's face, the eyes were familiar. An eerie feeling that he had met him before settled around him like a cold, wet rain. He shook the feeling off and bent down to the task at hand.

"O'Toole and his gang," Turner said, nodding toward the man Ryan had just tied up.

The silence that followed allowed Ryan to adjust to the sudden roiling in his gut. His stomach flipped, and his breath snagged on its way into his lungs. His gaze riveted to O'Toole's. No. It couldn't be!

"What's your first name?" he asked through tightly clenched teeth.

"What difference would it make to you?" the man demanded.

"None," Ryan answered, slowly rising to his feet. Bugger it. Had he spent the night making love to a married woman?

"Michael," one of the other men called out. "A fine upstanding Irish name!"

Ryan looked around at the shards of glass—all that was left of the windows—and splinters of wood—remnants of chairs and tables. O'Toole and his gang had shot the place to pieces, but it was what he had yet to find out that ate a hole in his gut. He needed to find out where Pearl and her girls were and what condition they were in.

"Ye bring shame to the proud people you've descended from," Ryan snapped, unable to keep from slipping into a heavy brogue.

Flynn nodded in agreement, finishing off the knots he was tying.

Reilly placed a hand on Ryan's arm, but he barely felt it. "You're not from around these parts?" he asked, already knowing the man was not, and all the while dreading the answer the man might give.

The man opened his mouth to speak, just as the front door burst open.

Ryan watched the imposing figure standing there stride into the room. He noticed the star pinned to the man's chest at the same time he noticed Mick hot on the man's heels.

"Mick? Why aren't you with your mother?"

"A fine name, lad," O'Toole said, before Mick could answer Ryan's question.

"Justiss?" Turner called out. "That you, Ben?"

The tall man nodded, seeming to take in the situation and decide his gun was one too many. "You might want to put away those guns now, boys," he said over his shoulder.

That's when Ryan noticed the Burnbaum brothers and three other young men he'd seen about town, moving up to flank the lawman. As a unit, the boys holstered their weapons, but not the unspoken promises of retribution etched on each one of their faces. The sound of someone crying snagged his attention.

"Where's Pearl?" he asked.

Turner nodded toward the kitchen. "I'd bet they're holed up in the kitchen."

Ryan headed in that direction, when a movement out of the corner of his eye redirected his attention. His gaze snapped back to the men huddled on the floor. He mentally counted and came up one short.

"I heard O'Toole had five men." His voice was tight with the need to shout.

Turner's eyes met his, and Ryan knew he had heard right. One had gotten away! "Justiss?" Turner called out.

The marshal slipped out the front door, but Ryan's gut feeling, and the echoing sound of pounding horse's hooves fading in the distance, told him it would be too late. The outlaw was long gone.

Ryan slipped quietly into the kitchen. Pearl sat at the kitchen table, white-faced and bleeding, from an evil-looking cut slicing across her cheek and from her split and swollen bottom lip. Pearls wasn't the one crying. In fact, he noticed she appeared to be oblivious to her injuries and was instead soothing the waif-like child sitting on her lap, clinging to her. Four young women, ranging in age from twelve to seventeen, hovered around her, trying to staunch the blood, but only one was crying. The other three looked mad enough to spit nails.

He cleared his throat, and everyone in the room turned to face him.

"Mr. Ryan?" Pearl sounded surprised; her voice was weak and thready.

"Aye, Miss Pearl," he said, taking off his Stetson and holding it in his hands. "Is anyone else hurt?" he directed the question to the oldest of the girls. She shook her head.

"What have you got there?" he asked, noticing the way the tiny girl on Pearl's lap burrowed deeper into Pearl's embrace.

"Emma," Pearl whispered.

Ryan wondered if Pearl was afraid of him. He'd met her once or twice before, after Maggie nagged him into riding out to The Ranch to lend a hand with repairs to the chicken coop, but she hadn't seemed bothered by him then. *Why now? Was something else wrong?*

He watched Emma tighten her hold around Pearl's waist and heard the woman's sharp intake of breath. Had she fallen and cracked a rib? "Girls, can one of you please take Miss Emma, while I have a look at Pearl?"

"Why do you want to look at Pearl?" one of the girls demanded, her eyes narrowing in suspicion.

"She don't owe you nothing!" another bit out.

"Anything," Pearl said, then addressed the oldest girl. "Amy, please take Emma."

Before the girls changed their minds, Ryan drew up a chair

and sat down next to their guardian.

"Does it hurt to breathe, too?"

Pearl's startled gaze met his. "How did you know?"

"I stepped too close to the southbound end of a northbound mule once." He intentionally kept his voice light, hoping to ease some of the tension in the room. "Blasted mule broke three of my ribs!"

"Oh, Pearl," he heard someone cry out from behind him.

He ignored the cry and focused on the woman. After a few moments of silence, and intense glaring on his part, she finally nodded. "All right then," he said with a nod of his own, gently probing her ribs.

She winced.

He grimaced. "Can you walk?"

"I dragged her in here," a tall girl answered.

He looked up at the young woman and saw the way the expression on her pretty face hardened. "They kicked her, Mr. Ryan." Tears sprang to her huge brown eyes. "When she refused to let them into the kitchen, they started beating her."

"I'm still here, Amy," Pearl whispered, placing a hand on the girl's arm. Ryan knew she had to be in a lot of pain, but she still sought to ease the girl's worry. "All I need is a bit of a rest."

"Ryan!" Turner called out, striding into the kitchen. He stopped dead in his tracks at the sight of the battered, bleeding Pearl. Ryan watched the way compassion slipped across his brother-in-law's face before it hardened into a mask of rigid control.

"Which one of them hit you?" Turner demanded.

Pearl shook her head at him, refusing to answer. Ryan thought he knew why. Though their backgrounds were different, he and his brother-in-law were cut from the same cloth. They both had a need to protect those weaker than themselves. Any man who beat a woman deserved to be punished, and he intended to see that O'Toole and his gang got what they had coming to them.

"Let's get Pearl out to my ranch. She won't be much good on her feet for the next couple of weeks."

Turner didn't answer immediately.

Ryan turned to one of the girls and asked her to pack a few things for Pearl. Amy again acted before the others and took a step forward. "We can take care of her just fine right here."

"Have you been out in the dining room?" Ryan asked. When the young woman shook her head, he continued, "It's going to take some doing to build more tables and chairs. Ordering replacement windows from the mercantile will take time, too."

"We still don't need your help," one of the other girls spat out. Ryan thought she looked to be around Mick's age.

"Daisy, please." Pearl was weak, but she still held some sway over her charges. "Mr. Ryan has kindly offered his ranch. Why don't we take him up on it?"

"But he didn't invite us," another of the girls blurted out. "Just you!"

"Did you think I would let you girls stay out here all alone after what happened?" Ryan was incredulous. But from the looks on their faces, the girls obviously thought he would do just that.

"What difference would that make?" another one asked.

"I'm sorry for the misunderstanding, ladies," he said, satisfied with the way the girls were now staring at him. "Pearl will need all of you with her, or else she'll spend too much time worrying about you, instead of concentrating on healing."

The girls stubbornly remained silent, waiting.

He was reminded of a certain dark-haired woman. And there, he thought, was the answer. They needed prodding along to get them moving where he wanted them to go. "Would you all please accompany Miss Pearl out to my ranch while she recuperates?"

"Why didn't ya just say so in the first place?"

Ryan just shook his head. Were all females as contrary as Bridget?

"You have five minutes to pack a few bags," he announced. "Mick can drive you all in the wagon—"

"What about Pearl?" Amy demanded.

Ryan shook his head, "Ribs are tricky," he said, looking at the very pale and very quiet Pearl. Her eyes were huge and glassy. He hoped she wouldn't suffer too much on the journey back to his ranch. "I'll carry her," he told the girls.

"Why can't she ride with us?"

"The wagon ride might be too jarring," Pearl explained simply.

As one, the girls slipped from the room and up the back staircase. Before he knew it, they returned with two large, bulging carpetbags.

Amy stopped to check the oven to make sure the fire was out. Satisfied that it was, she scooped the still-silent Emma up into her arms and nodded in his direction. "We're ready, Mr. Ryan."

# CHAPTER 20

"He'll be fine, Bridget," Maggie insisted.

"But he's just a boy!"

"Ye don't want to be sayin' that when Mick can hear ye. He's had to look out for ye, hasn't he?"

Bridget swallowed the words she had been about to say. Maggie didn't deserve the lash of her temper. Besides that, Maggie was right. Although her son's methods were questionable, he had done what he thought best.

"Aye, he has."

"And done a fine job of it, too."

The sound of horses approaching broke through the tension in the room. Bridget flew to the door and rushed outside. She had to see for herself that Mick . . . and James . . . were unharmed.

The sight meeting her eyes was not one her heart was ready for. James Ryan rode up to the house cradling Pearl in his arms, as if she were a precious burden. The greenest of envy swirled through Bridget like a vine, creeping into tiny unseen crevices, letting its roots take hold.

He had held her like that in his arms, just last night. Had it meant more to her than it had to him? Had she been so blinded by the intensity of his lovemaking, that she'd fooled herself into believing that James actually felt more than mere lust toward her? There had been compassion and caring, hadn't there?

"Bridget." Maggie's voice was close, but she hadn't heard her approach.

"Me brother cannot help his need to take care and protect others. 'Tis a part of him ye must accept if ye intend to let your feelings match the look in yer eyes."

Bridget's head snapped around to face Maggie. "I don't know what you're talking about," she said, stifling her need to strike out and hurt, as she had been hurt.

In that moment, while she and Maggie stood and watched, James carefully handed Pearl down to Reilly's waiting arms, she debated telling Maggie how she truly felt about James. But the need to confide her feelings was overruled by her need to learn more about the outlaws who had held Pearl and her girls hostage.

Ryan let Reilly carry Pearl into the house, unnerved by the similarities between Pearl's situation and Bridget's. Both women had been injured protecting the ones they loved. Though Bridget nearly starved herself in order to feed her son, Pearl had stood up to a group of soulless outlaws in an effort to keep them from hurting the girls she'd vowed to protect.

"Put her in the guest room," he heard Maggie order. She bustled about the kitchen, reheating the water he knew they would need to care for Pearl's injuries. Oddly, Bridget had not moved from where he had first spotted her, standing on the back porch. Had she heard the name of the outlaw? Was the man her husband? Bloody hell, he hadn't the time or the inclination to worry about her or their tangled web right now. There were five unhappy young women about to arrive, and the sixth stood wringing her hands by the foot of the stairs.

"Will she be all right, Mr. Ryan?"

He could tell from her red-rimmed eyes that Mary had been crying. He didn't think he wanted to listen to yet another of

Pearl's charges weeping. "In a few days, she'll be right as rain."

She seemed to accept his word as gospel. Mary sniffled a bit, wiped the backs of her hands over her eyes, then nodded. "What can I do to help?" she asked, eager to lend a hand.

"Why don't you go ask Brid—Mrs. O'Toole?" he suggested.

Maggie was telling Reilly how best to settle Pearl onto the guest-room bed when Ryan walked through the bedroom door.

"Don't be jarrin' her now," she warned.

"She may have a couple of cracked ribs, Maggie."

Her gaze shot to his. "And how would that have happened?" Ryan didn't want to tell his sister all that had occurred. She was carrying, and women in her delicate condition shouldn't be upset. Should they?

"Later," he said. Thoughts of Bridget lying in his bed, just last night, distracted him. He shook his head, hoping to dislodge the image. "Later," he promised before he fled the room.

The woman was addling his brain, and right now he needed it to be clear. He had to find out what Marshal Justiss knew about O'Toole and his gang . . . and whether or not O'Toole had ever been married.

Sam Paige, O'Toole's right-hand man, reined in his bone-weary mount, slid from the horse, and dropped to his knees in the soft dirt by the bank of the stream. His destination was only a few miles from here. He swept off his hat, scooped it full of clear, cold water, and poured it over his head.

Ignoring the way his horse's sides heaved, drawing in much-needed air after their all-out run from The Ranch, he set his hat back on his head and scooped up handfuls of the refreshing water and drank deeply. After a few minutes, his horse wandered upstream a bit and bent its head to drink.

"Dang fool," he spat out, thinking of the man he'd left holding the bag with the rest of the gang. "If I didn't want that mine payroll so bad, I'd leave him there to rot. Got to get to Slim's place, and see about a jail break," he mumbled to his horse, tugging on the reins. The animal ignored him in favor of slaking its thirst in the rippling stream.

Staring at the far horizon, Paige shook his head. "Can't believe O'Toole still thinks the fire at his cabin was an accident." He shook his head in disbelief. He hadn't meant to knock the oil lamp over; he'd been in a hurry searching for that blasted Bible and the safe deposit key. Once the flames starting licking their way toward him, he panicked and fled, never once looking back, never once thinking of the young woman who lay sleeping or the infant in the cradle by the bed. He wondered if O'Toole knew he'd fathered a child.

He shook off the terror of that fire, ignoring the lick of guilt swirling around where his heart should be. He still needed O'Toole to finish the bank jobs, and he needed Slim and his men to help him break O'Toole out of jail, or else they'd never knock off those banks.

Bridget buried the jealousy she felt toward her friend deep inside her. Pearl didn't need to be bombarded by Bridget's feelings of inadequacy and jealousy simply because they had been rescued by the same man. Even if that man had been the first one to touch her heart, or her body, since all those years ago when Michael O'Toole had swept her off her feet. Michael had confessed her eyes held the secrets of a wood nymph and he planned to spend the rest of his life discovering what those secrets were. James hadn't paid her elaborate compliments, but his beautiful blue eyes, questing lips, and tongue made her feel as if he had.

"Rest now, Pearl," Maggie told their friend before turning toward Bridget and motioning for her to follow her out of the room.

"Have ye seen to the girls?"

Bridget nodded, turning away from feelings she'd rather keep buried. "Amy and Mary are working out a schedule as to who will sit with Pearl, while the others help out in the kitchen."

"Good. Pearl needs her rest—"

Her words were interrupted by the sounds of raised voices coming from the kitchen. Bridget and Maggie hurried down the stairs to see what was wrong.

"Because I said so!" a sharp voice snarled.

Bridget took in the growing unease that was settling in the kitchen, like thick black smoke from a grease fire. "Girls, what seems to be the problem?"

After soothing the roomful of ruffled feathers, Bridget settled the girls back to their tasks. Amy grumpily washed off a pile of potatoes and settled down to peel them for the midday meal, while Daisy, the instigator, went back to sweeping off the back porch. The rest of the girls grudgingly went outside to pick more onions and carrots for the stew.

Putting the kettle on to boil, she and Maggie walked into the front parlor. "Do you think the man in jail could be your husband?"

Bridget's heart fluttered and her hands started to shake. To hide her fear, she started rearranging a mason jar filled with wildflowers.

"I don't know." The flowers were too far to the right. She fussed with them, centering them in the jar. "I never thought about it before, but it does seem strange that Michael's body was never found." For heaven's sake, now the flowers tilted all the way over to the left.

Giving up, she ignored the flowers and started pacing back and forth. The swish of her skirts was the only sound in the room. If he was alive, what did that make her? *Still married.*

"And just what do you think the head of the Committee will

have to say about that?"

Bridget's heart clenched in her breast. "I'm certain she'll have the entire Committee standing on your front porch demanding that you take those poor girls back where you found them, right before they ask Mick and me to leave town!" Bridget's chest was heaving with indignation at the thought of Sarah Burnbaum maligning those poor girls, or her son, in public.

Maggie opened her mouth to speak, but Bridget kept on going. "What about Pearl? Do you think the Committee will give up after one attempt to evict her?"

Maggie sat forward on the sofa, as if to speak, but Bridget kept talking. "It only took three attempts to get rid of Mick and me, before we took the hint." Bridget let her words fade, as she remembered their desperate situation. God, she'd been so scared Mick would starve right along with her! She shivered, reliving the nightmare. Somehow they'd survived. No. She shook her head. It wasn't *somehow*. It was due to the help of a generous, kind-hearted rancher that she and Mick had not only survived, but thrived.

But that was not the issue just now. She had to make Maggie see reason as far as Pearl and the girls were concerned. Sarah Burnbaum would not stop until she eradicated every last vestige of what the holier-than-thou do-gooder considered a blight on their town: The Ranch and all those involved with it. She could take care of herself and Mick, but Pearl and her girls needed help. They needed James's help.

"I think they should stay here," Bridget said in what she hoped was a firm voice. She really didn't like the thought of another woman sleeping in the bed she had slept in, being cared for by the compassionate rancher who had stolen her heart one tiny piece at a time.

Maggie shook her head. "With the barn being finished, Jamie

has more work than he knows what to do with. He can't spare Reilly or Flynn to stay behind and sit with Pearl."

A glimmer of relief shot through Bridget before she squelched it. Pearl wouldn't be all alone out at the ranch with her James— she liked the way that sounded and wondered why no shaft of fear chased through her at the thought of caring about a man. Had she changed that much? Had she gained enough faith in herself that she could trust her instincts when it came to men?

"I'll ask Mrs. Swenson if they can stay in town with us."

Maggie looked at Bridget, but the sounds of muffled laughter coming from the kitchen and the yard beyond had Bridget looking over her shoulder. Laughter was the best medicine for whatever ailed young people. It certainly seemed to help with Mick. So long as she kept a watch out, between Maggie and herself, they should be able to counter any attacks coming from the Committee for the next little while. Right now, she needed to pay a visit to the jail.

# CHAPTER 21

The rough board sidewalk was empty. Bridget's resolve wavered for a moment. Digging deep into her soul, she found the grit to go on. If there was a single grain of truth to the marshal's speculation that his prisoner was the same man who had walked out on her twelve years before, she had to know.

"Mick's well," she told herself. "He's happy," she added, blowing out a breath. Bridget bit her bottom lip. "I've raised a good son." Her heart warmed at the thought of him standing on the brink of manhood, no longer a man-in-training. Her eyes misted at the thought that her work was nearly done; only the fine-tuning was left.

She'd taught him to respect his elders, taught him manners enough that he wouldn't embarrass himself at a fancy sit-down dinner, but above all, she'd taught him to be honest. That trait, fortunately, ran deep and wide in him.

"Mick," she whispered, "I'm so proud of you." She hesitated outside the door to the jail. "I just hope you'll understand what I'm about to do."

Plastering a smile on her face and squaring her shoulders, she opened the door to the sheriff's office.

Marshal Justiss was alone and seemed surprised to see her. But the surprise swiftly changed to a look of speculation as he rose from his chair and walked around the scarred oak desk to greet her.

"Mrs. O'Toole," he rumbled.

Skittish, nerves dancing a jig up and down her spine, she focused on the sound of his voice, surprised at how it eased her worry.

"What brings you here?"

Though couched in pleasantries, she knew the question was not one to be sidestepped. The marshal expected an answer.

"After our conversation out at Mr. Ryan's ranch yesterday, I thought I would satisfy your curiosity and my own."

His eyes darkened to a deep, forest green and fixed on her for long enough that she looked away, uneasy. He obviously hadn't changed his mind. She hoped the marshal was wrong.

Bridget swallowed hard, trying to dislodge the lump of fear in her throat. Could it be written on her face that she'd been with James Ryan? "I'd like to see the prisoner."

Marshal Justiss leaned back against the front of his desk and crossed his long, lean legs at the ankle. "Are you sure you're ready?"

Bridget hated the fact that she was back to feeling unsettled. Wasn't it enough that she had come here to face her fear that the man locked behind bars was her Michael? Nerves be damned. For Mick's sake, and her own, she had to do it. She nodded.

He turned around and reached for the ring of keys hanging on the wall behind his desk. "All right." He paused, glancing over his shoulder at her, "If you're sure you want to."

His concern seemed genuine and lightened her heavy heart. No, she did not want to do this. "I have to," she answered.

He stopped again, barring her way to the back room where the prisoners were kept. "Before you go back there . . ." His voice was pitched low enough not to be overheard. "I just want you to know how much I admire your courage."

She shook her head back and forth, silently denying his words. "Courage?" she said. "I think not."

Marshal Justiss's eyes held hers for a heartbeat. "Let me do the talking," he advised.

Before Bridget could agree, they had stepped into the back room. Five men were divided between the two small cells. The two on the left side were lying down on their cots, facing the back wall. She looked over at the other cell. Two men lounged on cots, while the third stood at the bars. She started to look away.

"Son of a bitch!" the man at the bars hissed.

Soulful gray eyes ringed with thick, dark lashes widened in disbelief. As she watched, disbelief smoothed into recognition and spread across his familiar features.

"Michael?" The face had matured, but there was no denying the man standing behind bars in the Emerson jail was the man she had thought dead and buried these last twelve years.

He stood stone silent.

"You're alive?" Shock swept through her, leaving her knees weak and her head buzzing. Her eyes blurred in and out of focus. She could no longer feel her fingers or draw in the breath her lungs screamed for. She'd given herself just last night to the man she loved and planned on spending the rest of her life with. But now . . .

Though dazed, she felt a strong, firm arm wrap about her waist, as the marshal swept her back into the front room.

"Mrs. O'Toole?"

Dear God. Michael was alive? She couldn't quite get her thoughts to focus on anything but that. He was not dead. He was alive!

"Married," she murmured. Heaven help her! She was still legally married to Michael, the man of her young dreams, the man who'd swept her off her feet after just one look. The same man who had promised to love her forever. The man who had held a woman and her young charges hostage at gunpoint for hours.

"Mrs. O'Toole?"

Had he beaten Pearl, or had one of his men done it? His men! He was an outlaw! The man she thought she knew and loved now broke the law for a living.

"Mrs. O'Toole!"

Her eyes welled up with tears. It was all too much. Michael was alive, and she should be celebrating finding him after believing him dead all these years.

*"Bridget!"*

All she could think of was the fact that he was *not* the man she thought she'd known and loved. The man behind bars was a complete and total stranger.

"Drink this."

She found herself seated and a glass of amber-colored liquid thrust into her hands. Try as she might, she couldn't seem to hold it. Her quaking hands sloshed whiskey over the rim of the glass until a warm, firm hand steadied hers.

Marshal Justiss guided the glass to her lips, waiting expectantly while she swallowed the fiery whiskey. She was grateful for the trail of warmth burning its way to her quivering belly. God she was cold. So cold . . .

"You really thought he was dead." It wasn't a question.

Bridget forced herself to meet the marshal's intent gaze. "Michael said goodbye that morning." Closing her eyes helped to picture it, to remember. "Same as he always did. He kissed my cheek, touched the tip of his forefinger to my chin."

A tear welled up and broke free; she could feel it trickling along the curve of her cheek. "I loved him."

The marshal cleared his throat. "What happened?"

"He never came home."

"Not once?"

Bridget shook her head, fighting to keep a lid on the wild emotions rushing around inside.

"I have to ask . . ." The marshal paused, looked down at his hands, clenched them, and looked back up at her. "Is he Mick's father?"

Stunned speechless, Bridget could only nod. No one had ever questioned Mick's parentage to her face before—only behind their hands, when they thought she didn't hear them.

"You didn't realize you were pregnant the last morning you saw O'Toole?"

The implication was clear. Disappointment evaporated as white-hot fury bubbled to the surface, releasing her voice. She lashed out, "I don't know what kind of woman you think I am," she began, but before she could add that she'd never been with anyone other than her husband, thoughts of last night blurred her vision. She'd been with James in every way possible. Every position possible. They had been as close and connected as a man and woman could be. And she'd reveled in it. She'd given herself wholeheartedly to him. She could feel her cheeks beginning to flush. Oh, Lord. What could she say?

The marshal's gaze narrowed, but he didn't speak. He didn't have to. Bridget knew he didn't believe her. Well, maybe he did, but she was not going to give him any excuse to ask her point blank if she'd ever been with another man. Until last night, she hadn't, but that wasn't any of the marshal's business.

"I didn't realize I was carrying Mick until a week or so after Michael disappeared."

The marshal nodded.

Her hands started shaking again, so she clenched them in her lap to try to keep them still. Somewhat mollified by his acceptance, she continued. "I waited, watched, and asked everyone I knew . . ."

"And?"

"No one knew anything. He just disappeared." Bridget's hands started to ache, they were clenched so tightly. Still they shook. "I just knew something awful had happened to him."

Marshal Justiss didn't say anything, so she continued, "A few days after Mick was born, the cabin caught fire. I was—"

"During the day?"

"No. I was asleep and thought I'd been having a nightmare."

"But it wasn't a dream?"

She shook her head. "The smoke was so thick, and one whole wall was in flames."

"How did you get out?" The marshal was on the edge of his chair, waiting.

"I prayed, put a quilt over my baby, and ran through the flames."

"It's a miracle you or Mick weren't hurt."

"I didn't say that."

His gaze snapped back to hers, "Were you?"

She nodded, not wanting to have to tell him about the scars or the rest of it. James hadn't mentioned her scars last night. Hadn't he noticed them? Would it matter to her if he had? As if he understood, Marshal Justiss rose and stood before her, squatting down in front of her chair so they were eye to eye. He took her hands in his. She looked down at them, hers small and shaky, his steady and strong, and it was suddenly easier to tell him the rest.

"You don't have to tell me now."

"But you'll expect an answer soon?"

He smiled and nodded.

"My back is covered with scars."

"And Mick?"

"Not a one." She smiled. She'd done her best and protected her boy.

It was harder explaining the next twelve years, traveling from town to town, taking in laundry, scrubbing floors, all the while searching for word of her husband, but the marshal's steady silence eased her through it.

"For twelve years?"

Bridget let her gaze meet his. Compassion was a rare quality in a man. She saw and felt it with the marshal, as she had with James.

"It's easy to wonder why, but harder to explain. I looked younger than I was—"

"You still do."

"Traveling without a man . . ." Bridget sighed. "People talk and believe what they want to believe."

"And they believed what?"

"That I'd never been married. Mick didn't deserve to grow up hearing such talk."

"So you just moved on?"

Bridget nodded.

"How many times?"

"Thirteen times in twelve years."

"Are you going to run again?" His steely gaze challenged hers.

Bridget met the look and shrugged. "I don't know."

"What about Mick?"

"What about the man you have behind bars?"

"Let me help you," he said.

"How?"

"For starters," he began, "I know where your husband has spent the last twelve years of his life."

Bridget gulped, her stomach flipping. "I'm not sure I want to know."

"Yes, you do." Marshal Justiss sounded so certain of it, she almost believed him. After a moment of studying her, he added, "You'll want to know, because you'll need to face your problems for Mick's sake."

"Mick—" Her heart actually ached, thinking of her strong, proud son. "He'll never understand!"

"He's a good young man," the marshal offered. "He'll stand beside you through whatever comes next."

Bridget nodded her head. The confusion was seeping away as an image of her son standing beside her filled her mind's eye. A shadow of a taller man was standing beside him with his hand on Mick's shoulder. James had taught him to stand tall. James! Dear God, how could she ever explain this to James? He'd never believe her.

"Bridget?"

She looked up from their still-linked hands.

"I know we can get to the bottom of this."

Her instincts told her the marshal was a man to be trusted, while her heart cried out that she had already lost the trust of the one man she could have spent the rest of her life with.

What would James do once the truth about her was known?

"I don't know what to do. How will I tell Mick?"

"You need to put some distance between yourself and O'Toole," the marshal said. "Where can we talk privately?"

Bridget could not imagine having this conversation at Swenson's, or anywhere else for that matter. Thinking of the Committee, and unwanted gossip, she decided the best place would have to be the most public. "The hotel dining room."

"Let me buy you lunch over at the hotel," he urged. "I can start to fill you in. Once you know the facts, you can decide how to tell Mick."

Bridget could feel her strength seeping away. Her head swam and her breathing was far too shallow, too rapid. She had to leave before she dropped into a dead faint at the marshal's feet. That was something she wouldn't do, especially since the husband who'd deserted her was close enough to hear when her body hit the floor.

For Mick's sake, she'd go to lunch with marshal and find out what she needed to know. Then she'd be ready to face Michael again. For Mick's sake, she had to find out why the man who had vowed to cleave to her, until death parted them, had simply walked away from her and the life they were building together. For Mick's sake . . .

Michael O'Toole's hands gripped the iron bars caging him, separating him from the freedom he would die to regain. God help him, Bridget was alive! She hadn't died in that fire more than twelve years ago.

Relief washed over him. The Bible! Did she still have it? How could he ask? How could he convince her to come back and speak to him? She was obviously as surprised as he to find out their situation was not what either one had assumed. But what to do? How could he convince his *wife* . . . was she still his wife? In the eyes of the law, he couldn't say; he'd been gone for more than ten years. But in the eyes of the Church, they would be married, and he knew how much value his *wife* placed on the Church and its teachings.

Damn, but he'd give his right arm to get his hands on that Bible and the key to the safe deposit box, which he'd sewn into the back cover. Then the mine payroll would be his! After twelve long years, he'd finally be able to retrieve the money he'd stashed in the safe deposit box in Denver.

He wondered what type of woman the biddable young Bridget had grown into. She certainly was still a fine looking woman, although far too thin for his tastes. He preferred a woman with more to hang on to. But he had no problem trying to convince his wife he still cared for her if that's what it would take to get his hands on that Bible!

Once he got his hands on the money, he'd find a way to disappear again. This time, he'd stay gone.

# CHAPTER 22

"What should I do?" Ryan stopped mid-pace; his feet would not go any further. He had practically worn a path smooth on the cobbled walkway leading up to his sister's back door.

Turner leaned back against the newly painted porch post. He didn't appear any worse for the wear, even though Ryan knew how it felt to have a bullet rip a few layers of flesh out of your arm. But his brother-in-law seemed to be deep in thought, and for once did not have a ready answer. "Why don't you wait to speak to Justiss? I've known him for a few years. You can trust him to be honest with you."

Ryan nodded, taking in the wisdom of Turner's words. The dull ache in his chest where his heart should be tormented him. He had tried not to let himself care, but instead he'd somehow fallen head over heals in love with the widow and her son. Now that he had, what was he going to do about it?

The turmoil was driving Ryan over the edge. He blurted out the one question that plagued him. "Do you think O'Toole is her husband?" If he was, Ryan had already made up his mind that he would harbor no regrets about last night.

His brother-in-law shook his head, then stopped. "I wish I had the answers you need, Ryan." Turner tilted his head and stared at him. "Maggie is really fond of Bridget, and I am too."

Fond? Ryan mulled over the meaning of the word. His feelings went way beyond fond where the widow O'Toole was concerned. He had already lost his heart and was in jeopardy of losing his soul to her as well. But was his heart whole? After that long-ago night in Amarillo, he wasn't sure the frozen lump in his chest would be complete once it thawed.

"If she's in trouble, Maggie will stand beside her." Turner let the words sink in before adding, "So will I."

Ryan knew, without hearing the words, that his sister and his brother-in-law were prepared to stand with Bridget, no matter what. But where did that leave him? He wanted to believe that a man missing for more than a dozen years should forfeit the rights to his wife, but his staunch Catholic upbringing would not let him. If her husband was alive, the holy sacrament of matrimony still bound them together, whether Ryan liked it or not.

"Joshua?" He heard Maggie call out. " 'Tis time to have another look at yer arm."

The ex-marshal rolled his eyes heavenward before saying, "I think you have already made up your mind about Bridget, haven't you?"

Silence and confusion roiled around inside Ryan's head to the point that he wondered if it would explode. Gritting his teeth against the pain, he nodded to his brother-in-law, turned on his heel and left.

Unanswered questions, like so many wisps of fog, swept about him all the way back to his ranch. Had Bridget known her husband was alive? Was she truly running from the unfair gossip that seemed to surround her, or was she in fact running from a marriage that she would have everyone believe had ended with the death of her husband, a husband who at this very moment sat cooling his heels behind bars?

Ryan had removed the saddle and blanket when he heard footsteps approaching from behind him. He didn't bother to turn around. It would either be Flynn or Reilly.

"Where've ye been?"

Ryan ignored Flynn's question and began to curry his weary mount. The familiar feel of warm horseflesh quivering beneath the brush added a sense of normality to the otherwise surrealistic day.

"Have ye fallen on yer thick head and damaged yer already addled brain?" Reilly's question had Ryan spinning about to face his men.

"Well?" they both demanded, glaring daggers at him.

"And when have I ever answered to the likes of you two?" Ryan snapped, temper spiking dangerously close to the boiling point. He clamped the lid down on it.

"There was the time over in Oklahoma Territory . . ." Flynn said, scratching his chin.

"Wasn't that a grand fight, now?" Reilly said with a cheeky grin.

Ryan's fist clenched, and itched to connect with a target. Frustration nearly won out over the inner battle raging within him.

He patted the horse's strong neck and put away the grooming tools he had used on his mount. Checking to make certain his loyal friend had enough fresh water to drink and oats to munch on, he brushed his now-sweating palms against his dusty, jean-clad legs.

Facing his friends, he gave in to the overpowering need to talk to someone who would understand his very real fears. "How about a glass of the Irish?" They nodded and followed Ryan to the house.

Somehow the warmth of the smooth whiskey eased the tightness in his throat and loosened his tongue. His worries came pouring out. "Flynn, ye understand how it was?"

The redheaded man nodded.

" 'Twasn't as if I had a choice in the matter." He turned to look at Reilly. This time, Reilly nodded.

"Aye, Jamie, ye had no choice!" Flynn insisted.

"They would've kept ye behind bars until yer flesh rotted off yer bones!" Reilly's words only added to the intense frustration creeping up the back of Ryan's neck, cramping the muscles until they fairly screamed with tension.

"I never should have looked at Big John's daughter."

Flynn snorted. "As if the filly gave ye half a chance to ignore her."

"Twitchin' her silk-covered bustle in front of yer face every chance she had," Reilly added.

"Ye don't understand," Ryan rasped, looking down into the empty glass he cradled in both hands. "Ye never did."

Flynn poured more of the clear amber-colored whiskey into James's glass. "Always one to take on everyone's problems, ignorin' yer own," he muttered.

"I don't—" Ryan began

"Aye, lad," Flynn said knowingly.

"Ye do," Reilly finished.

" 'Twasn't about holding her in me arms," Ryan continued, conjuring up the long-suppressed image of the angel-faced blonde who had stolen his heart after one look.

"Oh, aye," Flynn readily agreed.

"She needed me." Ryan tried to explain what he was only just now beginning to understand himself. "Her father didn't understand that she only wanted to be married and live a life of her own."

"What the lass wanted was a patsy to take the fall when she and that overgrown ranch hand robbed her father's safe. So they left ye there to take the blame for it."

Reilly's words scored a direct hit. Ryan's heart still ached, thinking about that time in his life. But he'd gotten past it. He survived time in jail—well, not the full extent of the time he was due to serve.

"What yer sufferin' from now, lad," Flynn told him, "is guilt."

Ryan thought of the hours he'd spent trying to lose the thick Irish brogue, and when he had succeeded, the day he realized he also needed to change his name. Seamus Ryan Flaherty had become James Ryan overnight. Ryan now wondered if he'd lost a part of himself as well.

"Over Rebecca?" He certainly had felt guilty about not being there to stand up to her father for her, one last time.

"Have we given him too much of the Irish?" Reilly demanded of Flynn.

Flynn shook his head. "Not quite enough, if ye ask me."

He poured another round. "Now this may be borderin' on almost too much."

Ryan still hadn't unburdened himself; he still needed to get the rest of his worries off his chest. "Lads, ye have to listen."

Both men lowered their glasses and nodded solemnly.

" 'Tis Bridget. Do ye think she's telling the truth about her husband?"

Reilly didn't even hesitate. "I do."

Flynn nodded his agreement.

"How can ye be sure?" Ryan hated the way his words sounded, thick with brogue and slurred with whiskey. He shook his head, in an attempt to clear it.

"Think long and hard, lad. The answer will come to ye."

Ryan dragged his stiff and weary body off to bed. He toed his boots off, and left them where they landed. Not bothering to turn down the bedclothes, he drew in a deep breath and collapsed onto the bed, dead to the world by the time he exhaled.

"Should we at least loosen his belt?" Flynn whispered.

"He's too light a sleeper," Reilly answered. "Best to leave him be."

They turned as one and soundlessly made their way down the hall.

"Do ye think he'll figure it out by mornin'?" Reilly wondered aloud.

Flynn shook his head. "Difficult to tell. He's got a head twice as thick as yers."

Reilly snorted and wrapped an arm about his friend. "Sweet talkin' won't get ye out of yer turn makin' breakfast, boy-o."

"Yer a hard man, John Reilly."

"Faith, don't I know it."

# CHAPTER 23

Oh God, what a fool she'd been. So blinded by love, she'd believe anything her man told her. She'd believed it all. The plans for their future and the lies. He hadn't loved her. He *left* her!

Bridget's hands ached from clenching them in her lap. Marshal Justiss was patient with her, explaining as best he could. Her stomach churned. Trains robbed. Banks held up. Bile rose in her throat.

Mine payrolls hijacked. Innocent men killed?

She swallowed, clamping down on her body's reaction to the devastating news that her husband had spent the last dozen years leading a life of crime. Her heart didn't want to believe it, but a tiny piece of her brain prodded her; little things from the past that didn't seem right made sense now.

Michael leaving for days on end with no explanation as to where he was or when he'd be back again; the strange wound that looked an awful lot like a bullet had dug a groove along his arm.

Had Michael ever loved her?

As if sensing her inner turmoil, Marshal Justiss leaned across the linen-covered table and touched her lightly on the arm. "Don't be so hard on yourself, Mrs. O'Toole."

She lifted her gaze to his. "I don't . . . that is—" She lifted her hands up, unable to remember what it was she wanted to say.

Marshal Justiss nodded. "You are still in shock. You've thought him dead all these years. You've survived without him."

"Yes, but—"

"You have raised a fine son."

"Thank you, but—"

"Let me finish."

She nodded, trying to gather her scattered wits about her.

"Have you considered divorce?"

Shock had her gasping for breath. "I couldn't! What would people think? What would Mick think?"

And James. What would he think? Being a widow was one thing, but a divorced woman? She'd be one step up from the whores over at the Desert Rose.

A flash of understanding shadowed the marshal's deep green eyes before his eyes hardened. "People will think what they will. If we know in our hearts that we are living our lives to the best of our ability, then it really doesn't matter what anyone else thinks."

Bridget's head was filled to bursting with all the lies Michael had told, everything he'd promised. She had to leave and sort through it all.

"Thank you for lunch, Marshal Justiss." She rose from the table. "You've given me quite a bit to think about. I'll need a little more time before I talk to Mick."

Though every fiber of her being felt as if it had been stretched to the limit and she was in danger of coming apart, she held her head high and walked past the curious stares of the townsfolk, not stopping until she reached the boarding house.

"Where's Mick off to?" she asked when she entered the kitchen. He hadn't stopped when she called out to him. He seemed intent on his destination.

Mrs. Swenson shook her head and smoothed the starched white apron she wore. "I don't know. He didn't stop long enough for me to find out."

Bridget watched the dust swirling in her son's wake and wondered what had him running toward the sheriff's office like the devil was chasing after him.

*The sheriff's office* . . . She hadn't even had a chance to say hello to her son, much less tell him his father was alive—and cooling his heels behind bars.

She thrust her troubles away for now and instead focused on knowing she'd have to deal with Mick later—and then James. What could she possibly say to James? Forcing a bright note into her words, though she didn't feel cheerful, she asked, "How is Pearl feeling this afternoon?" Her world was about to come crashing down upon her head. She had accepted the marshal's word as the gospel truth, but having Mick find out the man responsible for holding up Pearl and her girls was his own father seemed beyond what her tired brain was capable of comprehending.

"Has little Emma eaten today?"

"She has, and I suspect she'll be right as rain soon," Mrs. Swenson promised. "She's upstairs playing with that little rag doll you made for her while she helps Susan keep an eye on Pearl."

"What are you girls planning on making for supper tonight?"

"Chicken and dumplings, with pie for dessert," Daisy announced.

"Well then, I can see Mrs. Swenson has everyone busy." Bridget nodded, satisfied everything here was under control.

"Idle hands . . ." the older woman began with a pointed look.

Bridget fidgeted under her gaze, wondering what Mick was up to. "Girls, why don't you all take a break and see how Pearl is feeling? Mrs. Swenson and I will bring up a pot of tea and some of my gingerbread in a few minutes."

The girls all agreed and tripped happily up the stairs.

When they had gone, Bridget slumped over, her head in her hands.

Mrs. Swenson sat down beside her and waited. When the silence got to be too much, Bridget looked up. She knew she could ride over and tell Maggie everything, but she didn't want to upset a woman in her delicate condition.

The tension tightened and built until Bridget felt as if she'd go crazy. "I have to tell someone before I burst!"

The older woman took one of Bridget's hands in her own and patted it. "I'm a good listener." Unable to hold back, Bridget told Mrs. Swenson what the marshal had to say about her husband.

"After all this time, he's alive?"

Bridged nodded and swallowed, nearly choking on the lump of anguish caught in her throat. "Mick's on his way over the jail!"

"Do you have so little faith in what your boy thinks of you that you think he'd judge you and find you lacking?" the other woman demanded.

Mrs. Swenson had hit the nail on the head. Bridget bit her bottom lip. She couldn't bear it if Mick judged her harshly. But worse, if her own son didn't believe her, how would she ever convince a certain black-haired rancher?

Bridget walked over to the dry sink and pulled the dipper out of the bucket of water. Pouring some of it over the pump, priming it, she then began to work the handle, filling the kettle near to the brim with cold, clear water. Her movements were slow and measured, the action soothing some of the coiled tension still filling her insides.

Once the kettle was heating, she pulled out a chair and sat down.

After a few minutes of intense silence, Bridget realized that Mrs. Swenson wouldn't demand that Bridget tell her the rest of what was troubling her; she would simply wait until Bridget started talking.

Before she could think where to start, words started tumbling out of her, and with it tears of anguish for the years she'd spent mourning a man who was never dead, and who wasn't worth her grief. "Can't you just imagine what the Committee for the Betterment of Emerson will have to say when they find out?"

"Widow O'Toole's husband is not dead. He's one of the outlaws in the town jail!" Mrs. Swenson said in a voice that mimicked Sarah Burnbaum's. "That'd be cause for talk. It'd stir those busybodies up like a tempest in a teapot!"

Inhaling the fragrant steam from her teacup, Bridget got up the gumption to ask, "Do you see why I can't talk to James?"

Mrs. Swenson shook her. "No. I don't."

"His standing in the community would suffer if he continued to associate with Mick and me." Bridget's voice cracked over the words.

"So you are thinking of James first."

"Aye," Bridget whispered, "and Mick."

"Do you really believe that a man like James Ryan would give a fig what those old busybodies have to say?"

Bridget wanted to believe that he would give her a chance to explain, that he wouldn't listen to the gossip that was no doubt, at that very moment, flying through the dusty streets of Emerson.

The older woman shook her head and took both of Bridget's hands in her strong, capable ones. "When are you going to do something for yourself?"

"Myself?" Bridget couldn't imagine why she should—or if she did, what that something would be.

"Why don't you slice up that gingerbread you promised the girls, and I'll follow you upstairs with the tea."

"But—"

"While you are sitting upstairs with those poor young women, why don't you think about where they might all be right now, if not for the desire to find a better life for themselves."

"Pearl was the one who saw to that."

Mrs. Swenson shook her head. "Do you truly believe that those girls would ever have had the wherewithal to escape the daily beatings or whatever else they are running from, if they did not have an overwhelming desire to strike out on their own?"

Bridget fell silent. She'd moved all those times for Mick's sake. Could she remember ever having wanted anything for just herself? She carried the sliced gingerbread, plates, napkins, and silverware on one tray, while Mrs. Swenson followed along behind with the tea.

Her stomach knotted in anguish when she realized that she *had* made a decision for herself, long ago, after Michael left. She'd been so wrapped up in feeling sorry for herself, she didn't care about living anymore. Miraculously, she'd felt the first fluttering of life stirring low in her belly, and everything changed. Her decision to live for her baby was the turning point. From that time on, she'd never done another thing that hadn't hinged on what was best for Mick.

She watched the girls fussing around Pearl. They seemed happy now that their friend was out of danger and being pampered. Bridget looked closer, but they still looked like ordinary children to her. Gram's words filled her heart: *It's what's on the inside that matters.*

"Well, yer biscuits broke the handle off my teacup!" Amy complained.

Bridget saw Daisy's face turn red. "I'm not the one who added so much flour to the gravy that you could cut it with a knife and fork."

Bridget opened her mouth to speak, but Pearl beat her to it. "If everything were perfect in life, why live it?"

Why indeed, Bridget wondered.

"So you're Mick?" Michael O'Toole said, scratching the day-old whiskers on his chin.

"Do I know you?" the boy asked, tilting his head to one side, studying the man through the bars of the cell that held him.

"Ask your mother if she remembers the forget-me-nots I picked for her bridal bouquet, then come back and ask me again."

Mick stumbled from the sheriff's office out onto the wooden boardwalk. He righted himself and stood staring off into space. Was the man behind bars his father? Had his mother lied about his father being dead? If his father was an outlaw, what did that make him?

With a sinking feeling, he remembered the flowers pressed in the middle of the Bible!

Mick dashed back to the boarding house, raced in the back door, and flew up the stairs to their room, mindless of the stares of the young women gathered around the kitchen table.

He found the O'Toole family Bible where his mother always kept it, right next to the bed. His hands shook as he lifted the book from the table and let it fall open in his hands. Tiny faded brownish-blue blooms marked his mother's favorite Psalm.

He knew the words by heart, but right now, not one of them reverberated through his pounding skull; all he heard was the echo of the outlaw's words. *Ask your mother . . . forget-me-nots . . .*

Mick slammed the book shut and held it to his heaving chest. He couldn't catch his breath or make his brain work. The outlaw in the jail was his father! *He had a father!*

Mick remembered living at the ranch with Mr. Ryan. He thought of the easy way the man had with his ranch hands, and the kind words Mr. Ryan always had for him. He remembered wanting very badly to be a part of the man's life. For a while, he had wondered what it would be like to have a man like James Ryan as his father.

But that was before he knew he still *had* a father. Mick raced back down the stairs, bursting through the back door on his way back over to the jail. He wondered if his father's blood was bad. If it was, did he carry the same bad blood in him?

"Whoa! Where are you headed there, partner?"

Mick skidded to a stop beside the sheriff's desk. He didn't want Marshal Justiss to know that the man sitting behind bars was his father. For the second time in his life, he lied. "I thought I'd share the Good Word with your prisoners."

The marshal narrowed his eyes and stared at him. Hard. Mick felt unease slide through his empty stomach. Did the marshal know he was fibbing? Just as he thought the marshal was about to boot him out of the building, the man nodded his agreement.

"Keep back from the bars. No telling what O'Toole or his men might try."

When Mick agreed, the marshal added, "I'll give you five minutes. That ought to be enough time. Then I expect to see you standing right back here in front of my desk. You hear?"

Mick swallowed against the growing lump in his throat. He nodded his head in agreement. Screwing up his flagging courage, he stepped into the short hallway and made his way to the jail cell.

"What brings you back here, boy?" one of the men demanded.

"Let him be," another muttered.

"What's that in your hands, Mick?" O'Toole's voice broke. Mick wondered if the poor man was so desperate to hear a reading from the Bible that he was getting emotional over it. Then shook his head. This was the man who'd held Pearl and her girls hostage.

"My mother's Bible."

"The O'Toole family Bible?" the man reached for the book.

Mick nodded, but kept the book just out of the man's reach.

"You wouldn't begrudge your father the chance to hold his own grandmother's Bible in his hands, would you?"

"I'm still not convinced you are." Something about O'Toole's eyes bothered him. As he spoke, his eyes had narrowed and grown darker, beadier. Mick shook his head, trying to dispel his unease. If the man was his father, then Mick should be more understanding.

Maybe it wasn't true. But the flowers . . . The proof that O'Toole spoke the truth was pressed smack dab in the middle of the Bible. He decided then and there not to wait to talk to his mother. He was going to be a man soon. Well, thirteen in a few months. And anyway, he figured he was old enough to make his own decisions without any input from his mother.

"What was your grandmother's name?" Mick asked, holding out for one last small bit of proof.

"Nellie Mae Flynn."

Mick's arms tingled and went numb, the Bible fell out of his hands, but the outlaw—no, his father—grabbed at it through the bars, snagging it before it hit the floor. The look of awe on his father's face was telling. The man nearly teared up with emotion, holding the leather-bound book in his hands, rubbing the back cover between his thumb and forefinger.

"I can leave it with you for awhile," Mick offered.

"You've your mother's big heart, lad," O'Toole finally said.

Mick nodded. The sound of boot heels scraping against the bare wood floor had him hopping. "I promised the marshal I wouldn't be long. I've gotta go."

The minute Mick left the room, one of his men turned to O'Toole. "Do you think Sam made it over to Slim's place?"

O'Toole nodded. "Should be on his way back about sundown."

"What's so special about that there book, O'Toole?" another of his men prodded.

"Didn't know you were so dedicated to reading the Bible."

He simply shook his head, not answering.

Later that night, as Bridget lay in bed, past events swept through her mind at a frightening speed. Not once since her decision to do her best by Mick had she thought of herself. Wasn't the last decision she'd made proof enough that she was incapable of making decisions for herself? She did a far better job of thinking about others, caring for others.

Flipping over onto her stomach, burying her face in the soft, lavender-scented pillow, she wondered if she was brave enough to even try to think of what she wanted from life. Rolling onto her back, she stared up at the darkened ceiling. If she had only herself to think about, only herself to be responsible for, what would she do? Where would she go? "What do I want out of life?"

The answer came as a soft snore from the bed next to hers, breaking into her train of thought. Mick mumbled something incoherent and kicked a foot out from under the covers. Bridget sat up, intending to go tuck her boy back in, but Mick mumbled again, and his foot slipped back under the covers.

*What do I want?* Letting go of all her worries for a moment. The answer was so simple and came so swiftly that her breath snagged in her lungs.

"James," she whispered aloud. "I'd want to be with James."

As soon as the words left her lips, despair flooded through her, leaving her weak and drained. In the eyes of the Catholic Church, she was married. For better or worse, till death . . .

So much for dreams of a happy future with the dark-haired

man who was never far from her thoughts. She was still a married woman, and she would stay true to her marriage vows, even if it killed her.

# CHAPTER 24

*Bigamy!*

The word swirled around in his aching head. How much whiskey had he had to drink last night? He couldn't remember. He started to shake his head at his foolishness, but the intense pain and accompanying roiling in his gut demanded that he stop.

He reached up and grabbed both sides of his head. Raking his hands through his hair, he clenched his fingers into fists and rested them at his temples. The pain of pulling on his hair was nothing compared to the ache in his head and the slashes across his heart.

If Bridget had accepted his proposal that day, they would have committed more than one sin. Though neither of them truly would have done so had they any knowledge that her first husband was alive. Remembering how it felt to sink into her welcoming depths haunted him, taunted him. Maybe he would have done it anyway. But the question that plagued him was: did she know? Had she used her weakness and her son as a ploy to get him to help them out of their dire situation?

The answers didn't come. His head was still clouded with too much of the Irish.

"Coffee. Strong and black."

"A gallon or so ought to do it," Flynn suggested.

Ryan turned around, slowly and deliberately. The movement didn't jar anything vital, and remarkably, his head began to clear. Reilly and Flynn had helped him get through more than one major problem. They had been with him for so long now that they were an intrinsic part of his family. Maggie seemed to take to them, treating them to the same clipped admonitions that had so often made him smile when she used them on him.

Why couldn't they just tell him flat out what they thought about Bridget? Why did they have to turn his question back on him, leaving him to answer it for himself?

"I've a pot brewin'. Care for a cup?" Reilly asked, watching him closely.

Ryan grunted in response. His head might have begun to clear, but it still pounded like the very devil.

"Put an extra bit of sugar in it, lad," Flynn advised with a sage nod.

Seated at the scrubbed oak table, Ryan slowly made his way through eggs, bacon, and biscuits before he looked up from his plate. The other hands had come and gone by the time he rose to place his dish, fork, and knife in the sink. At least the ranch wouldn't suffer, even though its owner did. The animals depended upon him and his men to feed them, to take care of them. He couldn't allow himself the luxury of taking a day to himself to nurse his hangover, or his foul mood.

Flynn stopped him before he could step down off the back porch. "Have ye decided yet how ye feel about her, lad?"

Reilly magically appeared next to Flynn; the two stood silent as stones waiting for his answer.

"I've no time to be thinking about women."

"He must have spent the night tossin' and turnin', frettin' over her," Flynn said to Reilly.

Ryan felt the first lick of temper flare to life. "I didn't say—"

"Poor man, he doesn't even know how far gone he is over the lass," Reilly confided to Flynn. Neither one seemed to be paying any attention to Ryan at all. That had his temper bubbling closer to the surface.

"I don't have the time—"

Flynn reached into the front pocket of his Levis and pulled out a dented silver pocket watch. "Half past nine."

Ryan couldn't stop the roar of anger that swept up from his toes as he slammed his fist into the porch column, cracking the wood. The previous owner had promised the ranch house was built to withstand any storm. Well, it had held up to the fury of Ryan's temper.

"I told ye we should have woken him up earlier," Flynn said quietly, watching Ryan through narrowed eyes. "Now he's missed his favorite part of the day, the milkin'. Now he's bound to be surly till noon."

Ryan clenched his fist again, only to feel a slick, wet substance seeping into his closed palm. Blood. He looked down at his hand. He'd split three knuckles and left a decent-sized gash across two fingers where they had connected with a knot in the wooden post.

"Too bad Bridget isn't here to care for your hand. She's got a way about her. Makes a man realize how lonely a ranch house is without a woman tendin' to the cookin' fires and the ones that could burn brightly within a man. If the woman is the right one."

Ryan turned on his heel and headed over to the barn. He had a ranch to run and no time for foolishness. Let his friends worry over women. He could live without them. He could live without Bridget. Couldn't he? Closing his eyes, he saw her lying on her back in his bed, her warm, dark eyes going blind with passion as he pushed her over the peak with his tongue. Would he ever rid himself of these memories? God, it had only been one night. *One night would never be enough with Bridget.*

He pulled a bandana out of his back pocket and wrapped it around his knuckles. He tied the knot, vowing never to see her again. But the thought ate a hole in his gut, leaving him feeling hollowed out, empty. What would it be like living with Bridget? The ghost of a smile swept across his face. Sunshine and rainbows, candlelight and tangled sheets immediately came to mind. He could imagine her standing in front of the stove cooking breakfast for him and his men. If he cocked his head to the side, he could almost hear the sound of her laughter for the next fifty years—as easily as he could imagine the nights they'd spend together.

Funny, whenever he thought of Rebecca Lynn he only imagined spending a hot, sweaty, sheet-tangling night or two with her. No more than that. With Bridget . . . well, with Bridget it was just different.

His heart suddenly tumbled over and his stomach followed suit. God, he wanted Bridget in his life. Not just to warm his bed, but by his side every day. In sickness and in health, for better or worse. He scrubbed his hands over his face. God help him, he was in love with a married woman!

He wondered what the law would say after twelve years. Bugger it, in the eyes of the Church, she was still legally bound to the man she had married a dozen years ago. What ate a hole in his gut was still that one simple question: did she know her husband had been alive all of this time?

His heart told him she hadn't, but his heart had been wrong before. Dead wrong. He'd gone to jail for believing and following in his heart. Well, maybe not for following his heart. Five years older and wiser, he realized his heart had nothing to do with the way he felt about Rebecca Lynn. But because his heart was truly on the line this time, he had to make certain he would never go back to jail again. No man or woman would ever force him back behind bars. He'd suffocate from the combination of the lack of freedom and his overpowering need to be outside breathing in the fresh air. Heart or no heart, he would never go back.

Marshal Justiss stared out the front window of the sheriff's office, his temporary home. A feeling of elation swept through him as he thought of the outlaw he had locked behind bars, a shout away, down the hall. Two years was a long time to wait. The wire he'd sent off to Marshal Brodie left him feeling well satisfied. He looked forward to receiving a reply, though the fact that O'Toole's right-hand man had escaped did continue to cast a shadow of worry over things. The man was notorious for acting without thinking, and, along the lines of a man who had no fear of anything, the very least of the man's thoughts would concern a hangman's noose.

What was left of the cup of coffee he'd poured a half hour ago had gone cold. He got up to refill his cup from the coffeepot kept warm on the cast iron pot-bellied stove.

The enamel cup was warm to the touch, even through the layers of calluses he'd built up over years of using his hands. Whether it was to hitch a plow, fork hay, hammer nails, or draw his Colt .45, the hardened layers of skin were as much a testament to the man as was his ability to pick up on what people were hiding from him; what they didn't say. Given time to think, he always figured it out.

Ever since he had arrived in town, all five of his senses had been on the alert. There was something about the rancher, James Ryan. He couldn't quite put his finger on it, just a feeling he had. Relaxed and with his feet propped up on the scarred desktop, he narrowed his eyes, gazing off into the distance, sipping the strong hot brew, and letting his mind wander.

*Seamus.*

The name popped into his head out of nowhere. Damned if he couldn't see the wanted poster in his mind's eye. A tall, rangy man, black hair, and light eyes with a go-to-hell expression in them. He slammed the empty coffee cup down on the desk, righting the chair as his boots hit the floor. In less time than it took to draw a breath, he was out the door, unhitching his horse.

It was time to have a word with retired Marshal Turner. He didn't think the former marshal knew the true identity of the convicted criminal hiding out in Emerson. If he did . . . well then, the former marshal was about to experience life from the other side of the bars.

Bridget sat with little Emma on her lap. She didn't think Pearl looked comfortable, but there was little left that hadn't been tried to ease her pain. Instructing the girls not to make Pearl laugh or bump up against her or the bed had been difficult for such a boisterous group of young women.

"Girls, why don't you ask Mrs. Swenson to take you over to visit Maggie?"

"But what about Pearl?" the oldest demanded, while the other girls nodded their heads in unison, awaiting her answer.

"I'll be right here."

"But what if you're downstairs and you can't hear Pearl calling you?"

Bridget could tell the girls needed a bit more coaxing, and a lot more hugging, before they would totally relax and let down their guard around her. She set Emma carefully on the bed, then stood and shook out her skirts before taking Emma back into her arms.

Scooting Emma over onto her hip, holding the little girl snug against her side with one arm, she turned to brush pale blond flyaway bangs out of Mary's eyes. She had a special feeling for Mary, if for no other reason than the way the young girl watched her son with an expression of total adoration.

Her heart swelled with pride, knowing her son was well on his way to becoming a man she could not only be proud of, but also one who would attract the love of a good woman. Something inside Bridget told her Mary might be the woman for Mick. The girl still had some growing up to do, but she'd worry about that later.

"Girls," Pearl called out from the bed.

Immediately a half dozen faces turned toward the battered woman lying on the bed.

"You know I trust Maggie as much as I trust Bridget and Mrs. Swenson. I'll be fine right here," she said with a half smile.

Bridget could tell she was in a lot of pain, and probably not admitting to half of it. But she was grateful Pearl had enough strength to speak up in order to sway the girls' thinking.

"Well . . . if you think so," one of the girls said.

"But we won't have any fun," another added, crossing her arms across her skinny chest.

"I don't want to."

"Bridget," Mrs. Swenson called out, walking into the room, "I was wondering if you'd mind if I drove on over to see Maggie." Her question effectively cut off any other protests or comments from the girls. "I've yet to see their new house. Well, not since the walls were nailed in place."

Bridget sent the woman a silent thank you. "Would you mind if the girls went with you? Maggie promised to teach them how to bake cream scones and soda bread."

Mrs. Swenson nodded. "I'll be leaving in about five minutes," she told the girls, who slowly moved, with varying degrees of reluctance. She turned back to Bridget. "Where's Mick? I was hoping I could convince him to hitch up the horse while I pack the jars of blackberry conserve I promised that darling husband of hers."

"He was up before me, but I haven't seen him yet this morning." Bridget worried over that fact, but then chastised herself. Mick could take care of himself. Besides, it was past time she started giving him more freedom. She would never know how he would treat that freedom if she kept him tied to her apron strings.

"Well then, I'll need a volunteer to hitch up the horse to the wagon."

The girls argued over whose turn it was, skipping out of the room and down the stairs. Mrs. Swenson turned back to Bridget. "Do you want me to find out where Mick is?"

"No. I'm sure he is fine. He needs some time alone."

"Have you spoken to him about his father yet?"

Bridget shook her head. "Every time I bring up Michael's name, Mick finds a reason to leave the room. At this rate, I'll never be able to explain what happened."

The older woman patted her on the shoulder.

"Your Mick is smart boy," Pearl said softly.

Mrs. Swenson agreed. "Be proud of him and wait it out. He'll come around, and when he does, he'll be more than ready to talk to you about his father."

Wise words from a woman Bridget had come to admire greatly over the past few weeks. She shook her head. Could so much time have passed since she'd arrived in Emerson? It had been nearly two months since she'd left the safety of the Ryan ranch. Just thinking about all that she had left behind made her stomach cramp. It was for the best, she told herself.

"I hope so," she agreed. "Time will tell."

"We're ready!" a chorus of voices called loudly from the foot of the stairs.

"Is there anything you need before we go?"

"We'll be fine." Bridget was always fine as long as she had someone to take care of.

When she was alone, with no one to tend to, she felt lost and without direction.

"Emma, would you like to ride out to see Maggie?"

Emma hid her face in the hollow of Bridget's neck and shook her head.

"We'll be home in time to make supper," the girls promised Pearl.

The quiet that followed the hustle and bustle of the girls' departure was unnerving. Bridget missed them already, but more than that, she was worried about where her boy might be. With a heartfelt sigh, she set Emma on her feet and took her hand. "Why don't we go see if there are any more daisies or violets left to pick for Pearl?"

Emma's solemn nod of agreement went straight to Bridget's heart and wrung it. One day soon, she hoped the little girl would string more than a handful of words together. She wanted to know how the child had come about those bruises dotting up and down her spine and on her face and chin. Her stomach tightened into a knot of revulsion, knowing the child had been abused when she should have been given hugs and kisses.

Noticing Pearl's eyes drifting shut, Bridget put a finger to her lips and tiptoed from the room. As they searched the back garden for the perfect flowers to add to the tiny handful Emma carried in her apron, Bridget wondered again what had happened to the man who had left Emma waiting quietly on the bench out in front of the mercantile.

Sarah Burnbaum had found her, and Millie Peabody had mentioned she'd seen the child sitting there, waiting for him to return, but neither woman had been willing to take the disheveled, bruised child in. By the time she and Mrs. Swenson had heard about the girl and gone to the mercantile, the child had vanished. It wasn't until a few days later that they learned what happened to her. Pearl had rescued yet another young girl, and taken the child into her home.

Two little hands cupping her face shook her out of her thoughts. "What is it, sweetie?" Bridget asked, noticing the troubled expression in Emma's pale blue eyes. The child laid her cheek against Bridget's, and Bridget's heart melted. It was the first open show of affection that Emma had offered. Bridget reveled in the sweetness of the act and the emotions that flowed through her. She sat down amidst the flowers and drew Emma onto her lap, burying her face in the whisper-soft, sunshine-colored curls.

The quiet moment was shattered by a thunderous explosion. Bridget grabbed Emma and pulled her behind her to protect her. The first blast was immediately followed by a second. This one was muffled, but more powerful. The ground rumbled ominously beneath them, sounding like horses' hooves beating the ground at a furious pace. Bridget was too afraid to look up. She simply gathered the precious child closer in her arms, praying that no harm would come to them or to the woman she was supposed to protect but had left sleeping upstairs

The rumbling sound grew louder, clearer, closer. Reason finally penetrated the fear that clutched her breast. Bridget rose to her feet, grabbed Emma, and began to run.

*Too late.* She and Emma were surrounded by a dirty, determined group of outlaws. Her life was over. It was the only thought that penetrated the shock of seeing her husband smiling down at her.

"Well, well," Michael O'Toole murmured. "If it isn't my wife." The way he drew out the word *wife* left the impression that he could barely tolerate saying the word, let alone the woman attached to it.

How could she have so misjudged the man? Or had time simply changed him? She lifted Emma into her arms. The child burrowed into her embrace and held on with surprising strength. Emma depended on her, and Bridget would not let her down.

"What do you want?" she demanded through tightly clenched teeth. Now was not the time for social niceties. It was time for some answers.

"You." Michael's words had the blood draining from the top of her head to the tips of her toes. She swayed, but reached deep and found the grit to hang on.

"Why?" Her voice cracked over the one word.

"Do the vows we spoke mean nothing to you?" he demanded, a hard glint coming into his narrowed, slate-colored eyes.

Of all the words he could have used, these were the ones she had no answer for. Her vows meant everything to her. She had honored them for years. Not once during all those years had she let any other man's attentions make her forget the fact that she was a married woman.

Until the night a few months ago when she'd given up hope of regaining her strength or living to see Mick grow to adulthood. A saint of a man had come to their rescue; a tall, black-haired rancher who had carried her into his home, promising to care for her and Mick.

Just the thought of all that James had done for them, and meant to them, gave her the strength she needed to regain her composure. "Where have you been for the last twelve years?" she demanded, her voice growing stronger with each word.

A muffled laugh and rude suggestions from two of the outlaws didn't shake her growing resolve. She needed to distract them. She had to do something to get them away from the house. Pearl was upstairs! She couldn't let them hurt her again.

"Have you missed me then?"

She gulped in a much-needed breath and nodded her head. To give voice to the words would have been an out-and-out lie. The action seemed to take a bit of the tension out of Michael's shoulders; they visibly relaxed. He turned and motioned to one of the men, who nudged his horse forward. Bridget tried not to stare at the hideous scar that slashed across the man's jaw, and steeled herself to wait and see what he would do.

Instead of speaking, he motioned for her to come closer. It was then that she noticed the horse he pulled by the reins. He motioned for her to get on it.

"What are you waiting for, wife?"

"I . . . that is . . . what about . . ."

A nearby shout interrupted them. The sound of horses fast approaching spurred the group of men into action. Before Bridget could think of anything to say, Emma was ripped from her arms, screaming, while Bridget was lifted onto the back of the horse.

"Please don't hurt her!" she began, only to be silenced by the leather-clad palm of her husband's large hand.

Emma's screams grew more gut-wrenching. "Please, Michael. I beg you!"

"Shut up, bitch!"

The words her husband uttered cut at her heart, leaving absolutely no doubt in her mind how he felt. Despite his crude words, a screaming Emma was plopped into her lap at the same moment another man whipped the hindquarters of her horse.

Her arms tightened around Emma, who immediately stopped screaming and settled into gut-wrenching sobs. Bridget wanted to cry right along with her, but wouldn't give Michael the satisfaction of knowing he had succeeded in scaring the life out of her. Jaw clenched, teeth grinding, she kept her emotions from bursting free.

By the time the group of outlaws had made it to the edge of town, the men following them had not been able to catch up to them or outrun them. Emma's wracking sobs had lessened into occasional hiccups and sniffles. Bridget tried to soothe the poor little girl, hoping against hope that whoever had set off the explosion had not injured anyone in the process.

The farther from town they rode, the more her worry increased. What had happened to Marshal Justiss? He must have been injured in the blast, or else the outlaws would not be free. Had anyone on the street outside of the jail been hit by flying debris? She would never be able to live with the guilt if anyone had been seriously injured—or worse. It would be *her* fault. Michael was still her husband, and she would carry the guilt with her to the grave.

Bridget closed her eyes, willing the thoughts to the back of her mind, and concentrated on the stranger she'd been married to. Why had he left? Did he always have it in his heart to cheat and lie, steal and kill? Even without knowing any of those answers, she couldn't ignore the fact that her strict upbringing would not allow her to think of breaking her vows. Bridget opened her eyes, lulled into a state of semi-calm by the horse's rhythmic pace.

She blinked, opened her eyes, and rubbed them. The sight before her had not changed. The tall young man sat straighter in the saddle. "Mick!" she cried out. "What are you doing here?"

His gray eyes, so like his father's, narrowed. "My father needed my help today."

Her son's words cut her to the bone. The wound ached. How could she have gone so wrong in assuming her son was on the right path? How could she have forgotten the morning she learned he'd tried rustling cattle?

*But that was to pay the doctor!* her heart silently cried out. *What is he doing riding with such a disreputable group of outlaws now?*

"Why, Mick?" she whispered, not daring to utter the words too loudly, not wanting her husband to overhear them. Her son gave her a long look before shrugging his shoulders and turning his back on her.

He took the reins from the scar-faced man and led her horse the rest of the way in silence. The cabin stood beneath a towering pine tree double the height of the cabin's roof. She silently pleaded with her son to answer her question, but he had yet to do so. Deciding to give it one last try, she asked him again. This time he answered.

"Like father, like son. Isn't that what people always say?" he growled out in a voice so like her husband's, her blood froze.

"Mick—"

"You should have married Mr. Ryan when you had the chance," he mumbled.

"But then where would I be now?" she demanded, knowing in her heart that she would rather spend her life on the run than ruin that good man's name and reputation with her own.

Mick reached up to help Emma down. Once the little girl was on her feet, he reached up a hand to help Bridget down. "You'd be safe, Mother."

# Chapter 25

The first blast shook the foundations of the mercantile. The second shattered the front windows. Ryan came to lying on the wooden boardwalk out in front of the store, with a ringing in his head and a stinging sensation on the left side of his face. He reached a hand up to rub the sting away, surprised to feel a sticky wetness there. All at once, his senses returned with a vengeance. He was bleeding. Someone had blown out the front of the jail!

The thought instantly cleared the rest of the fog from his brain. He shot to his feet and sprinted past the two storefronts separating the jail and the mercantile. The smoking pile of rubble that had been the sheriff's office looked ominous, but the mangled iron bars that had once securely housed more than one outlaw, and more recently the O'Toole gang, were a silent testament to the fact that not all men sentenced to remain behind bars would do so. A shaft of sorrow arced through him. By all rights, that's where he should be: behind bars.

"Justiss!"

Ryan heard more than one person call out to the marshal. God help the man if he had been behind the desk when the dynamite had been thrown through the front windows. There was no other explanation for the extent of the damage he surveyed. Putting those grim thoughts aside, he ignored the multitude of aches blossoming all over his battered body and bent to the task of carefully shifting through the larger piles of stone and lumber. He almost hoped they wouldn't find a trace of the marshal. He hoped the man hadn't suffered.

A distant rumble echoed toward them from across the river, from the direction of the town of Emerson. Turner stopped and patted the horse's velvety muzzle, soothing the suddenly fractious animal. Thunder? he wondered, looking up at the clear, crisp blue sky.

The second blast was more powerful, and more ominous. Thick black smoke rose up from where he knew the town to be. The front door of his house burst open and Maggie sprinted toward her husband and the marshal, who stood just outside the barn, unhitching the horse from Mrs. Swenson's wagon.

"What do you think—" Turner began, but one look at the marshal's thunderous expression, and he knew the thick black smoke would be all they would find of the former Emerson jail.

"Who did you leave in charge?"

The marshal shook his head, calling Turner's attention to the group of frightened woman gathered on the front porch. "Maggie—"

"Don't ye be frettin' over me now," she soothed, walking straight into his waiting arms.

"I'll be back."

"Aye, lad, ye will, or ye'll not get a bit of that blackberry cobbler the girls will be helpin' me make while yer gone."

He pulled her closer and breathed deeply. Lavender and rain. How had he survived the first two decades of his life without knowing what that combination could do to a man? He placed his fingertips beneath her chin, raising her face up to his. Capturing her lips in a kiss of silent promise, he added the whispered words that would ease her heart and mind. "I'll watch my back," he promised.

Satisfied, she stepped out of his embrace. With a hand resting protectively over the spot where he imagined their babe lay sleeping inside of her, Maggie bade him ride safely and to be sure and bring the outlaws back. Dead or alive.

Two miles down the road, he finally received the answer to his earlier question.

"I've never made a mistake like this before." Justiss swore ripely.

"Mistake?"

Justiss turned toward him, and Turner could read the anguish the man obviously suffered. "I didn't think."

"Think about what?" Turner urged.

"I didn't think at all!" Justiss replied, grabbing his reins in hands clenched with anger. "I was so certain that you knew James Ryan was a wanted man that I couldn't think beyond getting to the bottom of it. I didn't leave anyone on duty!"

"I already told you that I didn't know—"

Some of the agitation on the marshal's face eased. He nodded his head in agreement. "And I said I believed you."

"But not until you'd battered me with twenty questions. I never knew a man who could ask one question in so many different ways," Turner marveled.

"Hell, I learned from the best," the marshal said with a grim smile.

"Marshal Brodie is the best," Turner agreed. "I never had the pleasure of working with him, but there isn't a lawman in this territory or nearby who hasn't heard about the man's talent for tracking down outlaws and bringing them in."

"What are we going to do?" Turner asked, after another quarter mile of riding in silence.

"We are going to find out what's left of the jail. With any luck, the twin blasts will have blown the outlaws to Kingdom Come, but if not, then we'll track them down and bring them in."

Rounding the bend that led into town, Turner asked the one question he feared the answer to. "What about Ryan?"

"It's time for some straight talking."

"But what if he isn't—"

Reining in their horses in front of the smoldering pile of rubble that once housed the sheriff's office and town jail, Marshal Justiss swung his leg over the back of his horse and dismounted. "He is."

Turner hoped the marshal was mistaken. What in God's name would he tell Maggie? She'd never believe her brother was a wanted man! She'd never accept the fact that her brother had spent time in the jail in Amarillo. She probably didn't even know what state it was in.

A dark thought crossed his mind. The baby. He couldn't afford to upset his pregnant wife. He wanted Maggie to be healthy and whole, so that their baby would arrive healthy and whole. Every woman in town had offered advice regarding childbirth, and each and every one had warned that he needed to keep the mother happy and not to upset her. It wasn't good for the baby.

"Are you coming?" the marshal called over his shoulder as he made his way over to an all-too-familiar, dust-covered, broad-shouldered figure.

"Ryan!"

The relief that washed over his brother-in-law's features as he turned around to face them had Turner wondering just what Ryan thought he'd find, digging through the piles that littered the ground. Then it hit him: Ryan was digging for bodies.

"Justiss!" Ryan croaked out, swiping at the trickle of blood that seeped from a series of nasty-looking cuts on the side of his face. "We thought you were dead, man!"

Turner wondered if the marshal questioned the relief in his brother-in-law's eyes. A wanted man would shy away from the law, wouldn't he? Even after five or more years?

"Can anyone tell me what happened?"

Three men simultaneously stopped their digging and stepped forward, eager to fill the lawmen in, when a lone figure stepped out of the smoke. The woman swayed on her feet before collapsing in a heap not twenty feet away from where they stood.

Ryan was the first to reach to the woman's side. "Pearl! What happened? Why are you here?"

By the time Turner and the marshal reached his side, Ryan had the battered woman cradled in his arms.

"Bridget—"

"Why didn't she come with you?" Turner asked.

"Where is she?" Justiss demanded.

Ryan felt as if the bottom just dropped out of his stomach. "She isn't at the boarding house, is she?" He asked the question, even though he already knew the answer.

Pearl's eyes fluttered shut, then back open. She shook her head.

"Can you tell me what happened?" Ryan tightened his hold, stepping carefully around piles of shattered lumber and stone littering the road, making his way back to Swenson's Boarding House.

"She and Emma went outside to pick flowers, so I could rest."

"And then?" Marshal Justiss prompted.

"I heard a rumble, but thought it was thunder. The second blast rattled the windowpanes. That was no thunder."

Ryan leaned his shoulder against the partway-opened door, not waiting for either man to open it for him. He strode right through the kitchen. Before Pearl would answer his question, he had her tucked into Mrs. Swenson's best chair in the front parlor.

"Turner—"

Before Ryan could tell him what he wanted him to do, his

brother-in-law headed back into the kitchen. Sounds of water being pumped, and a teakettle banging against the cookstove told him without words that Turner had known what was needed. He should have figured out marriage to his sister would have any man trained inside of three months.

He started to smile, but Pearl's next words pulled him right back into the nightmare. "O'Toole and his gang have Bridget and Emma."

Ryan looked over at the marshal, who had been leaning against the wall, waiting to hear what Pearl had to say. He stood straighter, definitely ready for battle. Time to find the trail and track down the outlaws.

"Will you be all right, Pearl?" Turner asked, bringing her a cold glass of water.

"I thought you were making tea?" Ryan prodded.

"I was, until I heard about Bridget and Emma."

"Mick's gone," Pearl whispered.

"Have any of them been hurt?"

Pearl shook her head, though Ryan could tell it pained her to do so. "What are you trying to tell us, Pearl?"

"I think Bridget and Emma are all right. It's Mick."

Ryan felt every muscle in his body go rigid. If anyone hurt the lad, they would pay. "What about Mick?"

"I think he's riding with the outlaws."

"Ryan! Wait!"

Ryan heard his brother-in-law calling to him, but he couldn't stop, wouldn't stop. Not until he brought Bridget and Mick back home safely. Home. To his ranch. He needed to see Bridget with an apron tied about her waist, smiling down at him as she poured his morning cup of coffee while plying him with sweet scones and fresh butter. He needed her curled against him in the night after they'd love one another until their limbs were weak. The utter certainty that she had not lied to him about her husband filled him, giving him a sense of peace, a peace he needed to survive.

Though still a bit too thin and fragile-looking, the woman possessed a spine of pure steel, and a heart big enough to love a man like him. A sudden vision of Bridget with her hair tangled about her shoulders tightened every muscle in his body. Another vision quickly followed, this one of her brushing the hair out of Mick's eyes. He loved the way she cared for others; he loved the way she loved Mick. God help him, could she truly ever love him enough to forgive him for not believing her, for not trusting her with the truth of his past?

"Ryan!" he heard Marshal Justiss's voice ring out, but he kept going.

*"Flaherty!"*

The sound of his real name stopped him dead in his tracks. The world seemed to grind to a halt as he stood rooted to the ground, halfway between Swenson's back door and the barn. He shook his head, not believing it at first. He turned to face the men who were chasing after him, trying to get him to listen to reason.

Why hadn't he listened in the first place? Why hadn't he waited for Turner to catch up? If he had, how much longer would the marshal have kept Ryan's true identity a secret?

He stood absolutely still, his hands clenched into fists at his sides. Twin emotions raged through him. Anger was the first. He could handle the anger. He had learned long ago to keep a lid on his vicious temper, but the sorrow sweeping along in the wake of his anger was more difficult to handle. What would happen to him now? What of Bridget and Mick? Would the marshal still let him ride with the posse when he went after O'Toole?

His heart stumbled in his breast. There would be no future for him now. Bridget deserved better than him. His future contained a jail cell, and hers a difficult road back to the life she and Mick had led before O'Toole had been miraculously resurrected from the dead. He wasn't sure how he could help smooth their way, but he'd be damned to eternal hellfire before he let her go back to that lying, cheating, son-of-a-bitch outlaw husband of hers. Before the marshal escorted him back to Texas, he'd come up with a solution to her problem.

He could just hear Flynn and Reilly berating him for finally figuring it all out in his head, only to find he had lost the chance to offer the woman, who unknowingly held half his heart, the rest of it.

"So," he said, as the marshal came to a stop in front of him. "How long have you known?"

"Not right off, but something about your face just kept niggling at the back of my mind, like there was something I was forgetting."

"When will you be taking me back to Texas?" Ryan could barely handle the thought of leaving Bridget and Mick behind, let alone the men he'd befriended and taken in when his mentor died. He didn't doubt that his men would take care of the ranch while he was gone. It was the sinking feeling that he'd never see Colorado or Bridget and Mick O'Toole again that cut him to the bone.

"What about Bridget?" he whispered, not able to look Turner in the eye.

"Don't you want to know what happened to Rebecca Lynn Trainor?" the marshal demanded.

Ryan shook his head. "What about Mick?"

"Who's Rebecca Lynn?" Turner demanded, grabbing hold of Ryan's right arm, spinning him around to face him.

"We don't have time to go into particulars right now," Marshal Justiss said. "Suffice it to say, that your brother-in-law had more than one reason to change his name. At the very bottom of the list of reasons was the way Irish immigrants were treated when they arrived fresh off the boat."

"I'll go along willingly, Marshal, if you'll just let me ride out with you. I need to bring Bridget and Mick home safely."

"Home where?" Turner demanded. "To the boarding house?"

Ryan grimaced, then shook his head. "No, to my ranch."

"But she's a married woman!" Turner's voice reverberated with the anger that was obviously building inside of him.

Ryan thought to stem the flow of Turner's anger, wanting to spare the man he'd come to know and count on as a friend, but in the end he decided against it. What did it matter that he was about to lose another friend, when his whole world was caving in all around him?

When he was up to his neck in trouble, would he remember that the truth is the only thing that mattered?

"Turner," the marshal urged, "in the eyes of the church they are married, but how would you feel if it were Maggie instead of Bridget? How would you feel if, after a decade or more, a dead husband appeared out of nowhere? Would you expect her to honor her vows to her first husband? Would you expect her to divorce him, so that your marriage to her would stand up in a court of law?"

Turner's pallor changed from bright crimson to ash-gray. His silence indicated his turmoil. Ryan was grateful for at least that much. But why had the marshal spoken up for him? If he was a criminal, why would a lawman take his side on anything?

"We're running out of time," Ryan said, hoping to change the subject and move things along his way. "The kidnappers are getting away!"

"It's her husband, Ryan!" Turner shouted at him. "It can't be considered kidnapping!"

"What if she was forced to go against her will?"

"The man is still her husband!"

"I don't care," Ryan growled. "It doesn't matter what the law thinks . . ." The words died on his tongue. It did matter what the law thought. The law would put him behind bars. The law would separate him from Bridget and Mick. The law would take away his second chance at love. In his heart, he didn't think he deserved this second chance, but he'd be damned if he'd lie down and let this chance pass him by.

"If I promise to give myself up the moment O'Toole is back behind bars, will you let me ride with you, Marshal?"

For a heartbeat, the silence tormented Ryan. Then something flickered in the marshal's bright green eyes, eyes so like those of his brother-in-law that he looked from one man to the other. Both were tall and thick through the shoulders. Both were strong men, able to take care of his sister and the woman he loved. Here was the answer he sought. All he had to do to ensure the plan worked was to give up the woman he loved. Forever.

He'd go one better; he'd ask the marshal to take care of Bridget and Mick for him. He'd seen the way Marshal Justiss had looked at the lovely Bridget. She deserved to have a strong man by her side, an upstanding man, someone who wouldn't steal, cheat, or lie. He was guilty of all three evils. God help him, he was no better than Michael O'Toole.

The marshal nodded, and held out his hand. "I'd like your word on it, Flaherty."

Ryan held out his hand, and added one last request. "Only if you promise to look after Bridget and Mick. I need to know that someone worthy of them will be taking care of them while I pay off my debt to society."

Their gazes locked. The marshal didn't try to cover up his surprise. "I'd be honored to look after Bridget and Mick."

Ryan nodded and turned to Turner. "Will ye promise on your life to look after me sister and the baby? I may not get back up this way for awhile." He couldn't keep from slipping back into his brogue; he was nearing the breaking point of his control.

Turner grabbed Ryan's outstretched hand in both of his and squeezed it hard. "I pledge on my life that I'll never let anything happen to your sister, or any children we have, as long as there is still breath left in my body."

"Then you have my word, Marshal. I'll willingly give myself up when this is finished."

# CHAPTER 26

Bridget could not believe her son would willingly participate in her husband's corrupt way of life. She had to do something! But what could she do? Legally, she was still married to the man and bound to obey him. Maybe she could somehow convince Mick to go back to the Ryan ranch.

"Welcome to our new home," O'Toole was saying.

The words hadn't penetrated until she walked through the front door of the cabin and stood rooted to the floor. At first, she thought the only furniture in the entire cabin was the large brass bed standing against the far wall, with a pile of folded sheets lying at the foot of it.

But as she turned her gaze away from the bed, the sight unnerving her, she realized with relief that there was a battered three-legged table and two chairs next to the fireplace on the opposite wall. "I have a home with Mrs. Swenson."

"No wife of mine is going to live in a boarding house."

"But I—"

The blow to the side of her face should not have been unexpected, but somehow it was. Michael had never hit her before today, and this was the second time in only a few hours that he had struck out at her. He had definitely changed.

"Don't you touch my mother!" Mick shouted, lunging for O'Toole's legs and taking the bigger man down.

The scuffle was brief, but bloody. Mick's lip was split, and his nose bleeding, by the time his father hauled him up off of the floor. O'Toole gave him a hard shake for good measure.

Bridget took a step closer to Mick and laid a comforting hand on his shoulder, hoping to communicate without the need for words, that he should be still. For now.

"O'Toole!"

She heard someone shout from just outside the cabin door. Relieved beyond measure, she watched him turn on his heel and leave. Bridget drew her son into her arms. One arm around Mick's shoulders and another around Emma's back, Bridget felt her strength of purpose returning. She had spent her life doing for others, making sure others were taken care of. There would be time later to decide what she would do for herself, but right now she had a job to do. She needed to keep Emma and Mick safe, but she also needed somehow to convince her husband that she meant to honor her vows, even though the idea of lying beside him in that bed was the most repulsive thought she could imagine.

"You can't mean to stay with him, Ma."

The utter despair in Mick's voice tugged at her heart strings. "You were ready to ride with him." The words were blunt, but they had the desired affect.

"He said something about protecting his interests in Denver. I thought he meant a family, and I know how hard you've worked to take care of me. I thought if I helped him, then he'd help us."

She felt him quiver, and she began to rub his back, dropping her head to his broadening shoulder. "You've a kind heart, Mick, but not everyone is willing to put the needs of others before themselves. Your father must have meant something else entirely." She paused and lifted her head. She could not keep the tears from filling her eyes, but she blinked them away.

Brushing a hand across his cheek, she noticed that the peach fuzz was giving way to a much rougher, coarser type of hair. Yet another sign that her boy was becoming a man.

The pain of Michael's hand slapping her cheek was worth it, if it opened her son's eyes to the truth of his father's character. "I love you, Mick."

"Me too!" Emma piped in.

Shock had her stepping back and looking down into Emma's bright blue eyes. "I love you too, Mickey," Emma said, patting a tiny hand to his flushed cheek.

The sound of angry male voices carried in through the open window. Reality returned, and with it Bridget's fear for the children she loved.

"We have to get out of here," she said, dropping her voice to the barest of whispers. It wouldn't do to have her husband or his men find out what they were planning to do. For now, she'd let Michael think she was going to go along with his plans.

While they waited for him to return, she had time to think and plan how they could escape unharmed. They had to. Because the more she looked at that brass bed, the more she thought of James and the night they'd shared. If she had to hold on to the memory for the rest of her life, if that was all God was going to grant her, then so be it. Some people were just destined to be alone. But one thing for sure, she would never again be able to fulfill her duties as a wife to Michael. After a dozen years of believing him dead, to find out he was alive—and living a life of depravity—cemented her resolve. She had to protect Mick and Emma, and they had to escape.

The only thought centering her, keeping her sane, was the image in her mind's eye of James Ryan. The Irishman's shoulders were broad enough to share her load, his arms strong enough to protect them, and his heart big enough to care for another man's son. She hoped he had just a kernel of feeling left for her and didn't hate her. It was too much to hope that James believed her, but she wouldn't know until she saw him again. He'd captured her heart with his kindness to Mick and herself. She should have admitted from the first that she'd fallen in love with him, but now nothing, not even the return of her husband from the dead, would keep her from finding out if James returned those feelings. A feeling of rightness settled over her. She would grab at her own chance for happiness. Sometimes a body had to make her own chances in life. If a lifetime of kindness were all he offered, she'd accept it rather than lose his friendship, but she sure hoped for more.

What she felt for James could not be any more wrong than her husband's life of crime, could it?

The sun dropped lower in the sky, adding a hint of orange to the whitewashed log walls. Still she sat at the small three-legged table, staring at the bed her husband intended to share with her. She prayed she could come up with a way to convince him she never would, without putting Mick or Emma in danger.

A few hours later, her husband returned.

"Why are you so thin, Bridget?" he asked.

She didn't want to tell him how she and Mick had struggled to survive after he left them. She didn't want to tell him of the towns they'd moved from, staying one step ahead of the town gossips, in order to preserve her boy's chance of growing up proud of his name. Proud! Hah! What was there now to be proud of? Instead of discussing the likelihood that Bridget had never married, now the town would be able to talk themselves silly. She had a husband, all right: an outlaw. What difference did it make if she told him the truth or not? It was too late to stop the inevitable.

"I was starving myself."

"Why?"

"I didn't have enough money to buy food for two. The jobs I worked paid enough for food for one growing boy."

His gray eyes narrowed into slits of flint. "I don't believe you."

"It doesn't matter what you believe. It's the truth." She sighed deeply, drawing the sleepy Emma closer. "I really don't care anymore."

"*No!*" she heard Mick cry out, but she never saw the fist coming. It connected with brute force, snapping her head back, sending her into a spiral of graying darkness. Her last thoughts were of Emma and Mick. She prayed nothing would happen to them, and then the darkness claimed her.

"Mama, Mama," Emma pleaded. "Wake up. Please?"

Bridget felt something cool against her throbbing cheekbone. It felt wonderful. She opened her eyes and realized she lay on the cabin floor, with Emma crying and patting at her bruised cheek with her cold little hands.

"Where's Mick?" she whispered. Her throat felt dry, and scratchy.

Emma pointed to a dark form lying on the floor on the other side of the room. For the little girl's sake, she bit back the cry of anguish bubbling up inside her. She rose to her feet. She was shaky, but she'd do. But her heart nearly stopped beating when she knelt beside her son and saw the bloody gash across his forehead.

"Emma, who did this?"

The little girl's eyes rounded in fear, and Bridget was afraid she wouldn't speak. But Emma surprised her by answering, "The bad man who hit you."

It was the last straw. She'd find a way to bring him in herself, and come hell or high water, Michael O'Toole would pay for laying a hand on her son! She'd see to it that he spent the next twenty years behind bars.

The distant sound of horses rapidly approaching alerted her

to the fact that it was far too quiet. "Emma where did everyone go?"

The little girl looked up at her with complete trust in her eyes. "The bad men went outside."

"Did they say where they were going?"

"Uh-huh," she nodded.

"Where, Emma," she insisted, reaching down to tear a strip off her petticoat. It wasn't as clean as she'd like, but it was all she had at the moment. She gently blotted the bloody gash on Mick's forehead, breathing easier when it stopped bleeding. She tore off another strip and wrapped it around his head.

"To play in the trap."

Bridget shook her head, wondering just what that was supposed to mean. "What were they going to play?" she asked, hoping Emma would eventually say something that made sense.

Emma put a finger to her little rosebud-shaped mouth and whispered, "Shoot the lawmen."

Bridget shot to her feet and ran to the open door. The sun was nearly gone now, only a thin line of red-orange colored the horizon. There was no movement nearby that she could detect, but the sound of approaching horses was unmistakable. It had to be the marshal riding to their rescue. *Was James with him? Was Joshua?*

She had to do something to protect the children before she tried to warn the marshal and his men. She turned around and saw the bed, the big brass bed. She dragged Mick over and slid him underneath the bed; coaxing Emma to lie beside him might be a little harder. She placed a finger to her lips. "You must be quiet as a mouse, Emma."

"Are we playing a game, too?"

Bridget kissed Emma's forehead. "That's right, sweetie. You and Mick hide under the bed, and don't come out. Even if you hear gunshots." Bridget watched the child's face for a sign of understanding. "All right?"

Emma nodded, getting down on her belly, scrambling closer to Mick. "All right. I'll hide Mickey. I won't let him get scared or nothing," she promised with a definite nod that had her blond curls dancing about her little head.

Bridget quickly kissed the both of them again, and scooted back out from under the bed. Though still shaky, she ran out the front door. She didn't have a clue what to do. How could she possibly warn the men she hoped were headed their way? How could she be sure she wouldn't be running into the outlaws' crossfire?

She stopped and gasped for breath, nearly missing the answer to her silent prayers. The horse she rode in on stood a few feet away, still saddled, poor thing. As she walked over, intending to remove the saddle, she noticed the long leather scabbard attached to the saddle. She ran her fingers across the tooled leather and settled them on the butt end of the repeating rifle that somehow someone had forgotten.

Not caring who was close enough to observe what she was doing, or what they would do to her if she was caught, Bridget withdrew the rifle from its leather holder, and cocked it. Pointing it straight up into the air above her, she fired three times.

The sound of twigs snapping behind her had her spinning around to face her enemy: the man whom she had loved so long ago. For a heartbeat, she thought she saw a flicker of that feeling echoing in his eyes. All at once it disappeared, leaving only cold gray ice behind. Too late she realized that he held a gun, and pointed it at her heart. What would happen to Mick and Emma if she died? She had to do something to save them. She raised the rifle to her shoulder and fired again. The startled expression on Michael's face showed disbelief, then anger.

She had winged him! Blood trickled down his sleeve. Her arms started shaking; she couldn't hold the rifle still enough to fire again. This time when he raised the gun, pointing it at her heart, she stared right back at him, silently daring him to fire it.

"Don't think I won't shoot you, Bridget. I've come too far to give it all up now!"

"Give what up?" her voice sounded far away. She was getting dizzy again, and her jaw ached abominably.

"The money! It was always the money!"

"Tell her about the Bible, Father," Mick called out from behind her, startling her.

She wanted to turn around and demand that Mick hide again, but didn't dare take her eyes off Michael. Besides, Mick was an honorable young man, and he would die to protect her, just as she had been prepared to do for him. Maybe she hadn't done such a bad job of raising Mick on her own. One thing she did know: she would not let her son get in the way trying to protect her. She had to stall them. "What Bible?"

"The O'Toole family Bible, Ma," Mick answered, coming to stand by her side. He took the rifle from her hands, cocked it, and leveled it to a point right between his father's eyes. "Tell her," he ground out between clenched teeth. Blood seeped through the makeshift bandage she had wrapped around his forehead, but Mick's eyes looked clear.

"Mick brought me the Bible."

"Why?"

"It doesn't matter now," Mick spat out, "just ask him what was inside the back cover."

A growing sense of unease flowed through her; she didn't want to know. She looked at Mick's tight jaw and hard eyes and knew she had to ask, for his sake. "What was inside, Michael?"

He grabbed at his wounded arm, as if it had started to pain him. She thought he wouldn't answer her, but then he shrugged. "The key to a safe deposit box back in Denver. The box number was written beneath the words I wrote on the inside back flap."

"But I thought—"

"What? That I'd written those words just to you?" He laughed aloud. "You always were so naïve."

The words he'd written echoed in her aching head: *The key to happiness is in the hands of the one who holds my heart. M. O'T. 3\* 3\* 1 8 5 0.*

"I wanted you to think I'd written the words to you," Michael said slowly, as if remembering, "but the main reason was to hide the fact that it also contained the number to the safe deposit box."

Bridget drew in a ragged breath. "What is in the box?"

His slow smile was triumphant. "A mine payroll and the profits from two or three bank jobs." He rubbed his thumb and forefinger under his chin. "Thought I'd lost the money altogether—that is, until Mick mentioned you still had the Bible."

"You'd been robbing banks back then, too?" Bridget couldn't get her thoughts to work properly. She had misjudged him so completely. He had *never* loved her. "Have you no conscience?"

"None at all," he said with a smile.

"I guess I shouldn't bother to ask if you ever planned to come home."

"I don't think you really want me to answer that, do you, Bridget?"

Shots being fired in the distance startled her. She had forgotten their dire situation for a short time as she remembered all she had given to their brief marriage.

As the sound of gunfire echoed, still some distance away, she asked one more question. "Did you steal my father's gold pocket watch and my mother's cameo?"

His eyes narrowed, slid to a point off behind Mick, and then back again. Apparently whatever he saw there gave him no reason to worry. "I sold them for twice what they were worth. I needed the money to start over. Aren't you going to ask me about our marriage license?"

His words sliced her to the bone. She didn't think she could take any more truths just now. She didn't feel at all well. The stunning revelations her husband brought to light were more than she wanted to deal with. But she would, because she had to in order to get past them and move on to her future. She intended to have a future, and as God was her witness, Michael O'Toole would never be a part of it!

"You no good sidewinder!" Mick spat out, then startled her further by letting loose a string of swear words that curled her toes. Her boy had learned a few new words since they had last shared supper together.

He raised the rifle, but before he could squeeze off a shot, Bridget heard Emma call out from behind her. She didn't pause to think; she shoved Mick hard to the ground, spun around, and dove for Emma. Gunfire zinged overhead, and something sharp pierced her shoulder. As she lay there, listening as the shooting continued, she desperately hoped Mick had not been hit. Emma squirmed beneath her, but until the sounds of gunfire died out, she dared not move a muscle.

"Bridget!"

The welcome sound of James's voice had her opening her eyes, daring to confront what she had not been brave enough to do until he arrived. "Mick?" She couldn't put to words what she feared.

"Right here, Ma."

The sound of her son's voice, so strong and sure, was a balm to her aching head and troubled heart. Before she could rise up off her knees, she was lifted high into James's arms. She wanted to tell him that Emma needed her, but the words died in her throat as she looked up into the eyes of the man she would love for the rest of her life.

Somewhere in the back of her mind, it registered that Emma was talking excitedly to Mick. But her focus was centered on the man who held her close to his heart. "Bridget! I thought you were dead!" he murmured.

"Your face. Jamie, you've been hurt!"

"Never mind that now, what about you?"

"I'm fine," she started to say, but Ryan pressed against her shoulder and she couldn't stop the sharply indrawn breath that told him more than her words ever could. James demanded to know where she had been injured.

She ignored the demand, drew him closer, and kissed the hollow at the base of his throat and along the edge of the injured side of his face. She watched his pulse quicken. Bridget smoothed her fingertips across his warm, firm lips and sighed. There was so much she wanted to tell him, so much of their lives . . .

His hand reached up and squeezed hers, and she noticed the bandana wrapped about it. "James—" she began, but he shook his head. "What about, Michael, is he—"

"He's dead." Mick answered her before she even finished forming the question. She asked James to set her down. When he did, she turned toward her son. "Did you kill him?"

She wanted to know, although she would never hold it against Mick. How could she, when Michael had threatened to do the same to the both of them?

"Actually, he was caught in the crossfire. As soon as you pushed Mick out of the way, Justiss and I opened fire," a new voice answered.

"Joshua!" Bridget realized all at once that they were surrounded by men, but not one of them was a part of O'Toole's gang of outlaws. "Where are the rest of them?" She shuddered as her voice broke.

"The lying bastards are all dead," Mick answered with a grunt of satisfaction.

"Mick, you should never speak ill of the dead," she chastised.

"Even when they wouldn't have blinked an eye when their leader shot you or Emma down in cold blood?"

Bridget's heart fluttered, but she remained steadfast in her beliefs. "It isn't our place to judge others."

"You've a forgiving heart, Bridget O'Toole," Ryan said softly, drawing her back into his arms. She leaned against him, trying to ignore the throbbing in her jaw and the pain in her shoulder.

"Too bad it's wasted on you, Flaherty!" O'Toole hissed as he lifted himself up on his elbow and leveled his Colt at Ryan.

The impact of the bullet propelled him backward a few steps, but Ryan did not fall. Before he could draw his gun, Marshal Justiss fired off two quick shots. Bridget didn't have to look at her husband to know that, this time, he was truly dead. She was finally a widow! She would have her future, and she would thank the Lord for every day she spent of it in James Ryan's arms.

But something nagged at her tired brain and aching body. "Why did he call you Flaherty?" she demanded of James. "Isn't that Maggie's maiden name? But you don't look alike. I thought she was your step-sister."

"Nay, lass," he answered. The look of longing in his deep blue eyes had her taking a step closer. He shook his head at her, holding onto his shoulder to staunch the flow of blood where O'Toole's bullet had nicked him.

"But—"

"I'm ready to go back to Amarillo with you, Marshal."

"What's in Amarillo?" she demanded, walking right up to him, ignoring the way he shook his head at her.

He didn't answer her quickly enough; she turned to Joshua and asked him. "What do you know about all of this?"

Ryan's sigh was heartfelt and loud enough to have her turning back toward him, waiting expectantly. "No one knew anything, until Marshal Justiss put the facts all together. He recognized my face from an old wanted poster."

"Wanted—"

"Hush, now lass," he ordered. "Let me get it said, while I still have the strength."

She nodded, standing a breath away from him, hoping he would look at her and see that she trusted him and believed in him. No matter what he was about to tell her.

The shocked look that flitted across his handsome face told her he had just figured it all out. "You don't understand, Bridget."

"Then tell me."

Marshal Justiss had finished draping the dead men over their saddles, leaving it to Turner to tie the horse's reins to their saddles and then to one another. It would be slow going, but easier to get them all back to town that way.

"Before you tell Bridget about Rebecca Lynn, why don't I tell you the end of the story."

Ryan shook his head. "I've already told you I'd go with you. What more do you want from me?"

"I want you to listen," the marshal said through clenched teeth.

Ryan struggled with the need to go to Bridget. She looked so lost and alone, bravely standing there with blood trickling down the sleeve of her dress from a dark red hole. *Blood!*

"Bridget! You've been shot!"

"I have?" Bridget sounded surprised. Then all at once, what little color had been in her face drained. Before he could pull her back into his arms, her legs buckled beneath her.

# CHAPTER 27

Bridget woke to the familiar sight of lace-edged curtains and sunlight streaming in through the bedroom window. She breathed deeply. The scent of honeysuckle and roses welcomed her, and she smiled, knowing she was back in the guestroom at the Ryan ranch. When she tried to sit up, she found her arm had been bandaged and had absolutely no strength in it. Struggling to get her backside up against the headboard, using her good arm, she scooted back until she was sitting up straight.

A thin sheen of sweat beaded her forehead by the time she accomplished that much. She could hear voices from downstairs and wondered what James would be doing.

Everything came back to her in a rush of feeling. Anguish tore at her heart. James had loved another woman, and that woman had something to do with James having to go back to Amarillo, wherever that was, and serve the rest of his jail sentence. She did not know what he had done, or been accused of, but she intended to let him know she would wait for him right here at his ranch. Let him try to send her away!

Bridget gathered her strength and pushed herself up off the bed onto shaky legs.

Ryan looked up at the sound of footfalls lightly touching the steps. Bridget stood hesitantly on the bottom step with her hair tangled on her shoulders. She wore one of the robes Maggie had left behind before she moved out to marry Turner. It was made of thin, soft cotton, the color a dewy rose, the same shade that graced Bridget's flushed cheeks.

She looked around. "Where is everyone?"

Ryan cleared his throat. He wanted to take her in his arms and reassure her, but he would not put that on her right now. She needed to hear the truth and judge for herself whom to believe. Bridget would have to make the decision without any pressure from him. He desperately hoped she'd make one he could live with.

"Joshua headed on home to check on Maggie, Mrs. Swenson, and the girls."

She nodded.

"Marshal Justiss is waiting for me."

Pain, swift and sharp, speared through her, hollowing out what was left of her heart. "Tell me what happened, James."

He gently placed his hand to her good elbow and steered her to the chair he had pulled out for her. She sat and waited for him to begin. Nerves dancing along his spine had him getting to his feet and fetching the pot of tea he had set to steeping once he heard her feet touch the floor overhead.

"I don't know where to start."

Bridget placed her hand over his and squeezed it gently. "Why don't you tell me about Amarillo. Did you have a job there?"

In the end it was easier than he had thought it would be to sit down across from Bridget and tell her about his life back then. He told her of the fears he had conquered to cross the Atlantic, and how his roundabout journey led him to Texas. He continued telling her how, along the way, he befriended Reilly and Flynn, then the others. Somewhere in the middle of the story, he realized that they were no longer alone. One by one, his men had slipped quietly into the kitchen to listen to the tale he had never fully shared with any of them.

The part about being betrayed by Rebecca Lynn still stung,

but the trust and love in Bridget's gaze made it easier to bear.

"So you have to go back to serve out the last two years of your sentence?" she asked, after a long stretch of silence.

"Aye."

"Well, then," she said briskly, brushing the hair out of her eyes, "I'm sure Mick and I can keep busy tending the gardens here and cooking for your men while you're gone."

James rose to his feet, her words echoing through him. He wanted to be sure he heard her correctly before he grabbed hold of her and held on for dear life. "You'd wait for me?"

"Isn't that what a faithful wife would do?"

"But you waited before." The bleak realization that she would have to live through those feelings of abandonment all over again sliced through him, leaving him aching for the years she suffered, not knowing what had become of her husband. He didn't want to put her through that all over again.

She smiled at him. "James," she said, "you are nothing like the man I married. You're an honest man with a gentle heart." She took a step closer to him.

He backed away, shaking his head.

"You never turn from anyone in need, whether it be a man lying bleeding on your land," she said with a shy smile, "or a young boy rustling your cattle."

This time, she took three steps closer. " 'Tis past time you decided to do something for yourself."

The slow smile gliding across his handsome face had her entire body tingling. The jolts of pleasure increased when she took another step closer.

He stood perfectly still. "But you've a kind heart as well, lass," he said, finally taking that first step toward her, closing the distance between them.

She smiled and the lines of worry between her gracefully arched dark brows softened.

"I've never known a woman to work as hard as you, or one willing to give up her life in order for her own son to live."

"When is the daft man going to ask her?" he heard Reilly ask.

"He's workin' up to it. Don't rush the man," he heard Flynn answer.

Marshal Justiss stepped into the kitchen as Ryan pulled Bridget into his arms. " 'Tis time ye took something for yourself as well. We've both needed to shelter and protect those we care about, but I'm thinkin' we can find a way to add in what we both want and need for ourselves. I need you. I love you, lass," he said with a sigh of resignation. "If ye'd be willing to wait for me, I'd be honored."

"That's not how to ask her!"

"Not now, Reilly," Flynn said.

"But he didn't ask her proper!" Reilly wailed.

"Ask me," Bridget urged, her lips a breath away from his.

James hesitated, for a heartbeat, then smiled. "Will ye marry me and share your life with me, Bridget O'Toole?"

"Oh, James!" The rest of her reply was crushed beneath his urgent kiss. He didn't need to hear the rest of it; he needed to kiss her. His next breath depended upon feeling her warm and giving mouth pressed against his own.

"I love you, James Ryan," she finally managed.

"Seamus," he said with a smile. "Me name is Seamus."

"Are you ready, Flaherty?"

He drew in a painful breath and set Bridget away from him. "Aye. I am."

"Then have a seat."

Seamus looked confused. "But I thought—"

"I know you what you thought," the marshal said with a grin, "but you never stood still long enough to listen to what I had to tell you."

Seamus grudgingly sat.

"Rebecca Lynn Trainor came forward recently and confessed that she and one of the ranch hands, a big man by the name of Beaker, robbed her father's safe, but set it up to look as if you had."

"Why did she change her mind and confess now?" Seamus needed to know.

The marshal gave him an intense look. "It seems Miss Trainor found out Beaker had another woman."

"A woman scorned," Bridget whispered.

Seamus could believe that of Rebecca now, but five years ago . . .

"What about poor Jed?"

"Beaker admitted to panicking when the old man wandered into her father's study."

"Then he admitted to killing Jed?"

"No, he said it was an accident, but Rebecca Lynn swore on a stack of Bibles that Beaker pushed the old man."

"Then why do I have to go back to Amarillo?" Seamus demanded.

"It seems Big John Trainor wants to make it up to you."

Bridget rose to her feet and placed her hands on her hips. "Well then the man can just get on his horse and ride up here to Colorado and make it up to James . . . er, Seamus. My future husband will not be doing much traveling for the next few months."

Bridget turned toward Seamus. She was taking his advice, and holding out for what she wanted in life: him. "Will he?"

Seamus rose to his feet and hugged her tight. Before she could say another word, he placed his fingertips against her lips and shook his head at her.

She nodded.

He took her hand in his and got down on one knee. "Ye didn't answer me yet, lass."

"Aye, James . . . er, Seamus, I will marry you. I wish I could keep it straight in my head what to call you."

After a glance at the men gathered around the kitchen table, he smiled at her. "Seamus Ryan Flaherty, but you can call me 'darling,' " he said, sweeping her back into his embrace.

"Well now, the lad finally got the words out," Reilly said with a grin.

"Took a bit of time over it, but I'm thinkin' he has style," Flynn added.

"A toast!" the men cried in unison.

"To the prettiest bride-to-be," Reilly said, placing a kiss on Bridget's cheek.

"And the luckiest man in town," Marshal Justiss said, pulling her into his arms for a kiss.

"Here now, Jamie . . . er, Seamus," Flynn said. "Ye can't have anyone stealin' kisses from yer intended."

"I owe Justiss my life," he said simply, as the marshal released a blushing Bridget. "If he hadn't ridden into town hoping to pick up O'Toole's trail, I never would have found out that I don't need to hide behind a false name anymore. I'm a free man."

"Not any more, boy-o," Reilly said with a nod toward the bride-to-be, as he pulled the cork from the bottle of Irish he had been saving for a special occasion.

"He's slow to catch on," Flynn said, setting an assortment of glasses on the table.

"*Slainte.*"

"They started without us!"

Bridget laughed at the look on Joshua's face as he pulled a laughing Maggie into the room. She threw herself into her brother's arms and demanded, "Why didn't ye tell me?"

"And add to your worry about caring for Da?"

" 'Tis no excuse!" she said, pushing far enough out of his

arms to smack him on the back of the head.

He rubbed at the sting of it. "What was that for?"

"Aye, lass, save yer smacks for yer husband," Reilly said solemnly.

" 'Tis up to Bridget to smack some sense into yer brother," Flynn said, raising his glass.

"Ma?"

"Mick!" Bridget breathed a sigh of relief as she watched her son walking toward her. The bandage around his head was clean, with only a bit of dried blood on it. He was in one piece and, in fact, carried little Emma on his hip.

"What have we here?" Maggie demanded.

"Mama!" Emma squealed, launching herself into Bridget's arms.

"Do you think Pearl would mind if Emma came and lived with us?" Bridget looked hopefully at her husband-to-be.

He shook his head and smiled. "Don't you want to know what *I* think?"

Bridget surely hoped he was teasing her. She didn't think her heart could take being separated from little Emma after all they had been through together. "I'm thinking I like having my way," she said with a grin.

The heated look Seamus sent her curled her toes. *Getting what you want out of life is far better than leaping out of the way and letting life pass you by.*

Marshal Justiss held out his hand, taking Seamus's in his own and shaking it heartily. "You're a lucky man, Seamus. You have your freedom, the love of a good woman, a strong son, and pretty daughter. What more could you ask for?"

"Not a thing," Seamus answered, pulling Bridget back into his arms and kissing the breath out of her. "The day Mick O'Toole decided to rustle my cattle was the second luckiest day of my life."

"And the luckiest?" Bridget urged, though she thought she knew the answer.

"I've yet to have it," he said slowly. "But do you really want me to talk about such things in front of our children?" he asked, a devilish grin on his handsome face.

"I do love you, Seamus Flaherty," Bridget whispered, pressing her lips to his.

"I couldn't ask for more than that, lass."

"He didn't tell her he loved her!" he heard Reilly mutter from somewhere behind him.

"Ye weren't paying close enough attention," he heard Flynn assure Reilly.

"But—"

The voices slowly faded away, until it was just the two of them alone in the kitchen.

"I love you, Bridget O'Toole. Are you sure you won't change your mind?"

"About letting you going to Texas, or marrying you?" she teased.

"Never mind," he whispered, burying his face in her hair. "So long as you love me, nothing else matters."

Bridget reached up and placed her hands on either side of his face. "I plan to spend the next fifty years here on the ranch with you. Aren't you afraid people will talk if you don't marry me?"

"Maybe we could get married and not tell anyone in town for a week or two. That would give the Committee for the Betterment of Emerson something to talk about!"

"Just kiss me, Seamus," Bridget demanded.

"My pleasure, lass."

# ABOUT THE AUTHOR

**C. H. Admirand**'s love of the Old West began watching silver screen legends, Roy Rogers, John Wayne, and Gary Cooper, and was rekindled by a cross-country trip to Colorado and the Southwest. She attributes her love for writing to her seventh-grade English teacher, her love for reading to her parents, and her creativity to her Celtic roots.

She sold her first book, *The Marshal's Destiny,* to Avalon Books in June 2001. *The Marshal's Destiny* won the Lories Award 2002 for Best New Author/Historical and was nominated for the Dorothy Parker Award of Excellence for Debut Novel and the Francis Award for Best Author. When asked what is different about her stories, Admirand confides that she likes to draw on her eclectic background by using family names in all of her stories. She lives in New Jersey with her husband and their three "adult" children.